FORESHORE
RiverRun

ABOUT THE AUTHOR

Geoff Smith was ordained in 1969 in Sheffield and has been a curate, a vicar and a cathedral canon. Holy Disorder is drawn from the authors first hand experience of his work in the Church of England.

GEOFF SMITH

HOLY DISORDER

FORESHORE PUBLISHING
London

Published by Foreshore *RiverRun* an imprint of
Foreshore Publishing 2022
The home of quality fiction

www.foreshorepublishing.com

Foreshore Publishing
The Forge 397-411 Westferry Road,
Isle of Dogs, London, E14 3AE

Foreshore Publishing Limited Reg. No. 13358650

ISBN 978-1-7395930-1-8

Acknowledgements

In Memory of Janet Elizabeth Smith 1948 - 2017 and William Joseph Smith 1980 - 2018

Particular thanks to David Peak for his encouragement and his way with apostrophes which gave me the confidence to submit my manuscript to Foreshore Publishing.

Also to Phil M. Shirley and the team at Foreshore Publishing for their positive and professional support.

Holy Disorder

In the Church of England
you will find the sceptic at the altar.

(Oscar Wilde)

'After a discipleship of plain days
The first born of the bourgeoisie
It is disturbing to be offered this coast
For one's training as Messiah
(as the careful programme says)
The faithful will be few and the Heathen
Prominent, the change is quite important
There is to be a seascape out of dreams
And a city founded where tears fell'

EBG

The Ordination

His knees hurt.

Try as he might he could not raise his thoughts above this pain, this intrusion into what he was promised would be, and which was meant to be, the most profound spiritual experience of his life.

His knees hurt.

He tried to move his body; a discreet exercise regime intended to relieve the pressure on his knees. He remembered an old school friend who, on hearing of his plans for ordination, had pulled his leg about wearing out the knees of his jeans, but today it felt as though it was his knees that would not survive. If only he could stand and stretch, but the Bishop was edging closer.

His knees hurt.

He tried raising his feet, one ankle at a time, but that only made the pain that much more unbearable and knew that fidgeting would just draw the attention of the Bishop's Chaplain who had been watching him closely since yesterday's row with the Cathedral verger.

As the Bishop came closer he tried to turn the grimace he knew was clearly written on his face, into the semblance of someone in the embrace of a spiritual experience. But it was hard, what was he doing here?

How had all this happened?

The strange turn of events that had brought him from the back-to-backs of his hometown, the boring, routine work in the garage, the early mornings and later nights, the fighting, the drinking, the laddishness that had been his past and was meant to be his future – to this?

The soaring arches of the Cathedral, the clerestory lights high in the vaulting of the ceiling. This was poetry in stone, conceived and constructed by masons who had a story to tell, and for whom this was their worship. Even as they built, they knew that they would not be welcome amongst the Sunday-best worshipping congregation and the 'Barchester' clergy that would run the place. He had noticed the sign on the back of the chairs, 'Close Harmony'. How droll, how witty, given the lack of any sign of Christianity, not even love, just good manners, existing between the clergy in the Cathedral Close.

But today the Cathedral was full.

And today his knees hurt.

Next to him, Neil had nearly all his relatives present. His mother had spent hours sewing and crocheting the lace for his cotta, and now the family had turned out as though it was a wedding, which for Neil, in a way, it was. They were joined by the parishioners from his new parish, which was in the inner city, near the Cathedral, all keen to see their new curate ordained.

On his left knelt John, like him destined to serve his curacy in a village some miles from the city.

John's family had turned out in force also, clearly overjoyed to see him ordained into the ministry of the Church of England.

Sadly, David reflected, for all sorts of really rather poor reasons, why he was here on his own without the support of his family, who were more than preoccupied with the business of getting through each day, without having to spend money on a bus journey to the city. Neither was there support from the parish, which was not waiting to welcome him because they didn't in fact know that they were expecting a new curate. So he was on his own, much to the annoyance of the Cathedral authorities, who had reserved seating, assuming the usual degree of support and who now had empty seats in full public view.

And now his knees hurt.

At this moment that was all he could think of; that, and the fact that there was no one there to see him ordained. And when he left the Cathedral he must catch the train, which meant a rush, because there was only one train to the parish and his new life as curate of St. Agatha's.

The Bishop, preceded by his Chaplain came nearer, and now the words that accompanied the outstretched hands were pronounced solemnly and formally. The words of ordination from the old book, and that was that. Neil, now ordained as a deacon in the Church, seemed to relax -- and as he relaxed, seemed transformed, as though by a new and deeper spirituality, as if the words had made a real and actual difference.

Somehow it seemed that Neil was transformed, from the youth who had nurtured his dream of ordination for at least the whole of his teens, into a rather more serious, considered, and mature young man, the collar clearly suiting him.

The ordination retreat had been the most confusing experience. The group now kneeling along the altar rail had spent four days and three nights, in quiet reflection. A Chaplain had been with them and had preached at the ordination only a few moments ago, even though the pain in David's knee had made it seem that much longer.

The theme of the retreat had been the role of the priest as a bridging person. Pontiff, which gave the Pope his name, it had been explained, coming from the Latin, Pontifex, 'bridge builder'.

The retreat conductor had been well intentioned, kindly, but he was inevitably from another era. He was the classic study in the morning, visit in the afternoon, tea-and-sherry-before-supper kind of clergyman, whose very existence had been challenged at the radical theological college David had attended.

Silence was broken after the Bishop's Charge which had been a kind of valediction, "what has happened is preparation, now we are to discover, you are to discover, in your hearts, exactly what kind of priests you will be!"

As soon as all that was over there was only one topic of conversation, clerical dress. What to wear. Slip in? Slip on? Shirt? Stock? One inch? One and a half inch?

A strip cut from a fairy liquid bottle?

The following morning, after the evening sherry, which everyone seemed to think was fairly risqué, there was the revelation of black suits, brand new unyielding dog collars, necks marked with red stripes where the collar rubbed, and cassocks from evangelical Sarum style to Neil's fabulous walking Soutane with shoulder cape.

He had chosen a simple black polo neck with a pair of black jeans and his old jacket; the cassock was an old one that he had inherited at college and had held on to.

Now, out of the corner of his eye, he saw Neil's lips moving in earnest prayer and wondered what he might be saying, and to what God he might be praying.

The Bishop smelt of aftershave or eau de cologne. The scent was stifling and overpowered him instantly. He closed his eyes which had started to water, so strong was the scent, and tried not to breathe. He felt the smooth weight of the Bishop's manicured hand stroke his hair in an almost, but not quite, sensual gesture and as it lay there he heard the words again, this time spoken to him directly.

Take thou authority to execute the Office of a Deacon in the Church of God committed unto thee; in the name of the Father, and of the Son, and of the Holy Ghost. Amen.

And then the Bishop was gone.

David reflected on this momentous event. This event for which he had spent four years in preparation, which marked an abrupt change in his life. This event that meant for him, things could not be the same again, that meant that he was now a Deacon in the Church, Curate of St. Agatha's, and that the people of that remote seaside village of Drissburgh would look to him for support and encouragement in their spiritual lives. He would have the responsibility for baptising, marrying and burying all those who came to him.

He waited to see if the significance of the event would begin to transform him as it had clearly transformed Neil. He tentatively explored bits of his interior landscape, as though his tongue was reaching out to explore the cavity in a tooth, but really nothing, he reflected, felt much different. His cynicism was still there, healthy and unaffected, he even felt a bit bored, and when he tried to pray, the pain in his knee returned more fiercely than ever, causing him to grimace.

Which was when he caught the eye of the Bishop's Chaplain, who had been watching David, trying to read his mind and work out what was going on there.

He knew that the Chaplain had not been impressed by his performance during the Ordination Retreat, and yesterday's rehearsal, plus the fact that the Parish Priest of St. Agatha's, along with his whole family, indicated that they would not be turning up. This meant that the reserved seats were not needed, and as it was too late to reallocate them, that there would be spaces at the front of the Cathedral. This had done him no good either.

But he did try and wanted so hard to make a success of this career to which he felt strangely attracted, called even, but for which he also felt unsuited, even unworthy. Like now, when he should have been reflecting on the mystery of Ordination, and the awesome nature of the calling that God was laying on his heart, he couldn't seem to raise his thoughts away from his knee and the awful pain.

He really began to think he would never walk again, and it would be embarrassing when he limped shabbily away from the altar rail.

Perhaps it was as well that there was no one there to see him.

At the Ordination Retreat the Bishop's Chaplain had led a session on Vocation and he'd got them to talk about how their vocations had started and how the call to which they were now responding had first made itself known.

On reflection he knew he should have invented some story, because the Chaplain was one of those top-drawer career clergy, heading for a Bishopric from the day they leave theological college. Even now, in what was his second job, really just a second curacy, he was looking for people with whom, in due course he could staff his future Diocese.

But no, amidst the stories of people who were inspired by the lives of saints, encouraged by faithful vicars and school Chaplains who recognised and encouraged and nurtured their vocations, he told his (true) story.

Of how he went to the church youth club with a couple of friends from school and saw a girl called Susan Palmer, whose father ran a corner shop and who was from an altogether different social strata from himself.

Realising that he didn't stand any chance of her talking to him at the youth group, and hearing that she was in the church choir, decided to join the church choir himself in order to qualify for the choir outing to the seaside, with the hoped for possibility of getting Susan alone on the back seat of the bus on the way home.

From this fairly unlikely starting place he began to attend church regularly. Despite being thrown out of the choir because he couldn't sing to save his life, never mind praise God.

1966 was a pivotal year for his generation, and in a very personal way for his own development. He found himself somewhere between the ending, some twenty years earlier, of a war which had left a legacy of deprivation, poverty and hard work for little reward, and the sense that with the American confrontation over soviet missiles in Cuba, a real fear that a nuclear confrontation could escalate into conflagration.

Memories of that year still send tremors down his spine.

Of course there was the soundtrack – Walker Brothers, Manfred Mann and *Pretty Flamingo*, which always reminded him of holidays when he was very young, when his parents could afford holidays. The Four Tops, *Reach Out I'll be There*, Beatles and Beach Boys, Spencer Davies, The Kinks, Wayne Fontana and the Mindbenders, Dusty, Ike and Tina and always the Rolling Stones. *Paint It Black, Nineteenth Nervous Breakdown* and he was their number one fan because they were the number one bad boys.

He liked plenty of other music and musicians. The Beatles' *Paperback Writer*, The Who, the Small Faces and there was rubbish as well, but the soundtrack for that year was pretty amazing and considering it was made up of three-minute pop songs that weren't meant to last, the soundtrack for that year in particular, has endured.

It's odd how music speaks to your condition and situation, even if there is the usual exaggeration. For example, he didn't have one, never mind nineteen, nervous breakdowns, and he didn't develop a passion to become a paperback writer, but he did develop a passion, one which over time led him to the where, who, what, of now.

What did he know, and about what was he certain?

He knew that he wanted out. He knew that he wanted more. He knew that for a working class lad, stuck in a terraced house in his part of the city there weren't too many options. The army was one, but he had no desire to become a squaddie. Pop music was another, after all, as the Stones asked, what could a poor boy do but join a rock and roll band? But he couldn't read or play music, and he certainly wasn't a singer. Football? Again, not likely, he had never had much time for sports at all.

And then, the most unlikely thing of all.

If anyone had ever suggested the possibility, not that anyone had, he would have laughed uproariously. He certainly wasn't the kind of person to think about the church and all the God stuff. He was no creeping Jesus; he had never been an altar boy. He had, he thought, been baptized, his mother thought so too but couldn't be entirely sure. And then to find himself first in a youth club, then in a confirmation class, and then talking seriously to the new curate about how you 'offered', that apparently was the word used, for Ordination, was bizarre in the extreme.

David looked back over the four years that it had taken. Four years of study, tutorials, essays, reading, interspersed with holiday jobs in bars, cleaning windows, whatever he could get. He realised now that it had been an escape route from what working class future fate had in mind for him.

But it hadn't been a sudden brain wave that had set him on the path towards ordination.

Things had happened during this year of 1966 that had started a thought process which had changed him and shaped him.

1966 saw the trial of Ian Brady and his lover Myra

Hindley. They were known in the popular press, as the 'Moors Murderers' and they were indicted and found guilty and sentenced to life imprisonment for those so-called Moors Murders at Chester Assizes.

But David had a strong sense that there was more at stake in this trial than the conviction of two sad and dangerous people who had preyed on their young victims, before subjecting them to the most sadistic of tortures, then cruelly and cold-bloodedly killing them.

Somewhere in his heart he knew that his city was also being indicted. That the awful scenario which had played itself out was, in effect, the full grainy commentary in compelling black and white, with picture after picture of the two accused of the way in which life in the city had ceased to be fully and completely human.

There was a lack of humanity in removing these young people from their families, with all the distress that such an action caused. The tragic, tear-stained faces on the news, reflecting the disbelief and fury that such 'monsters' could have done such a terrible, terrible, thing.

There was the lack of humanity that actively allowed the torture of innocent children, with the man as the main protagonist, but egged on and actively encouraged, and this was the most shocking thing of all, by his female accomplice.

There was the lack of humanity in the disposal of the bodies, hiding them in shallow graves out on the moors, on the edge of the city – the murderers returning again and again to photograph themselves, picnicking with the graves in the background.

There was a lack of humanity in depriving the families of the right and the ability to properly mourn the loss of their children. This loss of humanity, loss of the simple compassion that human beings should feel for, and offer to other human beings, began in 1966, to be seen for the first time in the way in which the city played out the drama in the theatre of its streets, and squares, and alleyways.

He began to feel that things were not going well, that the post-war years in which he had grown up were giving way to a harder, less compassionate and altogether more dangerous world. As a child he had taken a make-shift tent out into the local park and spent long sunny days with his friends, with a few sandwiches and a drink.

Later on, along the deserted banks of the canal he had made dens, fished for newts and spied on courting couples. Throughout his childhood he had felt safe and at ease with himself and his friends.

Now, with the newspapers reporting the trial and the judge imposing three concurrent life sentences on the man, for what he called "three calculated, cruel, cold-blooded murders" and sentencing the woman to two concurrent life sentences for murder, that sense of feeling of ease disappeared.

As he reflected on the events he became more convinced that society itself was feeling less and less at ease with itself, and increasingly aware that the city may never recover the innocence that preceded the murders in a case that shocked the nation.

What was perhaps most shocking, after the age of the victims, was the ordinariness of the murderers, a stock clerk and a shorthand typist. They were arrested after they tried to implicate a family member, who shared the same name as David himself. This made reading the story in the newspaper that much more personal, even though he knew that they were different people, and had never met, but when he read that he, or at least his namesake, had called the police after witnessing a brutal murder he felt in a strange way a personal involvement in the story.

The judge praised the "utmost skill and thoroughness" of the police working on the case. They had discovered a left-luggage ticket in a communion prayer book which led them to a suitcase containing pornographic photographs and tapes that proved to be valuable evidence against the pair.

Two children, believed to be victims of the murderers are still missing.

David realised that if people in his community were ever to come to terms with these tragic events, and the monstrous nature of the crimes, which were made more shocking by the age of the victims, children of an age where every instinct of decent people was one of offering protection, then there needed to be a reconciling and a closure.

He had been working in an office job in the city centre, and tired of the continuous debating and arguing over the case he had tended more and more to absent himself at lunch time. Wandering around the city, staring into shop windows, calling into a record store to hear the latest music releases, buying the occasional LP and thinking as he walked, about the future, and where his life was leading him.

David occasionally passed a large, austere building in the centre, forming an island in the middle of a busy crossroads with traffic passing on both sides.

Something drew him and he found himself dodging the traffic as he crossed over and entered the building by a small side entrance.

The Church was dedicated to the Saviour. It smelt sweetly of what in due course he learned was incense. But there was also a back scent of beeswax and polish hiding a faint smell of human odours, sweat and socks, and something else that he couldn't quite explain.

He sat in the semi-darkness, which was only barely lightened by daylight filtering through windows high above the central aisle. The main aisle windows themselves offered little light due to the dark, stained glass that obscured the outside world, humming away gently in the background – a mix of traffic noise and human voices forming the rhythm section of the city.

Sitting there became a daily ritual. He would leave the office at lunchtime, refusing various invitations to share a drink, to play cards or football, and headed down to the traffic island, cross over, and enter the dark sanctuary.

He was completely untutored in religious matters, but as he read various notices and magazines, he began to understand the clues after reading the signs and symbols, and it dawned on him that this strange ritual environment, its darkened interior embracing him with its soft, gentle, scented air held a clue to the disease of which he was increasingly aware in the world outside.

The Saviour in question was the Jesus of the New

Testament and when he found a Bible and started to read, he became so engrossed on occasion that he made himself late for work. In fact his work colleagues began to tease him about his secret affair.

But in a world where it was possible for monsters to emerge who so denied their humanity that they could visit wickedness on innocent children, the question had to be asked how could this be and how could a God who claimed to be good, allow such a thing to happen? As he read the pamphlets, as he read the history of the church, and as he reflected on the idea of a Saviour he began to see that there was a connection between this large, warehouse of a building standing on its isolated and isolating traffic island, which had been dedicated, ironically in 1866, a hundred years before the events unfolding in this particular year.

It began to become clearer. He was untutored in all of this arcane material and so was working it all out for the first time for himself – that the goodness of God is partly that He is prepared to let people work things out for themselves, to get some things right and some things pretty dramatically and awfully wrong.

Then rather than come steaming in to put things right sends another person to share in the mess and try to sort it out as a human being rather than as a God type.

According to the pamphlets he found at the back of St Saviour's, this character is the Jesus whose story is told in the gospels. In a sense He was there to help people become human, to hold on to their humanity, and to ensure that humanity triumphs in the end, or as that weird and wonderful last book in the bible claims, in the end God wins.

So David reflected as he walked back to work: whatever evil comes along, our humanity is guaranteed because of Jesus. The cross was still a problem, and there was a lot that puzzled him, but if evil people have their way, then our humanity will eventually be eroded, we will be less and less at ease with ourselves and our neighbours and eventually evil will win. So it's not really all the mumbo jumbo or the hymns or the services or even the incense that matters, it's that this Jesus person continues to stand up for truth at any price, even the high price of dying and absorbing into himself, the sinfulness of even the moors murderers, so that it can't go on and infect the whole world.

A current song came into his head and he found himself humming along as he walked.

When I'm feelin' blue, all I have to do
is take a look at you, then I'm not so blue.
When you're close to me I can feel your heartbeat,
I can hear you breathing in my ear
Wouldn't you agree, baby you and me
got a groovy kind of love

London was a million miles away from his city. It could have been a different country altogether. But one story that kept appearing in the papers concerned a pair of twins who ran a protection racket in the East End of London.

There was still no arrest and the reporting was hesitant

because of the genuine fear instilled by the reputation of the Krays in London.

The story had broken in March of that year and had been reported on TV and in both national and local papers. A man who had allegedly been linked to the Krays had been killed in The Blind Beggar public house, Whitechapel Road. Intimidation had prevented any witnesses from co-operating with police.

This story linked with the story of the murders in his own city.

Human beings treating other human beings as though their lives had no value. But surely, he reasoned, human life is of the ultimate value? How could people do these things to each other and still live with their consciences?

The questions began to build up in his mind and he found himself reflecting again and again. What is the significance of this building, how does it relate to what is going on, the way that people are destroying each other, the lack of love?

He was still spending some lunch times in his building, he had to agree to spend some time with work colleagues, and some days the weather was too poor to be walking out and risking having to spend the afternoon in the office wearing damp clothes. But he still managed to get down to the church and to spend time in the semi-darkness trying to fathom out answers to the questions spinning around in his mind.

Sometimes he might read from the New Testament. Sometimes there was a new pamphlet in the small library at the back of the church, but sometimes he would just sit and reflect on the words of the pop songs that he so enjoyed.

Eventually a curate came to the parish, a man almost ascetic in his quiet commitment, and whose sense of pastoral care began to make an impression. Eventually the sense of vocation arose as an expression of how he could spend his life in the pursuit of the worthwhile work in which Fr. Hamer was clearly engaged.

The secret of Susan Palmer remained a mystery and his naive sexual experimentation was regularly forgiven by Fr. Hamer who counselled restraint but seemed able to live with the fact that his counsel was routinely ignored.

And it was this, that had in the end, made the most profound impression. That the Church, in the form of Fr. Hamer, could live with the shortcomings and failings of a community that simply couldn't achieve the high standards of premarital chastity, marital fidelity and honesty that the Church through its teachings required of people.

He imagined that, as Fr. Hamer had once explained, despite his natural appetites, lust for life, enjoyment of sex, precociousness, awkwardness, delinquency, and tendency to occasional expressions of violence, he had been loved into believing, and eventually into offering himself for the Church's ministry, for which to his great surprise he had been accepted. Despite the fact that he only rarely attended church, and at that time had no formal academic qualifications at all.

The Chaplain, with a raised eyebrow, archly responded to polite ripples of laughter from the others present, by observing that it had probably been a 'clerical error'.

The Cathedral was in the centre of the City. When he came down for the rehearsal he spent some time hanging out in a record store, listening to some new releases that he'd missed, and spending time chatting up the girl behind the counter before realising that he was going to be late.

When he finally arrived at the Cathedral the rehearsal had started and the verger, viewing his denim jeans and old sports coat, wouldn't let him in and would not believe that he was one of the new clergy being presented as Deacon at the ordination service.

He'd tried to persuade, explain, cajole and eventually voices had been raised in what he was distressed to realise was genuine anger, at least on his part. The commotion had attracted the attention of the Bishop's Chaplain who had been sent down to see what was happening and as he explained later, if necessary call the police.

The verger quickly realised that he'd made a mistake and that his job was on the line and so defended himself by protesting his innocence.

The Chaplain's view of the situation was easy to see, and David recognised that once the Chaplain's ambitions were realised, there would be one Diocese at least, in the Church of England, where David would not be welcome.

Unsound and unsafe. Can't manage people. Loses his temper. And, of course, the flaw that would prove fatal, he was not academic. He could see the entries on his file and he'd not even been ordained. What would they do with him when he was, and they could begin to exercise the authority that comes with the power that is exercised by any institution over people who are dependent on it for their livelihood, their housing and their career development? The pain in his knees was stronger than ever. He knew that it was muscles complaining that they were unused to maintaining the position for so long.

He much preferred to do his praying whilst he walked. He'd once mentioned that to his Tutor at Theological College as part of a justification for missing chapel for a whole term. The Tutor ,who was as mad as a hatter, had suggested that this particular form of praying could be justified because it was, as it were, a pilgrimage, a kind of wandering in the Desert of the Soul in search of the promised land of God's peace, which in time would be given to every genuine searcher and enquirer after truth. Well, he supposed, he was that if he was nothing else. By the time he came to leave Theological College he was clearer than ever that his career in the Church would be a short one unless he could find the right first parish and the right vicar to act as his mentor and in-service trainer to show him the ropes of ministry.

But who?

He went for two interviews. Both were awful. In one he was given a work schedule, that told how he would spend each day. The day would begin and end with an hour in Church, at which each member of the staff team would be required to give an account of their day, and plans for the evening. His one day off a week would be spent away from the parish and he was on no account to make personal friendships amongst the parishioners.

The other began with his arrival at the Vicarage on the Friday night, tired and hungry after a two hundred mile journey. David was shown into the study whilst the Vicar and his family finished their supper. It ended on the Sunday morning when the Vicar asked how he had enjoyed the Eucharist, and David told him clearly that not only had he not enjoyed it, but that he could think of a number of ways, from the greater involvement of lay people, to the use of modern music in which it could have been improved considerably.

The vicar in question, clearly very annoyed by this response, had written to the College Principal, asking for a reference on his spiritual life. It was at this point that EBG had entered the picture.

An old friend of the Principal, EBG was a man of tremendous humanity, a poet of some distinction, but tired and dispirited after a lifetime's ministry in the Church. This had left him unacknowledged and on the sidelines of the Dioceses' affairs in a parish that could never hope to understand the nature of the man they viewed as an eccentric, only to be humored.

As the principal acknowledged, it was a risky placement for a first curacy, but EBG was probably the only person who could survive having him as curate, and where he might stand half a chance of moving to the next step. After a year in the parish he would be made a priest and starting thinking about either a second curacy or possibly, if he did well, being given his own parish.

The visit had been a great success and the two of them had become slowly drunk on an excellent malt whiskey in the vicarage on the Saturday night. EBG had swapped poems for David's confessions about the sexual awakening of a young working class libido, some of which, as the whiskey took hold, were closer to fiction than fact and were mainly stories he'd heard his friends tell, transposed shamelessly to the first person.

To EBG's great delight David had overslept the next day and missed the early service altogether.

He left with EBG's strict instructions that he was to seek another Curacy, as St. Agatha's was totally unsuitable as a training parish, as was EBG himself to be a training Vicar. But David knew that he had made a friendship which would last for a long time to come.

Knowing EBG's disposition and view of the Diocese, he'd never expected him to come to the ordination, and as far as David knew, no one in the parish even suspected that they were about to get a new Curate. There was no house for a Curate and EBG had suggested that he had a room in the Vicarage whilst something was sorted out.

His family weren't there because his Dad's shifts meant that he couldn't get away, and it was an awkward journey from Manchester for his Mother and his two younger Sisters to make on their own.

The others at the Ordination retreat had understood. He knew he wouldn't see much of any of them after this but felt that they'd all been in the same boat and that there was an understanding, and one or two of them under other circumstances he could have sought out as friends. The Bishop had commented that he was disappointed that no one could be bothered to come for such an important occasion, and in a clear reference to the incident with the Verger, had made some reference to an ability to handle difficult churchwardens being a pre-requisite for a successful and happy ministry.

As the great service moved towards its conclusion and he could stand up and walk in procession back to his seat, the pain in his knee began to let up, and as he looked down the line he saw how pleased the others were and realised that it was time to make his farewells, take the Greek New Testament with which he had been presented, and leave.

He'd arrived plain Dave Saxon, known since childhood - although not at theological college - as Dazza. He would leave this great building and this impressive ceremonial, the music of Choir and Liturgy ringing in his ears, The Reverend David Saxon.

And, behind the choral refrain and the becassocked ceremony, the question was still there, persistent, pressing him for an answer, 'in what', it asked, 'do you believe?' 'In whom do you trust?'

Homage

Put out the bunting
Fly the flag
Declare a festal day
Celebrate in silent sound
The choral round
A fell wind stirs the dust
Dry leaves rustling
Whispered like the words
Stirred by the passage of time
Rhythm to the rhyme
The meeting trades in
In silent stillness
Steeped over time
The poet seeks to trace
The same silence in the space
Between words
Casts these dry
Ashes to the hunting wind
Where among the bones
Marked and laid over by stones

Children lark and swing
Under the shadowing tree
Calling the names
Haygarth, Wilson, Seddon
Handley, Metcalfe, Bunting
A timeless place
Where silence is carefully
Practised and tended
Children's rhyming games
Like spells stir names

EBG

Drissburgh

The Vicar of Drissburgh, EBG, had been in the parish for about fourteen years. In some ways he both hated it and loved it. Resented the way in which he had been sent here by the Bishop who had overruled any objections, insisting that he was the right man, and that this was his right job. But, at the same time he was also grateful that in accepting the post he had the wisdom to insist that he was given the freehold of the living. His fear was that when a new Bishop arrived, one whose theology and churchmanship was different to his own, he would set about clearing out the dead wood, as he put it. So, it was the freehold that was EBG's only defence against the politics and the bloodletting that had gone on in the Diocese, which had affected some of his close friends, many of whom had held diocesan jobs alongside their parish appointments.

Before he was ordained, EBG had been invited by the Principal of his college to attend an international Christian youth camp in Holland. It had been a tremendous experience with lectures, debating sessions, lots of wine and beer, and gloriously for the ordinands from England, it had been a mixed conference where young people of both sexes had the opportunity to mingle, develop friendships and debate what kind of future Europe might have in these early postwar years, as the rebuilding of bomb-blasted towns and villages was beginning, and the new postwar economy was beginning to heat up again.

Coming from England where many luxuries were still rationed, EBG found the culture of the conference exciting and stimulating, and it was unsurprising that one evening he found himself in the company of a young Dutch girl, Annya.

As they debated and talked with the other conference delegates, Annya began to tease EBG for his old fashioned attitudes and views, 'You English' she would say, 'you are so old fashioned, Europe is emerging from a dark and difficult period, but we are young and we should enjoy life more, we owe it to ourselves'.

EBG was enthralled by her and by her advanced views, which were like nothing he had heard expressed before.

He soon realised that he was spending more and more time in Annya's company, and that he was beginning to feel more and more drawn toward her.

At breakfast his eyes would scan the room and he would seek her out. Then, having found her, they would spend the day together, sitting together in the same sessions, attending the same lectures.

The other students from his college, noticed this growing intimacy and found it hard to understand. They attempted to draw him away from Annya's company, but the more they pulled in one direction, the more he found himself drawn along a different pathway.

It was still too early, and like many young men of his generation, he was uncertain of his exact feelings. He realised, however, that Annya had all the qualities that he had thought he would want in a companion. Somewhere at the back of his mind, he began to respond to the niggling feeling that here might be someone that he could share more than a few days at a conference with. All that, despite the difference in language, culture, attitude and nationality. Annya might make a wife that any young man would be proud to claim as his own.

Too soon the conference ended, and EBG and his fellow students headed back to college and end-of-term exams. But most crucially, preparations for ordination and the all-important first parish where they were to spend their curacy.

His last exam had ended and EBG was fixed up with a curacy in a northern city.

He was enjoying his last few days at college. Afternoons were spent in the small teashops around the Cathedral Close, rummaging in the bookshops, and window shopping for the right kind of clothes that a curate might wear. Grey slacks, sports jacket, clerical collar of course, and the clerical outfitters near the Cathedral were able to supply most of what he needed.

Having just bought a new shirt he was heading to the Corner Cupboard, a tea shop near the close, to meet up with a couple of friends. Suddenly, he went blind, or least his vision was severely restricted by a pair of hands which were clasped around his eyes, from the back of his head.

He felt that he could sense a familiar scent, and quickly realised that the hands were those of a young woman. Turning, he found himself face to face with Annya.

'What the…?' he shouted, 'Annya, where? How? I

mean, how can this be?'

Annya, let out a delighted chortle.

'I knew that you would be surprised, yes? But I wanted to see you again, and I knew that soon you would be leaving, but I have got a job and we can spend time together, you would like this?'

'Like?' he said, 'I could think of nothing I would like better, it would be smashing, to have you around, but where will you live? What job have you got?

It turned out that Annya had travelled with two other girls from their village near Amsterdam and were working at a local farm. She had Wednesday as her day off, and in her impulsive way had come to the cathedral town to find him, having remembered that he had described the Theological College, set in the historic precincts of the Cathedral Close.

'I am so glad, that I have found you' she said. 'Where can we go?' EBG instinctively invited her back to his rooms for tea. They stopped to buy meringues at the Corner Cupboard, EBG avoiding contact with his friends, and catching up with Annya, steering her by the elbow back to his rooms.

There they sat back, their eyes feasted on the sight of each other. Annya was as lovely as he remembered her, and she was sure that as crazy as it sounded, she was doing the right thing.

Suddenly she stood up, and lifted her blouse, up and over her head, unhooked her bra and faced him. EBG lifted a hand to her breast and caressed her, before taking her nipple into his mouth and kissing her.

It occurred to him in what followed that she was much more experienced than him, he was still a virgin, and that she led him gently but confidently to a point where he could enter her and consummate their relationship.

For EBG, certain things now fell into place. Sex, whether before, during, or after marriage, meant only one thing, and he invited Annya to consider the only possibility that he could now contemplate, which was marriage.

She, for her part, was much less certain than he was for his, but equally she had no desire to hurt him. She really did like this funny Englishman who, old before his time, had set his heart on being a parish priest in his church, in his country, in a grey, monotonous northern city, the likes of which she couldn't begin to imagine.

The problem facing them, and at least as far as EBG knew, the only problem facing them, was that according to the rules of the church at that time, ordination and marriage should be at least a year apart.

As the Principal of his College, advised him, 'either marry a year before ordination as a Deacon, or a year after you are Priested' – the Bishop will not make any exceptions I'm afraid'.

Explaining this to Annya, was even worse that EBG had imagined it might be, she simply could not, would not accept that anyone could be so stupid.

'We are in love' she raged, 'Isn't that enough, what more do they want?'

But no matter how she tried, there was nothing for it but to plan a long engagement.

So EBG took up his curacy.

St Philip's was a large, Victorian gothic mausoleum of a Waterloo church, set in a desert of terraced cottages, just outside the city centre in a bleak part of the town. From its vantage point on the slightly higher ground, it was possible to see the football ground from the church door, but that apart it was a loveless, hostile terrain, with small drinking houses, not even real pubs, with their dark, smoke-filled interiors.

The Vicar was a cold, hardworking man, whose only relationship with his curates, of whom there were three, was strictly formal. He was referred to by all three as Vicar, and the meetings in his study lacked warmth or humour.

EBG reflected at the end of his three years as curate in the parish that he had never set foot into any other part of the house and had only met the Vicar's wife at church and had never had a conversation about any matter of real importance.

Annya simply hated the City. She hated The North and felt her warm, European personality draining away into the cold, grey, damp atmosphere. The job she had found gave her no satisfaction and she was treated badly both at work, where her accent was sufficient grounds for suspicion. Was she German, was often the first thing asked. And her accommodation was poor, the room cold, with no possibility of EBG spending time with her, and certainly no chance of her spending time in his digs.

Bit by bit the attrition consumed what was left of their relationship and Annya felt herself disappearing, each time she looked in the mirror. There seemed to be less than there had been before. She was like a lake that was drying up and she knew that as much as she loved this man, as he did her, if she remained here she knew that by the time the Church would allow them to marry, she would have little or nothing left to give to the relationship; and that the girl whose life and energy, laughter and loveliness EBG had fallen in love with would no longer be there. He would be joining himself hopelessly with a lie.

So one day, without stopping to think or plan or explain she went into the city and bought a one way rail ticket to the port, where she took a ferry to Amsterdam. From there she wrote a letter to EBG trying to explain that if this was the life he had chosen, she had to be honest enough to be clear that it was not a life that she could share. She was afraid that if she did try, and she really had tried, that the life he had chosen would have killed her after it had killed their love for each other.

EBG had gone on to another curacy in the city, this one lasting four years, by which time he had become rather set in his ways and very much the confirmed bachelor.

In time a parish of his own had been offered, and from occasionally he had thought of Annya, and whether there was any possibility of a reconciliation. He dismissed the idea, thinking that in all likelihood she had met someone else and was by now married.

The letter offering him St Agatha's parish came at a point where one or two things in his present parish were coming to a head, and the idea of moving on, a change, a new challenge seemed rather unnecessary to him. So his first response was the standard, 'After much prayerful consideration…', but the Bishop was quite pressing and eventually EBG, not being the kind of person who found standing up to anyone, especially someone in authority, easy, simply said yes.

His first view of St Agatha's was in the rain. A damp sea fret, blown in by an east wind and he thought, no, Annya would hate this, but if it is God's challenge, then I must make the most of it.

The main street of Drissburgh ran down through the village to a T-junction where it branched left and right to run along the coast. Directly ahead a short track ran down to the long disused pier and the coal staithes.

Talk of marinas occasionally raised brief hopes of future prosperity, but it was only ever talk. The company that owned the pier and the staithes had long ago lost interest in this coast, and its property lay neglected. There were few visitors apart from the odd pleasure boat in the silted harbour, and one or two of the older men who still went fishing out beyond the small island beyond Whale Rock and kept the rumours of mackerel alive in the Mermaid Public House.

There were, give or take, a few derelict cottages near the old mine workings, a thousand houses in the village and a population of around five thousand. There was a Co-op store, a newsagent, a hardware store, an off licence, three public houses, a church and three chapels.

Near the centre of the village were some fine houses, double fronted, spacious accommodations that were being sold to off-comers as country retreats for people making money in the city.

These weekenders tended to be church, whilst the

majority of the local people were chapel.

Further out from the centre of the village were a number of council houses on three estates, where the majority of the villagers lived.

Further out again were some farms and farm workers' cottages which, whilst not in the village proper, were still in the parish.

St. Agatha's Church was a stone-built Victorian pile, built a hundred years before from subscriptions collected by a Mrs. Hudson, the wife of the mine owner. This remarkable lady had decided that Drissburgh needed a church of its own, that people should not have to travel the half-hour walk to Worsby. She had stood with her collecting tin with her two daughters each pay day, at the pit head. In this way she collected a thousand pounds which she then matched with a thousand pounds of her own money in order to build and endow the parish church of St. Agatha's named after her own mother.

The church was well situated on a bluff overlooking the sea, and in the lea of the church stood the vicarage, a well-proportioned stone house. Because of its isolation and distance from the diocesan offices, it had escaped the standard ecclesiastical vandalism which sought to renovate such houses in order to build a convenient, modern house to suit, as the blurb had it, the needs of the modern Vicar and his family.

The road past the Church ran up to a headland where it stopped.

There was a turning circle for cars and beyond that a glorious cliff top walk towards the next village up the coast which could only be reached by crossing a fast flowing stream that even at low water was above waist height on an average person.

EBG had arrived in Drissburgh fourteen years ago, and apart from an aside from the Archdeacon at a confirmation some four years before, there had been no indication that anyone in the Diocese had given either him or the parish a moment's further consideration.

Drissburgh was the height of his achievement and the conclusion of a career in the church, and as long as he was left alone to get on with his job as he saw fit, that was fine with him.

His daily schedule consisted of Matins, said in the church at seven, followed by a leisurely breakfast alone in the Vicarage with at least three mugs of tea, toast and Bacon. This was followed by three hours of 'study', which mainly consisted of reading the Times from cover to cover, and on Fridays the preparation of his Sunday sermon. Coffee was taken halfway through the morning, often with his verger Robert Edwards for company, which lasted until lunch. This was followed by a period of flat-out relaxation in summer in the sheltered garden, and in winter under the eiderdown but not actually in the bed itself. Then, at three he would take a well-watered whisky by way of fortification, before setting out on his parish visits. At six he returned to St. Agatha's to say evensong, when he might be joined by his verger Robert Edwards. His evening meal was taken in the Mermaid, by arrangement with the landlord's wife, and any evening engagements, like choir practice, Parochial Church Council, or Mothers' Union preceded his return to the rectory. Then a bottle of the malt whiskey, that was kept for him by the local Co-op, a special order of Talisker, at a special price.

Drissburgh was one of those small semi industrial villages that were scattered along this coast. It was originally a fishing village, reliant on the rural economy, but with the hunger for coal, and the discovery of vast reserves only half a mile or so inland, the village had grown dramatically. It became a major export centre for the coal from Drissburgh pit, with wagonways running directly from the pit head to the staithes, where the wagons were offloaded into small coastal steamers for the journey down to the foundries further south.

Now that king coal's reign had ended, the village was experiencing something of a post-industrial renaissance as the scars of its industrial past were slowly disappearing, and the off comers were arriving to weekend in their semi-rural retreats only an hour's drive or so from the city. Even the Co-op whose most extravagant line had been EBG's Talisker, was beginning to stock an increasing variety of luxury items and had only a matter of weeks before taking delivery of a coffee grinding machine in order to dispense freshly ground beans to its new and more discerning clientele.

This change was having its effect in the life of the church. Many of the off comers were of a church-going inclination, associating church attendance with the quality of life that they were seeking in, and from, Drissburgh. There had recently been pressure from some of the young mothers, for a family service on the Sunday in place of

Matins, 'possibly even a Parish Communion, Vicar?'

Robert Edwards was astounded by the temerity of the request.

'Talking to you like that Vicar' he raged, after all it was well known that no one could talk to the Vicar 'like that' except him. 'Stunting is what I call it, the traditional service has been good enough for us since sixteen sixty two, and now it's not good enough anymore, well I know what Cranmer would say, he wouldn't like it, wouldn't like it at all'.

EBG had long since learned to smile at Bobby's outbursts, knowing that anything he said would only make matters worse. Evensong having finished, they walked from Church back down to the village toward The Mermaid, where Bobby would walk further to his house on the council estate. There he lived with his wife, who was the PCC Secretary and Treasurer, and their forty year old son, a diabetic, who needed constant supervision.

As they walked EBG realised that this might be the opportunity he needed to alert them to the imminent arrival of David, the new, and as yet unannounced curate, whose ordination on Sunday meant that he would be arriving in the parish in time for Evensong on Sunday.

He also realised that if he mishandled things, not only would his life be a misery for months to come, but David's ministry might be blighted from the start.

EBG knew that he needed Bobby's support because he would make sure that the churchwardens cooperated, and that the church council accepted the news without the kind of full-scale declaration of hostilities between themselves and the vicarage that had accompanied some of EBG's less well-handled or less popular decisions. One such was the introduction of candlelight at the service of nine lessons and carols. This was 'stunting' at its worst, and the fact that the church had been full, and that many of the new people who had spent Christmas in the village, had attended with their children had no effect whatsoever on Bobby. Especially so when he heard from the cleaners that there was wax on the pews, some of the hassocks and the nave carpet.

Eventually, after a heated debate, the PCC had ruled that the 'experiment' had failed, and that next year the service would be lit in the normal way by electric light. EBG thought that he must have imagined hearing the phrase 'As God intended' but wasn't sure.

Of course on hearing the news, the young mothers, who had formed a kind of young wives' group in opposition to the Mothers' Union had proposed a counter resolution, and it was only after considerable effort on his part, and the exercise of what he thought of as consummate chairmanship, that EBG had managed to effect a compromise by introducing a Christingle Service. This gave the young children their candles, and to which the PCC couldn't object too forcefully because the collection would go to the Children's Society. This would help the parish reach this year's Missionary giving target. There had been a shortfall in the last two years' total, which had resulted in a difficult, time-consuming correspondence with the Diocesan Secretary.

Sensing the importance of getting things right EBG

steered Bobby into the lounge bar of the Mermaid and bought him a pint. His own well-watered whisky, The Mermaid kept Glenmorangie on one side for the Vicar, being served without his asking.

'Hilda won't mind this once and there's some important church business I need to discuss with you'.

Bobby in The Mermaid was a sight rarely seen, and his presence attracted some comment from the regulars, but they were left alone. EBG spelt out the problems as he saw them, the pressure on his own time, the changes in the village, the new people with their modern ideas, with which in the most part he was out of sympathy, the divisions that were emerging within the Church and within the village. All of this, he explained, had led him to the conclusion that the parish needed some new blood.

As he hoped, he could see that Bobby was beginning to think the worst, that he was being told that EBG was about to resign and leave. That would mean all sorts of dreadful things, not only diocesan interference, because the Bishop was Patron of St. Agatha's and had the right to appoint whoever he chose as Vicar.

Far worse it would mean a visit from the Archdeacon, and the parish, really meaning Bobby himself, having to surrender control of some of the peculiar ways that were part of their unique administration of the parish. Worse still, it would also have meant having to control and manage the enthusiasms of a new man, a man whose churchmanship might not suit St. Agatha's, or worse, someone who would take the side of the new people against the old members who had faithfully served the church for years, hundreds of years it seemed in some cases, EBG thought ruefully.

'No' said EBG, in anticipation of Bobby's question, 'I'm not leaving'. And he went on to explain that he had been contacted by an old friend of his, Harold McMillan, who was Principal of a Theological College in the South.

Harold had told him about this promising young man who was looking for a first curacy. The man, David, had achieved an awful lot, in succeeding at theological college especially, since he had come from a fairly poor working class background. David had made the transition without losing his sense of perspective, and Harold thought that he would have a great deal to offer a parish like St Agatha's with its unusual social mix.

Harold had suggested that David should join him as curate of St. Agatha's. The diocese had miraculously, agreed both to ordain and pay this new deacon and licence him to serve as Curate of St. Agatha's.

Bobby would, EBG was certain, recognise that this was quite a feather in St. Agatha's cap because it meant that it was seen as a training parish for new clergy.

The only problem was that the parish had to find a house, but as the man was single he had agreed to stay in the Vicarage to start with.

EBG could see that he was doing a good selling job, because Bobby's only question was about when the man would start, 'He's coming on Sunday', replied EBG, 'and he should arrive for Evensong'.

Bobby sipped his pint and thought carefully. 'What will it cost us?' he asked, EBG knowing that that was the first question he would be asked when he got home.

'Possibly some expenses' EBG replied, 'but the Diocese is bearing the cost of the stipend, and the rent for his accommodation', he added as an afterthought.

It would certainly help us, Bobby thought, what with the new people and their constant demand for new family-friendly services, a youthful new curate would be an ideal addition, and it would take quite a load of the Vicars shoulders.

'Well, Vicar' he said, 'I'll talk to Hilda, but I'm sure she will agree, if you think it's right for the parish'.

There was no doubt that EBG had sold the idea well, and Bobby finished his pint, lit a cigarette and went off home to tell the good news to Hilda.

EBG enjoyed his supper that evening, it was the landlady's specialty, beef and mushrooms with dumplings in red wine gravy.

There was no meeting that evening and EBG returned to the Vicarage thinking that an evening with Mr. Talisker, a book of poems, Auden perhaps, and Radio Three would bring the day to a good and well-deserved conclusion.

Poetry is all artifice and tricks

Poetry is all artifice and tricks
Making new art from old licks
Poets inventing pain they are not feeling
From the work of others, unaware they must be stealing
Sometimes they read the writing
And transfer as they are reading
Emotions, stresses, heartaches and strain
You cannot fairly steal another's pain
So round they go these written verses
Each adapting to renewed purpose
Quite leaving reader and writer out of breath
Like a stunt rider on the wall of death

EBG

First Days

The train from the City left at 3:40 in the afternoon and pulled into Drissburgh at around 5:30. It was Sunday, and there were few other passengers, so David had a compartment almost to himself.

He had very little luggage, a suitcase and a rucksack, a few books and a change of clothes. As the train pulled out from the station there was a sense of relief and he felt himself relaxing. He pulled a book from his rucksack and settled to reading.

The train wound its way out through the suburbs slowly. This being Sunday, there were the inevitable engineering works, and as the train crawled along David became aware of the changing landscape. The concentric rings of urban development, change, decay, and regeneration. Staring into the backs of houses and gardens. The ornamental ponds, the pigeon lofts, the neglected gardens of the houses in multiple occupation, the tidy gardens of the retired and the family gardens with their mini football pitches and basketball courts.

Eventually, the city fell away and the landscape gave way to small villages and isolated farms and cottages.

Each stop felt more isolated, more rural, and for David a growing unease over what he had done, leaving his job, his friends and his family for this strange new existence as a curate in a forgotten and isolated part of the diocese.

Drissburgh Station was about a mile away from the

village centre and David set off at a purposeful pace thinking that if he could, he would arrive in time for evensong and sit with the congregation in order the better to get a feel of what the church was about, and how (if) he might fit in, to this new life he had chosen.

Arriving in good time, the bells were still ringing as he came up the church path, the sides-man on duty looked him up and down carefully, too carefully David thought.

'Is the Vicar around' David asked?

'There's a service about to begin' came the stony reply, 'The Vicar's busy just now, but if you want to wait outside …' and the sidesman's response tailed off to nothing.

David realised immediately what was happening. He had been mistaken for a traveller, an easy mistake as he was carrying two bags, and travellers, especially young single men, asking to see the Vicar before a service, usually meant that they were asking for money, or somewhere to stay.

David wondered whether to explain, but some deep seated, inchoate feeling of anger arose from somewhere deep down in the pit of his stomach, and which was not about to be easily controlled. It seemed to take over and respond before he could offer the simple explanation that would help make a poor start better.

'Could you just tell the Vicar that there is someone here to see him' he began.

But before he could finish, the door was opened, and the voice tremulous with barely concealed emotion, 'be a good lad, eh? Let's not have any trouble, it's a nice evening, now why not just wait outside?'

David's anger now began to rise, he felt his face redden,

and then just as he started to square up to the sidesman, a small grey haired man, wearing a cassock came out of the vestry, he came across immediately with a questioning look on his face, 'Is there a problem?' he asked.

'No, Bobby' the sidesman replied, this young man is going to wait outside for the Vicar, 'aren't you' he muttered to David between gritted teeth.

David thought to himself this is going from bad to worse and was about to reply when the cassocked man asked,

'Are you David?'

'Yes I am'. David replied.

'Good, the vicar is expecting you, but didn't think you'd get here until later'.

The sidesman looked puzzled and only partially relieved that he had been rescued. But he let it go and David was escorted through the back of the church, under the tower and into the vestry.

'David' said EBG, 'glad you made it, will you preach for us?'

David looked aghast which made EBG laugh. EBG continue, 'no, relax, maybe for tonight you can sit in the congregation and see how we do things at St Agatha's.

After the service they headed back to the vicarage with the sides-man's churlish farewell to EBG and a look of straightforward hostility directed at David's retreating back.

Doubtless he would be interrogating Bobby whilst the collection was being counted and the silver returned to the safe.

And so the first days of his new life began. There were services, a first funeral to be taken, visiting to be undertaken and one extremely grumpy sidesman to be avoided.

Nothing had prepared him for this change. Certainly not Theological College, which whilst it had pretty much always been both enjoyable and challenging, had failed to reckon with the reality that was life in the local parish church. David smiled to himself. What would people say if he began to explain some of the ideas and theories that had abounded amongst the staff and students at college.

What struck him was what EBG had called the 'hands together, eyes-closed approach of so many of the congregation at St Agatha's. There was an approach to, and an understanding of religion, that was not even in any meaningful sense, folk religion.

EBG had told him recently that one of his regular sermons, preached about every eighteen months or so, was a sermon which he had originally based on the first New Testament lecture at theological college. There it had been called 'The Synoptic Problem', but in Drissburgh and in EBG's previous parish it had been called Mark One – that is until a clothing store of that name had opened in the nearby town and EBG had renamed it Mark First.

David realised that he was going to have to rethink his approach. He had thought of himself as an ordinary person, working class, certainly, someone who could communicate with his own people in a language that could be understood. But after his first sermon, an elderly lady had told him that he was 'too clever for us, you should be at the cathedral or somewhere where people can understand you'.

So he began to experiment, not only with his language, use of words and illustrations, but also to make sure that his one point was made, reinforced and restated before he sat down.

It was also clear that his less orthodox ideas were best kept to himself. For some time at college he had played with the idea of light being a metaphor. Whether it was light as it shimmered on the water, or light falling mysteriously and radiantly through a window, with its refracted colours and the dust suspended glistening and glittering. Light was both illuming and dazzling. Light was his God and it was light he worshipped. Light that both gave and sustained life.

So much of his early life had been in darkness. He realised that his family was simply too poor to afford large electricity bills and lights were switched off if no-one was in a room and sometimes even when they were. On one occasion when he was trying to pull together the certificates he needed to get into college he was studying alone in the front room, which was rarely used, and according to his mother had to be 'kept for best'. Suddenly the door opened, his father glared at him, and then switched the light off and shut the door.

When he had told EBG this story the vicar had laughed and said, 'well, you know how to tell the difference between the vicar and the curate, don't you?'

David had played the straight man as required and asked the naïve question.

'The curate goes round switching the lights on and the vicar switches them off' chuckled EBG.

Each morning David walked to church to say the early service with EBG. It was only a short walk from the small cottage below the church, which the parish was renting as a temporary curate house since he and EBG had agreed that his sharing the vicarage was not going to work for either of them.

Every morning as he walked he noticed the quality of the light shining on the water. Walking up to church, with a sun rising behind him, his slight figure casting long shadows in a morning sun, he would find his gaze drawn out across the ocean to the play of sun on water.

Such endless eternal brilliance, even on dark and overcast days, seemed to him to suggest that somehow the created order, nature itself, was the celebration that demanded a response. Not some faded, philosophical construct, but nature itself, which even now was slowly reworking and renewing the damage done by man's poor stewardship of what nature had given him in trust.

And in church each morning for the service he would find his heart uplifted by the light that filtered through the high windows at the top of the central aisle. It was, he thought, a sign of hope for a troubled people at a troubled time.

After the early service he would join EBG for breakfast at the vicarage. This informal session enabled them to stay in touch with what the other was doing, and to bring some semblance of planning to what was effectively a chaotic pastoral and parish administration. This administration was often held together only by the intervention of Bobby Edwards, who would always know before either of them when it was time to change the liturgical colours, when a saint's day was in the offing, who was sick and needed visiting, and when the sick communions were due.

He realised that some of what he had been warned about at college was beginning to come true. His days lacked a pattern or a structure. Often he would spend the morning at the headland staring out to sea, or other days with a book curled up in the small front room of his cottage.

At EBG's suggestion he visited some of the main members of the congregation of St. Agatha's. They were mainly people whose association with the church went back years, but all he gained from this exercise was a strong sense that people thought that it was time the vicar moved on and that Bobby Edwards should have less influence at the Vicarage. Sharing these revelations with EBG simply brought a scarcely veiled smile to his lips, and the sense that, of course, he knew what his young colleague would hear and that was the point of sending him on these visits in the first place.

For David, after three years at theological college, the first few weeks in the parish were claustrophobic in the extreme. He had moved from a small but cultured community, many of whose members were openly gay, to a largely elderly community where any enjoyment of sex, and the laughter that was the only sensible response to religion taking itself too seriously, had been swept away by the austerity of life and the winds that blew in from the ocean.

David had chosen St. Michael's Theological College as the place for his theological education because it was beautiful. The day he'd visited had been a warm, soft, summer's day. David hitched down from Manchester the night before and changed into his John Collier's fifty shilling suit in the toilets in the Market Place. He then walked across the ancient close, dominated by the magnificent spire of the Cathedral, and knocked hesitantly on the college door.

He'd contrasted the sheer beauty of the Close and the magnificent Cathedral, with his own street in Manchester and had thought how it would be if he could spend three years in such a marvellous place. Just to be surrounded by beauty on this scale after Beswick was a prize in itself, even if it came to nothing. But if it did, he imagined that he would return to the industrial north in due course to spend his working life as a priest, so why not enjoy his studies in such a fine place.

The door was opened by a clergyman who greeted him with a broad north-country accent and introduced himself as Harold McMillan the Principal. Taking him by the arm, which he gave an affectionate and hardly necessary squeeze, Harold introduced him to the staff who were having their coffee in the Senior Common Room. This was before taking him through to the room where some of the students were sitting talking and taking their mid-morning break. He was put in the care of two students who were to show him the college, and the town before bringing him back for lunch and his formal interview.

The interview was over almost before it began and Harold, commenting on the three years' work that had gone into acquiring 'O' and 'A' Level successes, had suggested that work in the college would be less arduous than that, and that if he showed the same commitment at St. Michaels as he had during his pre-theological studies he should complete the course satisfactorily.

His journey back to Manchester was a journey into the past. Not into some metaphorical past that had existed and gone, but a past that was being lived as present by its inhabitants. It was a past of cobbled streets glistening with rain, of small factories and workshops belching out the pollution that covered roof tops with the grimy soot that dulled the sun's light when it shone on the slates. It was a past of hard, back-breaking work that killed those who were forced to participate in its rigorous disciplines, simply because they had been born here and fetched up there.

For David, he realised now, the letter of acceptance when it came was received with all the pleasure that a prisoner might know when he received notice of his parole.

The church, and theological college, meant a release from the inevitability of this life. Whilst it was true that society at that time was in transition, and that the cold war and nuclear weapons meant that international crises caused people at all levels of society to fear for their safety and for their future.

Alongside this public anxiety there were new technologies, increased personal affluence, foreign holidays, and new music emerging from northern cities and from London, repackaging and introducing, blues from the American South.

David recalled the first time that he had heard The Beatles sing 'Love Me Do' on the Radio, Two-Way Family Favourites, and he was enthralled. Here, suddenly and without warning was a music that spoke to him of his own life, his own dreams and his own ambition.

Fr Hamer, for whom David had been a source of considerable pleasure and pride as his vocation had blossomed, received the news with mixed emotions and it was only later, as David was leaving, that he was able to express what he really felt in wishing David well for the future.

It concerned an incident that had happened early in David's time at the church. He had been attending the youth club which took place with the reluctant agreement of the PCC after Evensong on Sundays.

David had not been the only ordination candidate in the parish, an older man, a teacher at the local grammar school had offered himself a few months before David and the PCC had welcomed and approved his candidacy.

Fr Hamer had voiced some misgivings as to his suitability but had been overruled by both the PCC and the Rector.

Unfortunately the man had been turned down, and he had somehow blamed the curate for this failure as he saw it.

When Fr Hamer had then supported David, against the advice of both the PCC and the Rector, who made it clear that they thought he was wasting his time and energy on someone who wouldn't ever make it through the system, which was seen as fairly rigorous, Julian, the man in question took it as a personal affront.

One Sunday evening after evensong, during the youth club meeting, Julian arrived and asked to speak to Fr Hamer. They sat in a corner of the large hall and spoke quietly so as not to be overhead. Suddenly, to the consternation of the young people, Julian's voice was heard shouting and as he stood up suddenly he knocked his chair backwards.

Fr Hamer also stood up and at that moment Julian raised a fist to strike the curate. Without stopping to think David ran across the room, caught Julian' outstretched arm and his clenched fist, turned him abruptly, caught him by the front of his shirt and tie and marched him backwards out of the hall before dumping him unceremoniously on his backside in the gravel.

Julian was furious, but before he could storm back into the church hall to finish what he had started, David made it clear in uncompromising words that could not be mistaken, what the consequences would be if Julian ever tried such a trick again.

Fr Hamer was visibly shaken and thanked David for his intervention. Later that month David was taken to meet Fr Hamer's own theological college principal, and if he was not mistaken, offered a place. But in the end he had chosen St Michael's.

St. Michaels was not a disappointment. The lectures and seminars were stimulating and there was a good deal of freedom. David quickly made friends with a couple of like-minded people who, like him, were in the first year, and settled down to a life that any normal undergraduate would have recognised but which for David was both revealing and startlingly decadent at the same time.

He quickly mastered the art of scaling the close walls after the gates were locked at 11:00 pm, and on more than one occasion managed the feat whilst holding a pint glass and not spilling a drop, even when jumping the last three or four feet to the ground. He even, for one spell, managed to acquire a key, quietly letting himself in via the kitchen door rather than going to the lengths of arranging to have windows or fire escapes left open by the less adventurous students.

The key was reclaimed when he met Harold one night, leaving college to return to his own house, by the same door that David was entering long after the cathedral clock had stuck two.

The group of friends that worked there through the three years of theological education, together formed a close society. Drinking, womanising, borrowing cars for fast drives to the coast, and on one occasion borrowing a car that was not insured and ending up in the St. Michael's Magistrates Court. They were all on various charges related to driving the vehicle, but mainly for the unspoken offence of being in the south with a northern accent. This was not helped by answering the arresting officer without the respect he felt he deserved from these future 'gentlemen of the cloth'.

There had been an affair. It was love at first sight for David and he'd tried hard to save it when it started to fall apart. They met when he was walking through town one morning, and Sarah was walking into work. David's daily routine was to walk out after breakfast to look in the bookshops, read the magazines in W H Smith's, before heading back for his first lecture. This morning with his friends he was admiring a shirt in a new shop that had recently opened. The shirt was purple, and David rather liked the idea of wearing purple when the bishop of the diocese, who was the colleges' visitor, came on an official visit later in the term.

As he was admiring the shirt, he saw a young girl's reflection in the shop window and turning sought her opinion. She was very open and quite unlike the giggling girls that David remembered from his Manchester days. His friends made a discreet departure heading back for college and David decided that he could catch up on the Chaplain's Old Testament seminar at a later date and asked if he could walk to work with her.

She worked in a boutique in the touristy end of town, where the half-timbered buildings were half standing, to the delight of the American tourists that descended on the town by the coach full in the summer. Arriving at the shop, she invited him in for a coffee, and they chatted, until her boss arrived at ten.

He asked if they could meet later, and they agreed to meet for a drink when she finished work at six. For David the arrangement meant missing evensong and his evening meal, but he didn't care. At six he was sitting by the door of the Old Tavern, waiting, and at ten past she came in. After buying their drinks they sat and chatted like old friends.

Without seeming to plan it, their relationship quickly

became physical and intensely intimate. For David it was a new experience to meet someone who simply enjoyed the physical expression of love so obviously and without guilt. Any thought of morality seemed out of place because their love was the most moral thing he had ever experienced, and when Sarah brought things to an end he was heartbroken -- the more so because he didn't lose her to someone else, but to the knowledge, which she faced more honestly than he did, that she was not prepared to share his life as a curate's or a vicar's wife.

He saw her from time to time after their relationship ended, and when he left college sent her an invitation to his ordination, but she did not reply.

After Sarah, there were a couple of other girls but his heart was not in the business of giving or receiving love; so after a couple of evenings these new relationships would lapse. David sensed that if he was not careful he might find himself defaulting into the solitary life.

Now that he was in the parish, after the initial excitement at the arrival of this unexpected and slightly strange young curate as a colleague for EBG, a couple of the older ladies began to invite him for lunch and for supper. But the younger and more eligible female members of the congregation remained aloof, maintaining a safe distance between themselves and the curate.

His reputation for strangeness started almost immediately after his arrival. Sometime before, when he was at St. Michael's a well-known radical clergyman, renowned for his espousal of radical causes had arrived to lead a college conference on religion and politics. Of his various recommendations, including renewed support amongst theological college students for the armed struggle, he'd suggested that once in their parishes the students should read two papers. These were *The Times* as 'work' and *The Mirror* 'in order to understand how working class people were thinking and feeling'. David had been taken by this suggestion and immediately recommended that the college subscribe to the *Morning Star* as one of the papers delivered each day to the common room. Once in the parish, in fact on his first morning, he had gone down to the local paper shop to order *The Morning Star*, much to EBG's genuine amusement, to be delivered to the Vicarage.

At the paper shop it was assumed that this young man in tee shirt, jeans and sandals was a relative of the vicar's, in Drissburgh for a holiday. Accordingly she had been pleasant and welcoming and it was not until the following Sunday when she was introduced to David as the new curate that she sensed, as she complained to EBG later, that she had been shown up because she had treated David like he was an ordinary person and not given him the respect due to one of the cloth.

EBG's view of this was his usual amusement at the effect that his new colleague was having, as he told David, 'you're like a barium meal, revealing some of the truth that this place wants to hide about itself'.

For David the seeds of doubt about his vocation, calling, and the way of life he had chosen, were sown in these first few weeks in the parish. It was inevitable as he knew, a whole range of new experiences, new faces, new people making demands on him, new skills to be learned, sermons to prepare and preach and no one to share his feelings with and thrown more and more onto a dialogue with himself to understand what was happening and what was possible.

And these dialogues were conducted with himself while on long walks across the roaring headland. There, he could shout into the wind, which would tear his language from him and give him in return only the echoing silence. He would sit at above the bay and watch the fish swim in search of food. Occasionally he would look down into the water, which on calm days would sometimes be almost completely clear, and he would see one enormous fish which would swim in wide sweeps around the bay, just flicking its tail idly. It was as though it was in search of something, some secret or some knowledge, that once known would make sense of the world and the purpose of existence.

He began in time to come to terms with the sense that being was as important as doing. He began to be given, and to accept, more responsibility as curate of the parish as EBG recognised his fast developing maturity in the job.

David realised that the priestly vocation is one of enormous privilege, that at its heart there lies a trust in which, and by which, the priest is invited into the lives of his parishioners as an honorary member of the family; when that family is undergoing some crisis, celebrating a new birth through baptism, creating a new family unit, through marriage, or undergoing the trauma of loss and bereavement.

For David, this ministry of acceptance and blessing of the lives of his parishioners was worthwhile. What he found difficult, as he tried to explain to EBG, and occasionally to Bobby Edwards, was the congregation, which seemed to collect together all the misfits and hopeless cases in Drissburgh, throw them together in a cocktail of psychologies and pathologies, and then compound the felony by referring to them as the Body of Christ. A less likely or less attractive body could you hope to find.

For EBG, who quietly agreed with his young colleague, but who felt loyalty to the congregation, some of whose members at least he counted as friends. The tension of the vicar curate relationship was not entirely a healthy one. But he found David strangely attractive and his company and sermons at times enormously compelling, and so found himself defending David when the Bishop's Chaplain came to interview him about how things were working out now that David had arrived.

The Chaplain's visit marked the end of the first period of David's ministry and preceded a special conference for the newly ordained clergy from the diocese.

'I rather think' opined the Chaplain 'that David will be the sort of priest whose ministry will be of value to a certain kind of person outside the church'. EBG retorted sharply that in his view there was only one kind of priest, and that was the priest who exercised a ministry of word and sacrament, a ministry that David was fulfilling with remarkable maturity for one as young as he was.

But he knew, as he spoke, that the man in front of him had already made his mind up about his curate and that

David's future, like his own, was in the hands of a self-seeking career clergyman whose star was in the ascendant, and about whom bishops would write letters to each other saying how pleased they were to have him in their Diocese. His photograph would appear in the *Church Times* with nauseating regularity as he wormed his way through the system to the very top of the barrel of rotten apples that represented the higher reaches of the Church of England's full time ministry.

St Agatha's Churchyard 1967

Silently, ghostly figures
Assemble, in the churchyard
Beneath the cedars to raise a merry
Carolling to celebrate the birth of Christ the king
Stabled, mangered, blessed
And worshipped now as then
A soft breeze stirs
The canopy as the Cedars brace
Themselves for the coming storm
And a mid winter evening sun
Sets on this ancient ground
Solid, comforting
Weathered, persisting
The church is dedicated
To place and purpose
In the graveyard
The names of villagers
Memorialised in stone
Who have passed this way

Rest now their names
Sifted through Yorkshire earth
Becoming one with time and place
There is a pattern of celebration
And of grieving, of life's, the year's
Beginnings and endings
Recorded in the dusty books
In registrars ink, stored
In the oak chest in the vestry
English names which when spoken
Signify the peopling of this earth
This place, this time

EBG

The Uncertainty
Begins

———

For David, the life he was now embracing, seemed to have less and less in common with the life he had imagined.

Following that first hearing of the Beatles, like many young men of his generation, he had almost unconsciously emulated the look, in particular of the lead singer.

When David attended his selection conference the chairman had greeted him affectionately and at the first meal, had patted the empty chair next to him. 'Do sit with me dear boy', he had said by way of an invitation, which was at the same time a command.

There had followed a long, and at times difficult-to-follow conversation about music, music groups, church music, hair styles, monks and black polo necks as the must-have uniform of the next generation of young clergy, especially if they had a white roll neck.

David laughed politely at the jokes, some of which he understood, and some of which he definitely did not, and he remembered wondering what was underlying this far too familiar and at times overly familiar atmosphere.

The chairman, in his interview had asked David how he would approach the chairing of a PCC. David had only had one experience of such a meeting, when he was asked along to explain some accidental damage which had happened at the youth club, at a dance night, where there had been a real band.

The meeting had wanted to close the youth club immediately and Fr Hamer had asked David to come along and explain just how important the youth club was for the young people.

That first experience had appalled him and now here he was at his first PCC meeting as the new curate.

David had entered the church hall to be greeted by Mrs Jones and Gina, her daughter, who had been in Church on the Sunday when he had been introduced to the small congregation, and on every Sunday since as far as he knew.

As he crossed the hall to find a chair at the back, he could hear a couple of the members that he'd not yet seen in church, and who had not been on EBG's visiting list, asking who he was.

'The new curate' declared Gina, 'isn't he dreamy?' she asked. 'He's my new friend'.

The meeting was a tedious affair; it was clear to David that EBG hated the whole business and Hilda Edwards as Treasurer and Secretary dominated the proceedings, assisted by Bobby who throughout the meeting, referred to his wife as Madam Secretary or Madam Treasurer.

Any suggestion, proposal or contribution to debate what she disapproved of, was met by a scornful response and the ultimate sanction which effectively stopped any proposal in its tracks, was the threat to withdraw her cooperation completely. 'As long as they're prepared to do _all_ the work themselves, let them get on with it, but you can count me out vicar' she would say. In the silence that followed EBG would move on to next business.

David could see why EBG's whiskey consumption went up on PCC nights.

The meeting was scheduled to start at 7:00 pm and EBG arrived breathless at 7:01 pm. David knew that his whole day had been spent in preparation for the meeting, that he'd spent the morning writing poetry, and that after lunch and his afternoon nap he'd had a long and idle bath until four when had David called with a message following an afternoon spent visiting. EBG had missed evensong that day, which was unusual for him, and most of the three hours immediately prior to the meeting had been spent playing the piano to calm his nerves, finishing in time to rush round to the Hall just one strategic minute late and open the meeting with prayer.

Throughout the meeting Gina kept turning round to smile at David and it was no surprise when after the meeting, Mrs Jones came over to invite him to Sunday lunch, David thought it wise to plead another commitment.

The meeting had gone reasonably well with no major upsets or fallings out until the item of the new curate was reached.

At this point Hilda Edwards reported that the new curate's arrival would mean an extra expense to cover the rent on the Shooting Lodge, a small one-roomed cottage on Front Street overlooking the sea.

The cottage was in a prime location in the Village and had belonged to an elderly man, something of a recluse, who had lived there until his death earlier that year. At one time the house had been on the market and a number of bids had been received from people seeking to acquire it as a holiday cottage. Eventually the Estate Agent handling the sale had bought the cottage as an investment property, and had advertised it for rent just around the time that EBG and David were agreeing that David needed a place of his own, as they both valued their privacy.

Hilda explained that the modest rent meant that the PCC budget needed revising to cover an extra £200 a year, but as David's stipend was being paid by the diocese, and his expenses, fortunately only a pound or two a month, were being borne out of his own pocket, the parish was being given a real opportunity to develop the work in the parish.

EBG, knowing that his high-handedness in inviting David to come before getting the agreement of the PCC, could be properly criticised, was strangely quiet. A question from the back of the meeting was then asked by one of the people who had asked who David was when he arrived, 'Wasn't it' they asked, 'the PCC's job to ask the diocese for a curate, and shouldn't they have been consulted before the decision was taken?' In the silence a number of people turned to stare fixedly at David as much as to say, 'you'll see lad, who's boss in this parish, it's the ones as pay'.

The discussion that followed rapidly became heated and EBG and the Edwards found themselves quickly isolated. For David it was a thoroughly humiliating position to be placed in, and he felt himself reddening with embarrassment and anger in equal proportions.

Eventually a compromise was reached, which meant that David was on probation for his first year, when the situation was to be reviewed by the PCC. A final motion was passed which made the decision to have curates at St. Agatha's a matter for the PCC to decide, although it was acknowledged in an amendment that the choice of person should be left to the vicar.

As the meeting was breaking up one elderly man took him by the arm and muttered, 'nothing personal, lad'. Another person who he had seen serving in the Co-op store asked if he'd heard of the tragedy being suffered by the Blackburn's. 'They had' she explained' 'been a big church family but they'd fallen out with EBG and had started going to the Chapel'. It appeared that the son was dying of a brain tumor at home and the whole family was there with him, 'I'm sure they'd appreciate a visit from you, just so they know the church cares'. David took a note of the name and address and promised to visit next day.

So, the next day he found himself standing at the door of the small, neat bungalow, with its well-tended garden, waiting for someone to answer the door.

The elderly man who answered, looked angry and close to tears. David explained that he was from St. Agatha's, that he'd heard that the son was not well, and had called round to offer his support and prayers.

The man had simply exploded on the doorstep. 'Fuck off', he'd shouted, 'fucking church, we're not fucking interested in church or God or fucking Jesus, they've not helped us and we're not wanting any help from you or from the church, so fuck off and leave us alone!'

David was stunned. Nothing at St. Michael's had

prepared him for a reaction like this. His pastoralia classes had taught him that when you went visiting, people welcomed you, and your ministrations were valued. But the people who taught these classes at theological colleges were hardly the most experienced priests. As there was nothing he could do, he turned and started back down the path.

The slamming of the door was immediately followed by its being opened again and a woman's voice calling after him. 'Please, don't go. My husband's just upset, our son's dying you see, and we're frightened, we've never had anything like this happen before'. Catching him up, she clung to his arm, 'please come in, say a prayer with us, please'.

David turned and went back toward the house. He noticed next door's curtains flutter as he stepped inside. The man who had answered the door stood back to let him in, saying nothing, but staring dully as he passed. Inside the room there was a bed with a shaven-headed man, lying apparently asleep. Sitting around the bed were a young woman with a drawn, tear-streaked face, and two bedraggled children. As he came in the man opened his eyes and asked who he was. Before he could reply the older woman, who had followed him into the room said, 'it's the curate Bill, come to see how you are'. The man smiled weakly 'I'm dying' he said, 'anyone can see that'.

'No' said the older woman, 'the doctor says you're getting stronger everyday', but the man looked blankly back and made a gesture in David's direction as if to say, you don't need me to draw a picture just look.

David could see that the man was on the very edge of life, clinging desperately, and relying on enormous reserves of willpower to survive. He wasn't sure what he should do next, and he could feel their eyes on him as though expecting him to say or do something miraculous, as though he might restore the man to life and to his family.

David was aware that the silence had lasted too long, but before he could speak, the young woman let out a ghastly shriek and threw herself onto the prostrate form of the man, hugging him in a tight embrace and kissing him feverishly, and all the time crying 'don't leave us, don't go'. Her words tailed off into a wail of distress that made her sound like a wounded animal, and as she lay there the man reached out and pulled at the front of her clothes so that her breasts were exposed and leaning forward appeared to be sucking from her nipple as though he was desperately trying to discover a source of the renewing of life from his wife's body.

The scene, which was clearly a repeat of some continuing drama being acted out in this tragic house, brought an immediate response from the older couple who dragged the wife away, desperately trying to cover her up as they did so. The father tried to console her whilst the mother used her hand to soothe her son's brow. David heard himself saying, surprised by his presence of mind, and in a way quite impressed with the way he was handling himself, 'let us pray' and to his amazement the group bowed their heads, put their hands together as though they were in Sunday school and waited for him to lead them.

Later, walking away from the house, he kept reflecting on the scene, and thought of his fellow students and what they were experiencing. Lost in such reflections he was startled by the sound of a motorcycle pulling up next to him and a voice shouting above the rasp of the engine 'well, curate, and what're doin' then?' Turning, he recognised Sam Trader on one of his collection of vintage motorcycles.

Sam, was a local character who made a living buying and selling old, and sometimes genuinely vintage cars and bikes. David had already come across him when he tried to buy a car so that he could get home to Manchester more easily to see his own family. Sam had tried to sell him an old VW that had seen better days and which was a dubious prospect for the MOT. Eventually he had acquired an altogether more reliable, but less interesting Mini, in which he was planning his first visit home after Evensong on Sunday for a couple of days before returning for his first post-ordination conference.

Having established that David was not busy, Sam persuaded him to climb into the side car, which needed the ballast provided by David's weight, to stabilise the outfit, and together they roared off out of the village away from the coast and out on the Worsby Road.

As they drove along at what to David seemed a frightening speed Sam kept up a shouted commentary most of which was swept away by the wind. What he gathered was that the bike was a 1937 Brough Superior, fitted with a 1000cc JAP engine. Not JAP thought David, surely there were no JAP motorcycles in 1937. According to Sam, such a bike as this had established a world speed record in 1937 at nearly 170 mph. David imagined from where he was sitting in the sidecar, that they were in danger of exceeding that record at any moment.

They returned to the village by way of a narrow lane that finally entered the housing estate where Bobby and Hilda lived and became in effect, a fairly suburban street. Sam dropped him off by The Mermaid and he decided to stop in for a drink before heading for home.

Sitting in the corner of the bar were a couple of the women he recognised from the group of younger wives that were trying to effect changes at St. Agatha's. David, having got his drink, wandered across to their table and asked if he might join them.

It turned out that they were discussing a fashion show which had been one of the items on last night's PCC agenda, and which Hilda had reported rather frostily as a disappointment 'in more ways than one'.

The show had been sponsored on behalf of a catalogue that one of the women subscribed to, and she had donated her profit from the clothes sold on the night to the Church. This generous gesture had produced around fifty pounds for the church, which as David reflected was a quarter's rent for his house.

The women were now enjoying telling the tall tales that had surrounded the show and thought that it was an opportunity to pull the new curate's leg and to test him a little bit to see if he was easily shocked.

The main source of amusement concerned the third person, Gilly, who David had not seen before. It seemed that she had recently moved to the village into the family's holiday home in order to get away from her husband. They were not getting on and had agreed that they both needed a cooling off period. So Gilly had moved away with the two children who were both under school age.

Now, amidst gales of laughter from the women, she recounted how last night she had been persuaded to act as one of the models and had been squashed into two outfits that were at least two sizes too small. In fact one of dresses, a sparkly evening number in which she had struggled out onto the small stage taking tiny steps in order not to put any strain on the seams, had slipped allowing most of one breast to pop out completely. The women, as they retold the tale of how the performance, and in particular the modeling, by Gilly again, of some slightly risqué French-style underwear, had outraged the older members of the Church, and they were enjoying their new-found reputation as the cause of scandal in the small community of church and village.

David found himself warming to Gilly and to her naïve, knowing innocence which reminded him of Sarah. Although she was older, and clearly had suffered more than Sarah. Too soon Gilly said that she must go back to relieve the babysitter who was doing her a favour. She didn't want to create the impression she was taking advantage of the girl who was the daughter of a neighbour. It seemed to David quite natural to leave at the same time and to walk back down through the village to her house, and to wish her good evening. He then turned back up the hill to the vicarage, and the meeting of the magazine committee for whom he had prepared an article about life in theological college which was being considered at their meeting in fifteen minutes.

Later that evening, after the magazine committee had finally disbanded, having agreed to accept David's article, and agreed the other contents of that month's magazine, consumed their tea and coffee and set off down the hill to their respective homes, calling their farewells, EBG had indicated to David that he should remain behind.

For EBG, the decision to open up what he knew would be a sensitive area of discussion with his curate was a difficult one; but he considered that it was his duty, as far as was possible, to act both as guide and mentor to the young man.

Indicating to David that he should pull an overstuffed armchair closer to the fire, EBG set a bottle and two glasses on the table between them and motioned that David should feel free to fill his glass as required.

For a long while the two sat staring into the fire as the flames flickered and danced. David had no desire to be the first to speak, and in any event it was clear that EBG had something on his mind, so he waited.

EBG on the other hand was not sure how he would raise the subject and had only half a sense any way of what it was that he was wanting to tell his young colleague.

'Your arrival here' he began, 'has been good for the parish, and for me. You've brought some fresh air into the proceedings, and that's good, excellent...'.

He lapsed into a semi-musing silence and David waited.

'But' EBG continued 'you've ruffled some feathers in the diocese and that's not so good. The Bishop's Chaplain was here. It seems that he's got it in for you and nothing I said made much of a difference. So, if you want my advice you should watch your back, and particularly as far as he's concerned. He's an ambitious bastard and if he doesn't get you on the way up he'll get you on the way down, I'm sure of it. He thinks you were a mistake all the way round... that you slipped through the net when his back was turned, and that you'll not make the kind of priest that they can trust'.

It was a long speech and David knew that it came from somewhere deep and close, and was intended to be heard with the same affection with which it was delivered. He also knew that it was true that the man was out to get him and that whatever he did would make little difference over the long term. He was a marked man.

As if reading his thoughts, EBG, speaking partly to David and partly to the fire, went on to say that in his view, the file that was kept on each priest in the diocese, and the report that went to Lambeth indicating a man's suitability for promotion, was yet another example of how deeply corrupted the system that held sway in the church truly was. The patronage that was exercised made certain that only people like us became people like us. The whole thing so far removed from the Gospels and the Acts of the Apostles in which the replacement for Judas, Matthias was elected by throwing lots, he couldn't imagine.

David was intrigued, 'You mean there really is a file? I thought that was one of those theological college paranoias that kept people up at night worrying, and that was all.'

'Oh oh, noo', EBG's reply was quite deliberate. 'The way it works is that each bishop has to fill in a report each year, and the report sets outs which clergy in his diocese should be considered for promotion under the headings of Residentiary Canon, Archdeacon, Suffragen Bishop and Bishop. That report is sent to Lambeth Palace and kept on a file or in a Book or something, so far so good, but now it gets really good.

'What happens then is that when a diocese has a vacancy, the bishop has to consult this Book or File, and a list is sent out from Lambeth. Of course, all he does when he gets it is open it, and lo and behold what names does he recognise? That's right, the ones he put in. So you see, you can bet that our bishop has put his Chaplain's name on the list already, so it's only a matter of time before our friend is on his way and then he'll reward his own cronies by putting their names in the book.'

David expressed surprise that any system so obviously corruptible and corrupting could be maintained in an organisation that claimed through its systems of PCC's and Synods to be democratic. EBG was developing what was obviously a well-trodden theme, as the effects of the Talisker began to warm his blood, he renewed his attack.

'I had a friend once' he went on, 'who became a bishop'. The person who appointed him had known him for years and had appointed him onto the staff of the Cathedral, which is when I first knew him. Then the said bishop headed south, and not long after, my friend received a letter asking him to come south also, as a Suffragen. It

The Uncertainty Begins | 79

was a classic case of the patronage of liberalism. My friend
enquired about Lambeth's view of the appointment only
to be told that if Lambeth had a view it must be positive,
otherwise why was his name on the list they had circulated.
The answer, of course, was obvious because this bishop,
who was a nice well-meaning chap, I can vouch for that
because he'd been my bishop as well, had put my friend's
name on the list in the first place. Of course that bit was
never mentioned by either of them, why knock a system
when its favouring you?'

David was thoughtful. Clearly, if he was going to have
a future in the church he needed the support of these
people. But at the same time the chaplain and the people
he represented, were such dreadful people, establishing
their careers by sucking up to the right people, being in
the right place at the right time. In many ways the liberal
establishment represented the worst of all possible worlds.
It was clear to him that what it represented owed nothing
to the gospel, and that the Jesus of the gospels and the
disciples would never have been invited into membership
of the liberal club. Yet if he stood against it he wouldn't
ever succeed in changing it, and would simply find himself
railing against a system that was too powerful to fight.

EBG, as he'd already admitted to David on the night
they first met, had taken refuge in Drissburgh, and the
Parish of St. Agatha's, and poetry. He sheltered from the
establishment behind the parson's freehold, safe in the
knowledge that neither the bishop or his chaplain could
require him to surrender his living against his will, as
much as they might like too.

It was the only certain place where the liberal establishment could be resisted. For David it was still some distance away, and to achieve it he needed the patronage of the very people he despised.

EBG's silence seemed to indicate that there was not much else to be said about the matter, but as he reached for, poured from, then offered David the bottle, it was clear that there was no hurry to leave.

As they sat in the warm, comfortable silence David's mind went back to his earlier conversation with Gilly. She wasn't pretty, yet she had the strong distinctive features of a woman who knew her own mind. In their brief walk to her house she'd told him about her husband who was running his own business, and how, as the business had taken off her husband had become increasingly distant and tense, snapping at her and the children. Now that she was living on her own, she found life so much more relaxed.

She knew that her husband was seeing someone else, and that at first she'd not worried, but under the pretext of business he'd taken to staying away for nights at a time. She'd felt insulted at first, and then one day when he was meant to be on a business trip to Scotland she'd met him in the street. He was with the girlfriend, and had tried to cover his embarrassment as he introduced them.

For Gilly that was the final straw and she'd taken the children, babies really, and moved into the cottage they'd bought in happier times a couple of years before, and that was it. She'd not seen her husband since, and all she knew was that he was still paying the bills, although for how long she wasn't sure.

Suddenly his thoughts were interrupted by EBG, 'well young man', he was saying, 'maybe we're worrying unnecessarily, maybe if you stay here and keep out of the diocese's way, in due course the bishop will move you to a better parish, or even, if you're luck, a parish of your own, and then you can get on with the job you were ordained for.

David raised a questioning eyebrow, which EBG picked up on.

'I know', he said, 'the job you were ordained for, it does have a ring to it, rather a grand way of putting it. The thing is David, you, as a young working class lad, should know a thing or two about subversion and really, that's our job. Subverting the way things are in order that they can be better, improved, just make life more enjoyable, for folk, more fun'.

David raised his eyebrows again. He was unsure where all this was leading or whether it was just the whisky talking.

As EBG warmed to his theme David was thinking to himself, that he wasn't entirely sure what that job was, and as he could see clearly enough, EBG himself did little enough, spending most of his time with his poetry books and his writing.

But EBG continued, 'Subversion is, and always has been the main weapon of working people in the class war. They have always undermined the organisations' they work for, so that instead of serving the bosses' purposes they serve their own. Workers have always done this, in a variety of ways some relatively insignificant, making things for their own use out of the firms materials, undertaking bits of private work, using tools from work, clocking each other in and out, you know the kind of things that go on', David nodded, remembering how work was a constant battle between the boss, who wanted productivity and the workers who wanted a quiet life.

EBG continued with his theme, 'that's where we come in as clergy, we are in all sorts of ways, subversives. We pretend to belong to the establishment' and some of us don't even pretend, thought David, as he remembered the Bishop's Chaplain, 'but in fact we stand for values that put us at odds with the system', EBG continued. 'Take the communion service as an example. Every Sunday the church, in the face of a society that is all about getting and possessing, storing up treasures on earth, house, car, TVs, things, sets out it's table and claims that sharing is the key to human happiness and individual fulfillment. Take Jesus, here is a man we preach about to people who are fixated on success, in their jobs, their lives, their children's achievements, who ended his life a complete failure, that's what clergy are. They're the people who stand against the values of the people they minister to, a small, weak, insistent voice, raising questions about the meaning of life, the true, meaning of life, that is; at least that's my understanding of what it means to be a priest. And it's what keeps me going'. As the whisky took hold EBG picked up a notebook from the small side table that he kept next to his chair. 'Anyway, enough of that I've been playing with a new idea for a poem ' he smiled, 'I've got a couple of verses finished'.

'Read them' David invited. 'I'm always interested in the latest work from the pen of EBG the poet vicar of Drissburgh', glad that the subject had changed before he had to find an intelligent response to EBG's commentary on the true significance of priesthood.

Caught in the web of languages
The philosopher smiles as he deconstructs
Taking the words of the sentence, he rearranges
And what he knows, from the sum of knowledge, deducts
Particularising the source of meaning, he says, yes
knowing that night will soon fall
but clearly his yes is bound to relativise
And be without particular meaning at all

'So what's it called' asked David, hoping that the title might shed some light on the poem.

'The Philosopher', EBG replied, 'but I'm having trouble with the last verse, I've got as far as this,

The sounds of shared distress can be heard,
the rattling of sabres and definitions.

'But such agonising is clearly absurd now, I need something to round it off and that will rhyme with definitions.'

David laughed, 'well don't ask me' he said, 'I'm no poet'.

EBG, ignored him, trying, inspirations, concatenations, nations, relations, before David offered,

'Discovering the meaning of life in sexual relations' which EBG ignored. Before David mentioned that he must really

be going, that he'd heard that it was bad luck to finish the last drop in the bottle, or was it bad manners, something his mother had warned him against anyway, and EBG thought that was just superstitious. Together they'd agreed that superstitious was the word, and then EBG had come up with, *'As it revolves around ancient superstitions'* which had seemed like the final word to both of them.

The Philosopher

Caught in the web of languages
The philosopher smiles as he deconstructs
Taking the words of the sentence, he rearranges
And what he knows, from the sum
of knowledge, deducts
Particularising the source of meaning, he says, yes
knowing that night will soon fall
but clearly his yes is bound to relativise
And be without particular meaning at all
The sounds of shared distress can be heard
the rattling of sabres and definitions
But such agonising is clearly absurd
As it revolves around ancient superstitions

Conversion
and
Vocation
_____

As he left the vicarage and set off down to his cottage, David reflected on his life, and how much it had changed in the few years since he'd left school and started his first job. He'd swept the forecourt in a local garage on Hyde Road in Manchester, and now here he was in Drissburgh, drinking Talisker and heading back to his little cottage, complete with its view of the ocean and that marvelous light that shone across the water in the early morning. Even now, in a bright moonlight, it had a light that tracked across the ocean to the distant horizon, creating a dark stain on a sky that was showing the first streaky signs of dawn coming up out of the east.

There was a good deal in their conversation that night. That was summed up by EBG's poem and its last line. All their talk about the church, and consequently those who exercised and abused their power and position, were really the high priests of a cult. Then there was the mystery and power of language itself. He knew what was happening within himself -- the mystery and power of sexual attraction. Sex, power and language were the themes and currency of superstition, and superstition was the business that he and EBG were in. Superstition is what they traded in, it was their currency and superstition is what kept them in business.

People's fear, and as he knew only too well, the psychologies and pathologies of the congregation, were really just an open ward. Out here on the streets, unattended, on the loose and even in the PCC, in church on a Sunday, in the Magazine Committee, it was capable of doing immense harm, of destroying people with its bitterness, fear and paranoia

What was that line? The sounds of shared distress. That's what he heard on a Sunday morning in the prayers and in the hymns, and in the responses from the congregation. The sounds of shared distress.... agonizing... around ancient superstitions.

It was this that the Bishop's Chaplain could see when he looked at David, and why he knew that David was dangerous. Because David would blow the whistle if he was left alone and not dealt with. He would tackle that whole mess head on. The Chaplain recognised that David was a deconstructionist, and what he would deconstruct is what legitimised the Chaplain's stranglehold on people's souls.

A vocation has two active ingredients. The sense of being called has to convince the person whose vocation it is, or whose vocation it will become, but the vocation has also to be objectively recognised, in this case by the church. That's where the selection conference came in.

Looking back on the conference from the perspective of having graduated now from theological college, and from his experience of both the ordination retreat and his post-ordination training, David was amazed that he managed to scrape over all the hurdles that had been erected.

It was clear to him, as it had been to his friends, that

he was a one off, a freak; someone who would always offer a challenge to authority, and that this was the burden that he would have to live with throughout his ministry.

Always a people's clergyman, never a clergyman's clergyman. Oh well, he thought, so be it.

Before turning in, he decided, on the spur of the moment to visit his friend Neil. It was some weeks since the ordination and they had both had time to begin to adjust to this bizarre life they had both embarked upon.

Reaching for the Diocesan Yearbook, David called Neil's number, a groggy voice on the other end of the line answered.

'Hello, Neil here, how can I help'

'Hi Neil', David began, 'How are you, how's the parish, I thought that I might pop over for a visit, see how things are going, is tomorrow a good time for you?'

'Who is this?' Neil began, then as the penny dropped, 'David, do you realise what time it is?'

'It's two in the morning and you have just woke me up, I've got an early service at 7:00 am. David, this is not remotely amusing, I need to get back to bed'.

Before he could put the phone down, David interrupted. 'Neil, wait, sorry about the time, but, you know, I just thought that we could meet in town, have lunch, something. I'd really like to know how it is working out for you. I'm sorry about the time, I only just got in, but I'd been with the vicar, EBG you know, and we'd had some whisky, and I wasn't feeling sleepy and… I'm sorry, but are you free tomorrow?'

Neil agreed to meet, somewhat grudgingly David

thought, and put the phone down. 'Till tomorrow then', David muttered into the beeping handset.

The early train pulled into the city just before 9:00 the next morning and David set out from the station to walk to Neil's flat which was in the clergy house, next to the church.

After Drissburgh the city felt busy and bustling, much more to David's liking, he thought. There's life here, the city is open for business, he thought.

As he walked through the city centre, he found himself drawn into the shops and before long he found what he was looking for, a record shop displaying the latest hits and a bookstore with a couple of new novels and a poetry section. He had hoped to find a paperback poetry book as a gift for EBG to pay him back in some small way for all the whiskey David had drunk in their evening sessions, when whiskey, women and words had been the eponymous subjects of their various tall tales and claims.

After checking the A-Z he set off for Neil's flat, which was on the edge of the city in a parish which had its feet in the city centre but its head in a depressing, dirty, disheveled inner city area, which was part red light district part no go area, especially after dark. It was the first point of arrival for the many immigrants who arrived here looking for work, and a new start in a new country. This was signified by, amongst other things, a small Russian bakery and any number of secondhand shops.

Finding the church was relatively easy, and soon David was knocking on Neil's door. There was a loud crashing from inside and the door burst open. From inside the flat a scary, and scared looking character came bursting out, pushed David to one side and hurtled down the street. He was followed by Neil looking drained and exhausted.

'David, thank goodness it's you. I think you saved my life'.

'What's going on?' enquired David, appalled by what he had just witnessed.

'Let's go upstairs' suggested Neil, still very shaky from the experience.

Upstairs, Neil told David what had happened that night. He had gone off to bed at 10:30 after the news and had been sound asleep when, at about 4:00 am he heard the sound of breaking glass. Going downstairs to investigate, he entered the parish office, which was the room from which the intruder had exited and pushed past David.

Neil had been confronted by the youth who having broken in was looking for things to steal, money mainly.

Neil had walked straight into a situation for which nothing had prepared him, certainly not his three years at university or his two years at theological college.

He tried talking to the youth who was extremely threatening and managed to position himself between Neil and the door, he then proceeded to threaten Neil if he didn't give him money. Neil's flat was upstairs, and so was what little money he kept for his fairly limited and simple needs.

'Try explaining that to a hooligan with a knife'. Neil was clearly deeply distressed by the whole experience, and it took a couple of cups of strong coffee, before he started to come round.

David gathered that from four in the morning until he had knocked on the door at ten, Neil had effectively been held hostage in the parish office.

'You're lucky not to have been hurt' said David, 'I'm going to call the police, where's your 'phone?'

'No', Neil panicked. 'No, I promised I wouldn't, just leave it, it'll be okay'.

'But you can't stay here' said David, 'it's clearly not safe, you could have been killed, the parish will have to move you, or at least improve the security, and if all else fails, next time lock the door of your flat and call the police'. This last comment was lost, because he could see that Neil was not listening to a word he had said.

And then it all came bursting out. Neil hated the parish, the people, and especially the vicar a pompous man, who spent most of his time on courses and diocesan committees. He was extremely ambitious to move on, and was careful to cultivate the right contacts. The vicarage had been let to a local social care group, the vicar living outside the parish in a pleasant house in one of the leafy suburbs, but insisted that the curate lived in the clergy house. He'd told Neil in one of his pompous, self-justifying comments, that was what separated the clergy from 'mere' social workers, they actually lived in the communities they served.

David, immediately decided that practicality was called for, so 'first things first' he said, 'phone book?'

'What for?' asked Neil

'To phone a glazier, at least we can get the window

replaced.'

David looked around, 'better get a locksmith too. You need to lock the inner doors from the inside, that will keep people from getting into the whole house, if it happens again.'

Having established that despite having a parish office, there was in fact no parish secretary, it was just another bit of the vicar's PR, and a way of not having to let anyone in the parish know his address, David made the necessary calls.

It began to dawn on him just what a profound deceit lay at the heart of what was happening to all those who had been ordained just a few weeks before. Neil was sent out into the sticks where he was a fish out of water. He was a kindly, soft-centered suburban boy here in the city, where he was a fish in hot water. Doubtless the others were similarly ill placed, in parishes where they were ill-prepared and unsupported. Who'll be the first to crack? David thought. Looking at Neil, he didn't give him long.

Apart from having spent the past six hours in his pyjamas, and being held hostage by a madman with a knife, Neil was also deeply distressed by his general treatment. His parents and family had seen his vocation as a genuine call from the loving God they met every week at their suburban church.

The smiling vicar had encouraged Neil and nurtured his sense of calling to the ministry. It's a great thing, he had assured Neil. You will be rewarded with a fulfilling life, serving God's people.

Some reward thought David, stuck here in this hell

hole with another self-seeking, self-serving, pompous idiot whose only aim was to get out of the rank and file of clergy and into the hierarchy.

David felt that he hardly needed to ask Neil how things were going, but he was wrong. Once Neil had changed into his dog collar, black shirt and black trousers, David noticed he began to relax. Neil described something of the area they were in, some of the problems it offered and even began to highlight some of the positives. Which were its multi-culturalism, its liveliness, and the genuine warmth he experienced from local people. Although living in the clergy house meant that he had no neighbours, and was cut off from the people around who lived in a mixture of tenement housing, flats and terraces.

Since his ordination Neil had begun to enjoy his new life, which was a real change after university and college. Given that he had never had a job, it was a real change of life. His day, he said, began at 6:30 am when the alarm went off, and then he had to meet the vicar in church at 7:30 for Matins. Twice a week they had a communion service, which Neil was really looking forward to celebrating when he was to be ordained as a priest next year.

After the service the vicar gave him his tasks for the day. These were mainly visiting, getting to know members of the congregation, visiting the hospital, and once he was more experienced, visits in the local prison, whose forbidding walls topped by razor wire, Neil had noticed, on his way from the station.

David noted the difference between his situation and Neil's, a list of duties was the last thing he would expect from EBG.

'So how does he know what you have actually done?' David asked.

'I report to him every day after we have said evening prayers in church, and before we decide what meeting I should attend that evening.'

David was shocked by this description of the routine that had set in so quickly, and that Neil seemed to accept it unquestioningly. When he asked the obvious question he discovered that today was in fact Neil's day off, and that if David hadn't asked to visit, Neil was planning to drive across to his parent's house for the day.

It was left to both their imaginations to reflect on what the vicar might have done if Neil had failed to turn up for morning prayer and been found being held hostage by a young tearaway. What do you think he wanted Neil asked. Money I should think, said David, probably for drugs, it was clear from the expression on Neil's face that this thought had not even crossed his mind.

They were saved from further discussion by the arrival of first the glazier and then the locksmith. Both were soon hard at work repairing the damage and improving security. When Neil asked them, it seemed that they had both contacted the vicar for his approval for the work, 'to be on the safe side', as they put. It left David wondering that there had been no call from the vicar enquiring as to Neil's health.

David was outraged on Neil's behalf, but as his friend seemed traumatised by the events of the previous night, decided that there was little to be gained either from boasting, as it might appear, about his own rather privileged life, or encouraging Neil to dwell on the what-might-have-beens of the situation.

'Seems just as well that I turned up when I did' said David. 'Your friend has left, the repairs are underway and we can go out and enjoy a quiet drink, but for God's sake take that bloody dog collar off.'

'I can't' Neil replied, 'I have to wear it in the parish even on my day off, vicar's orders' he added somewhat shamefaced.

David laughed, 'well, I'm not going out for a drink with a bloody vicar' so we'll just have to go somewhere outside the parish, 'there's a good place near the Cathedral, The Mitre, let's go there.'

Having agreed their destination, the two curates set off like brothers in arm, determined to enjoy the rest of their day before David's train took him back to Drissburgh, and a life markedly different than Neil's.

Entering The Mitre they found a back room where they could take their pints in relative privacy, and continue their conversation. Like any new recruits in a job there were both stresses, such as Neil's early morning encounter, and pleasures. Not the least being the subject of such huge gratitude expressed by parishioners, often for just turning up. 'Oh, Father Neil, I'm just so glad that you were able to find the time, I know how busy you are.'

The afternoon passed reasonably pleasantly. David began to feel quite mellow as pint followed pint, Neil had passed on a couple of rounds, but even he seemed to be relaxing after his ordeal. He seemed to accept David's advice, which had become more insistent. 'Always, if you hear anything suspicious, lock your door and ring for the police, that's their job. Once they've locked him up him and he's no longer any threat you can always visit him in prison if you really want to save him.'

Neil looked cautiously at David, uncertain if he was joking, and thought better of making any reply.

They still had a couple of hours to kill and David suggested that, given that he was out in the sticks, they should go to see a film. He knew that Woodstock was showing just around the corner, and that he would have enough time after Jimi Hendrix had brought the film to its epic ending with his version of Star Strangled Banner, to catch an early evening train back to Drissburgh.

As they were leaving The Mitre, laughing at David's unsteadiness, they walked straight into the Bishop's Chaplain who was entering with another clergyman that neither of them recognised.

There was an awkward silence and the Chaplain's muttered greeting sounded less than friendly.

'I didn't know you two were friends' he said, addressing himself directly to Neil, 'don't let him lead you astray' nodding vaguely in David's direction. And then more ominously, 'I have a meeting with your vicar this afternoon, I'll pass on your greeting.'

Once outside, encouraged by the drink they both laughed uproariously and walked unsteadily in the direction of the cinema.

Neil looked genuinely concerned as he turned to David. 'Be careful with him, he's out to get you and he's got contacts and power at his disposal.'

The film was everything David had hoped, and apart from falling asleep briefly, a result of the drink, and needing the loo twice for the same reason, he whispered to Neil on his return from the second visit, 'you don't buy your beer in The Mitre, you rent it'. Soon, Jimi Hendrix played the finale and they left, Neil to his newly secured home and fascist boss, and David to Drissburgh.

At the station David invited Neil to make the journey out to visit him when he had time, teasing him with a strong reminder not to wear his bloody dog collar or 'you'll embarrass everybody', without stopping to define exactly who the everybody referred to.

As the train pulled out of the station, David thought about his friend with real concern. Neil was far too naïve to be in such a difficult and exposed situation, with a man who would sacrifice his curate's future to his own overriding ambition.

Why are we doing this? wondered David. He thought back along the path that had brought him to Drissburgh, his time at college, his friendships, his early days growing up in the inner city, the two years of night school as he tried to compensate for his spectacularly disastrous school days by acquiring the basic qualifications to get into college.

And now, ordained and with EBG, a good man and one who cared about the parish and its people, who was not driven by ambition, but simply a desire to be available when people needed him. EBG didn't do visits, found PCC's enormously difficult, was much happier sitting writing in his study, or walking, or drinking his whisky, but when he was called upon would offer all the support he could to those who were going through a difficult patch.

And for that he was admired. His parishioners thought well of him, and he was pretty well adjusted, as he had said himself. 'I only ever wanted to be a parish priest and that's what I am, and that's good enough for me.'

David wondered if that would be good enough for himself. At one level he was sure that it would, but at another, deeper level, he was not so sure.

It was early days yet, he had been ordained for only a few weeks, he had a further year of training as a deacon before he went back to the cathedral to be made a priest, and before that he had months of sparring with the Bishop's Chaplain, and months of post-ordination training, implying that they were all children who could be patronised with impunity. And then, of course, there was the difficult decision about what came next, his second curacy, back to the city? Stay in the sticks? Or try a suburban parish or even as had been suggested a more specialised form of ministry as a diocesan officer.

Well, David thought as he settled further into his seat, there's time yet for those decisions right now I need to think about what on earth I'm going to preach this Sunday.

But it just does not end there. For David as for many young clergy the process of growing into the priests they will become takes time, and as many young clergy have recognised, continuing conversions, as their faith either deepens and matures or the questioning becomes increasingly more disquieting.

For David there was a strange mixture of both processes at work. Certainly, in the daily round of parish life and activity, there was a continual deepening as his commitment to people grew and strengthened.

People made in the image of God, good people and bad, saints and sinners, the simple souls and the complex and scheming individuals, but for all the difference and variety for David, the longer he stayed in Drissburgh the more difficult it would become not to feel a deep sense of affection for the people.

He knew that he would never be a clergyman's clergyman but he liked people. He was interested in what they had to say, he listened to them as they expressed their convictions and he could see the intrinsic goodness that shone through. This was his first conversion and it was a conversion to the human.

Later, of course, he came to realise that to support and encourage people, and to represent their interests and concerns, it was not enough to work with them at the local level. The structures that influenced their lives and made the biggest changes possible were structures that existed at another level of society altogether from this place, and these people of Drissburgh.

For David, in due course, politics would become a way forward. It was here in the campaigning and organizing work that he would take up what was able to effect the biggest changes on behalf of the people he cared so deeply for. This second conversion, shaped his ministry, his life and his work in the years ahead, but all that would come later. It would be, as is often said, another story.

The third conversion which had an immediate effect on his life, and challenged him to take action, was the corruption he saw at work in the church itself.

People like the Bishop's Chaplain needed to be challenged. And David saw that for himself there was an emerging, and quite new vocation, of the prophetic which he found himself wearing in his deepest innermost thoughts like a blanket.

Imagine this

Imagine this
A picture painted with words
A distant landscape
Figures pressing forward
A progress, crowds
Obscuring the central
Character, dust, a hazy sun
Imagine drawing
Closer, hearing
Sound carried on still air
A cry of pain an angry shout
The sound of leather tearing flesh
A wounded animal scream
Imagine drawing nearer still
Imagine the smell
Of sweat stained bodies
Mingled scents
The smell of raw wounds
The cloying sweetness of blood

Imagine blinking
Missing the final scene
The body lifted High,
the puzzled Onlookers, uncertainty
At what is taking place
Drifting away
Imagine, from a safe
Distance, looking
Back at the scene
Three figures on three trees
And at the foot of the middle tree
Two kneeling, a man
And a woman weeping
And a voice:
If you sing, sing my name
let your words echo my virtue not my shame

EBG

Mr. Saxon
is a
Humanist

———————

The Curate's Discussion Group was the last place that David might have expected a prophetic confrontation. The group had been started in the first place as a support group. EBG had thought that there would be value in David receiving support on a regular basis from a mixed group of parishioners. Not exactly a 'peer group', but a meeting where the members were invited to meet as equals with, rather than sit at the feet of, the clergy.

The group met on the second Wednesday of every month, sometimes in David's cottage and occasionally in either the home of one of the group members or in the pub. In fact they had only met in the pub on one occasion, when the meeting became rather more open than planned, and was gate-crashed by a couple of locals who had rather more to say in their drink-fuelled way than was helpful.

For David, the problem with the group was not so much who was in it, but that he was not given to simple, definitive answers to complex questions.

So the group would fix on a subject, and expect him, as the clergyman, to be able to comment with some authority on whether their view was right or wrong.

More than once David had been wrong footed by Phil Ashby, who had stated emphatically that this or that was right or wrong, and then invited David's agreement. When David had not agreed Phil had used the opportunity to suggest that as a clergyman who had been trained to know right from wrong, should not be so afraid to speak clearly.

Every time it happened David would try to gently turn the conversation, and raise the possibility that some things might be more a matter of degree, more relative, but Phil wanted certainty, and would look disappointed, crestfallen even, if David failed to support his extreme views.

One evening after the discussion had started, as it often did, with a story from the daily paper, the group found itself in the middle of an increasingly heated debate about the rights and wrongs of the American war currently being fought in Vietnam.

For Phil who was a flight sergeant in the RAF, based at a local base that occasionally provided facilities to the USAF, it was a simple matter of black and white. The war was being fought legitimately, and it was not for them to argue the rights and wrongs of a conflict which was simply the concern of the American Government.

David tried to get the other members of the group to share their own views, and to see whether Phil's opinion was generally shared. Eventually, as happened only too often in the group, David found himself on the opposite side of the argument with the bulk of the group occupying the silent centre ground.

Phil became increasingly belligerent, shouting David down. It seemed that for Phil the issue turned on authority, and taking orders. David tried hard to be reasonable, but eventually observed that the latest American excursion into Cambodia could not be justified on either moral or military grounds. It was wrong. The Cambodian government's sovereignty had been compromised and the Americans had no chance of winning the conflict. David heard himself rehearsing a rather cod version of the just war theory as Phil became increasingly angry, eventually rising to his feet and heading for the door. As the door slammed, David heard him shout back into the room that he was no better than a 'bloody humanist'.

The rest of the group was visibly shocked, but they were also clearly torn. Phil was one of them, and they respected his views and his normally disciplined approach. To see him driven to a degree of desperation and anger upset them. They were both sympathetic to Phil and equally angry with David for pursuing the argument as far as he had.

It was clear enough that the evening had ended and individually each member of the group refused David's offer of coffee before excusing themselves.

David had a feeling that the group had come to the end of its natural life but he was quite unprepared for what came next.

Apparently Phil had gone home directly and in the heat of the moment had written a letter to the Bishop accusing David of exceeding his authority, misleading the group, sharing his misguided ideas and justifying them by his humanist beliefs.

Phil had ended his letter by suggesting that David was not fit to be made priest, which was the next step in his career.

Inevitably the next day the phone rang. The Bishop's

Chaplain had received the letter and thought that, perhaps they should meet to discuss the implications of Phil's complaint.

An Evening Concert

Deep voiced, chorale
Set against soprano
Lute and fiddle
Songs echo
Late spring, winters steady
Refusal to retreat
Intermittent showers of snow
And rain, sudden sharp rivers
Running deep and slow
Past these village churches
James and John and Agnes
As though it were the last
Of England
Not the heart the last of song
Not the start.

EBG

Ginny

The next day dawned wet and miserable, and to make matters worse David woke too late for Matins. His plans for the week coming, such as they were, ended with his projected trip to Manchester to see his family, after which he would travel back to attend the first of his post-ordination training sessions with the diocese before returning to Drissburgh in two weeks' time.

He dragged himself from his bed, his head felt remarkably fragile (had he really drunk so much again last night?) and his mouth felt as though something had crawled in and died. He washed and cleaned his teeth. Meanwhile, the kettle boiled for his morning tea, with which he washed down the couple of slices of Marmite toast that passed for breakfast.

Having consulted his diary he noted that there was nothing pressing today, no preparation for Sunday, and the work that had to be completed for his course he could safely leave until he was in Manchester.

Looking through the window he could see that the weather was clearing, and out across the ocean the sun was burning off the cloud, and stretches of blue sky were appearing, auguring well for the afternoon.

So David decided that the best he could do with the day was to take some thinking time, and so he set out to a walk across the headland, at least as far as the river, where, if he felt hardy, he might even swim over to continue his walk along the coast to Swansley. There, he could get a drink before heading back.

He had acquired a small backpack into which he placed some bread, a piece of cheese, a small tin of meat paste and a can of beer, which had somehow been overlooked at the back of the fridge. Leaving his house he headed up the road toward the coast, stopping to buy a Mars bar from the newsagent, still a little frosty with him when he came into the shop.

Thinking that if the weather continued to improve, he might take a diversion up to the old fort, he set off.

The fort guarded the headland, and from a distance looked authentic enough. Close up it was revealed as a concrete fortification, built as part of the coastal defences against a possible invasion during the 1939-1945 war. The flat roof of the structure provided shelter for sunbathing, and because the fort was as isolated as it was, there was little chance of being disturbed.

As he walked up toward the road's end and the turning circle, he turned things over in his mind. His conversation with EBG, his realisation about the Bishop's Chaplain and the danger he represented to David and his future. These thoughts wove in and out of other thoughts related to Manchester, and his forthcoming visit home. He wondered how his mother was keeping, and whether his father would behave reasonably, or whether they would end up, as usual, arguing angrily over some ridiculous proposition that his father would insist on putting forward for debate. Propositions supported with a mixture of half-truths and prejudice dressed up as fact. In and out of his thoughts drifted the image of Gilly, who in his imagination had become even prettier and more intriguing. He kept dismissing her image because, pleasant as he found the memory, it was clear that if he pursued this line too far he would come across a sign that read 'here there be dragons' and any further he would be deep in the danger zone.

At the turning circle he headed out across the headland to the bay, pausing to see if the fish that he'd first seen a few weeks before, and which he thought of as his own, was still there. He stared down into the water, which was clouded with sand and mud, stirred up by a storm somewhere out at sea. He could dimly make out the shape of the fish, swimming, with powerful strokes of its tail, around the bay. He wasn't sure what it was, and thought maybe it was a salmon, it was certainly large enough, but it could have been anything and he really had no knowledge of fish and their various types.

Nevertheless, he spent a few moments idly watching as it swam, enjoying the sight of a free creature at ease with its environment, this was definitely one fish that was in water.

Then, with a last glance at the creature as it swam out of view, heading apparently to the mouth of the bay and the open sea, David turned and headed up the cliff path toward the tower. As he walked, he tried to empty his mind completely, thinking of nothing, yet no matter how he tried the image kept returning of the small, typed pamphlet that EBG had given him, reluctantly, and only after extracting a firm promise that it was returned.

The pamphlet was entitled The Complete Poetical

Works of EBG, The Poet Parson of Drissburgh. It contained a number, about six, poems which according to EBG represented the sum total of his published works. Each poem, necessarily he supposed, had carried the possibility of various meanings; not all that profound but somehow together they added up to a bleak testament that the future of the human race was clearly in doubt.

As one poem spelled it out, the watchers and the watched were bound together in a competitive relationship as they vied with each other for scarce resources. In that poem, as in the others, there was the suggestion that it would be the watchers, the natural things, like his great fish, that would be the inheritors of the divine promise that the world, which was good, would reach a conclusion out of which goodness would triumph without the help of the human race.

It reminded him of some words he'd come across in a book he'd read at college. The author, an American, Ernst Troeltsch had a deeply pessimistic view of the human project suggesting that 'as the beginning was without us, so will the end also be without us'. Such thoughts left David both depressed and reassured. Depressed that ultimately, humanity was without purpose. Despite his strong sense that he should be a priest, there was real doubt in his mind that God was anything more than a humanly authored attempt to provide some purpose. He took a sneaky delight in knowing that no matter how they tried, people like the Bishop's Chaplain would share the same fate, eternal, unending, oblivion, as him. They might have a moment or two of success in their lives, but ultimately it would amount to nothing, and he and they would be on a level with each other.

As he walked he felt a powerful sense of revulsion at the thought of the Bishop's Chaplain. He was a man who carried within himself such a strong sense of his own significance, which instead of reassuring David, although it apparently reassured the Bishop, left him with the thought that he had been in the presence of, and the only word he could think of but which was perfect, was smarminess.

The man left an oil slick in his wake. He was the sort of person who if you saw him in the second class compartment of a train you would automatically redirect him to the first. This was not because of any quality he possessed of himself, because as far as David could see he possessed none, but because he would be communicating a sense of being in the wrong place. He had a studied unease with his situation that would read like 'I'm here, but of course I'm intended for better.'

Out to his left as he walked, the ocean settled and shifted under its own weight as the water swirled up the coast. The currents following the channel, once busy with a whole flotilla of ships carrying coal and freight to the once busy ports up and down the coast, the ocean was now deserted, nothing from here to the horizon as far as the eye could see.

This was the original shape and pace of life. It was a shape that had for thousands of years been explained by theologians, those servants of the queen of the sciences that had been displaced by, and had still not come to terms with, Copernicus and Darwin, whose explanations of the origins of life, and the relative place of the earth in relation to the observed universe, had made the explanations that looked back to Genesis as no more than the collection of myths they were. Not just misleading, but failing to explain adequately what people could see for themselves, was an apparently purposeless creation; cruel, accidental and wasteful.

The sun was stronger now and he removed his sweater, then turned up to the tower, thinking that he might look out to Whale Rock in the hope of seeing the seals that sometimes could be seen swimming off the coast of the small island.

As he neared the tower he thought he could see someone, a figure stretched out on the concrete roof of the ruins. Coming closer he realised it was a woman. She was sunbathing, and he thought probably asleep in the warm sun having chosen a particularly sheltered spot.

Instinctively, and almost in a schoolboy-like state of tension he found himself trying to make as little noise as possible as he neared the sleeping figure, which by now he could see was both female and wearing very little. In fact, as far he could see, she was sunbathing in the semi nude. It was only then that he recognised that it was Gilly, and that her clothes, jeans and sweater, were in a neat pile serving as a pillow as she stretched out in her bra and panties.

Suddenly he panicked. Who would be the most embarrassed, her being found in this state of undress, or him at being discovered creeping up on her in this way like a guilty schoolboy. So, he coughed to attract her attention and warn her of his approach. Looking up she smiled, and in what seemed to David, slow motion, sat up, slipping her sweater over her head but leaving her jeans where they were.

'Don't worry, she said. I saw you ages ago. I didn't think there was much danger, well...' she said, seeing the look that crossed his face, 'what I mean is, I don't suppose someone in your position makes a habit of leaping on women.'

'No', he admitted, 'at least not till we'd been introduced properly'.

'We were.' Her reminder caused him to flush, and his face already red from the exertion turned an even brighter red, which simply made her laugh.

He sat down at her invitation, and she told him that the children had been left with a neighbour. She needed to have some time on her own to think. He offered to leave, but she said that the things she'd been thinking about were not easy, and maybe she needed to talk them over with someone like him, who as a clergyman might have some help to offer. And, because he was young, would perhaps be more understanding than the old vicar. David felt just a little guilty thinking about EBG as he agreed with her.

Things had not been going well in her marriage since her last child, the youngest. She'd not wanted it and had tried everything to cause a miscarriage, but she'd gone full term and had the baby. Part of her distress had been the knowledge that all the time she'd been carrying the baby, her husband had been carrying on with another woman. And not just one either. It had seemed that he'd become insatiable and because she was ill, and tired, she'd not wanted to respond. So he found people who would. Even when she was in hospital having the baby he'd been with someone else. She wasn't sure who, but it was someone he worked with.

She'd felt so awful that it seemed easier to put up with it, but things had got worse recently because he'd got this idea that they should open their marriage. This, as she knew, was just him saying that he wanted to conduct his affairs in public, and with her permission so that he needn't feel guilty. Anyway, she'd agreed, and one night he'd brought this couple home. He knew them through a contact at work, and they'd had a few drinks and then her husband, his name was Alex, had suggested that the woman came upstairs with him. As soon as they left the room the husband began kissing her. At first she'd put up some resistance, but it seemed easier to give in, and finally he undressed her and they'd made love, or what would be better called lust.

Alex came in just at the end as she was still naked, and whilst he was smiling she knew that he was angry. That night he'd hit her and hurt her before saying he was sorry, and insisting that they made love. She'd stayed awake most of the night, feeling confused, angry and dirty, and left next morning. She wasn't sure what was to happen, and hoped that Alex would contact her.

David, sitting next to her, wasn't sure what to say. He rehearsed a couple of thoughts, but nothing made sense and knew that the less he said now, the less would need to be unsaid later.

By now Gilly was crying and it seemed only natural to David to slip a comforting arm around her shoulder, and they sat together for a long while, David staring out to sea and Gilly, with her head on his shoulder.

As they sat, David sensed that what he was feeling had more in common with the natural instincts of his sex in relation to a young, pretty and vulnerable woman than with a sense of the higher calling associated with his vocation and ministry. But then he knew about one, and was only just beginning to learn about the other. It seemed to him in the absence of anything better he should trust his instincts, and his instinct was to kiss her.

Looking back on their meeting later that day as he walked towards Swansley, he found himself amazed that someone as sensible and full of confidence as Gilly seemed to be, should have allowed herself to be put into a position where she would go along with the things she had described to him. After all, she was a well educated, intelligent young woman and her husband had a good, well-paid, responsible job, yet somehow they had allowed their lives to get into such an awful mess. A mess that neither would tolerate from others in their professional lives.

As he walked he was haunted by a recurring image of Gilly, with some faceless man, standing naked and vulnerable as her husband came into the room. He saw the three of them there and tried to imagine what might have passed between them. What might have been said, and the image of Gilly, naked, remained as he walked.

For some reason he knew it caused him pain, the kind

of pain that is felt between lovers as they seek to protect and shelter each other, and it was a pain that he had not felt for some long time.

Getting on with it

My faltering, dog-eared dreams
My heartaches, plans and schemes
Are all rolled up and counted in
Here's hoping the good outweighs the sin
I fly the kites of constant hopes
Continually bouncing off the ropes
But for all my constant battling
Success remains just staying in the ring
Don't claim too much for me
There's no real clarity I'm all at sea
The comings and goings, ins and outs
Getting on with it despite the doubts
So how do you rate success
Keeping straight avoiding the mess
Life is simply not well planned
So let us publish and be damned

EBG

**Training Conference
for
New Clergy**
_____

The training week for the new clergy was run for the diocese by the Bishop's Chaplain, who was himself a relatively junior member of the Bishop's Staff. He had only recently been appointed to the job following his move from a curacy in one of the university parishes where he had spent most of his time. Having finished his doctoral thesis, now as the Revd. Dr, he was the blue-eyed boy of the diocese. Indeed the bishop had been overheard at a Synod meeting telling one of the archdeacons how the diocese had been fortunate to keep him.

The Chaplain was an ambitious person. He had no intention of remaining a parish priest, and had some years before outlined his game plan. He'd told a friend at theological college that he wanted to be a bishop by the age of forty. The plan involved acquiring his doctoral thesis, creating an aura of confidence around himself, ensuring that he was a person who could be trusted to deliver by the simple expedient of refusing no request, as long as it came from a member of the hierarchy. This would establish a rounded career profile, with academic and parochial qualifications to the fore. Then, seeking an appointment, any appointment to the staff of a cathedral, any cathedral, from where, as he explained, he would be sure to be noticed.

Part of the game plan was to be above reproach. So he made sure that he married and fathered a number of children, but not to be encumbered. He would marry someone, who it appeared to his colleagues and parishioners, made no demands on him whatsoever, so that to all intents and purposes the work style that he maintained was that of a bachelor, his wife taking full responsibility for the running of the household.

Visitors to the chaplain's household would be greeted at the door by his wife, tired and drawn, carrying a child with one or two more clinging to her skirts. They would be shown into the study where Sadler Lane would sit surrounded by his books, apparently unmoved by, and uninvolved in the business of domestic management. That was conducted off stage to a soundtrack of crisis and imminent disaster, from amongst which tea and cake would miraculously appear. It was served in china cups on silver trays which had been bought in the local antique shop to imply inheritance, connections, and good family.

The Chaplain had managed in both his jobs to acquire houses that were splendidly Barchester like, which was simply another way of ensuring that he was seen in a setting appropriate to his Episcopal ambitions.

The setting for the training week was the diocesan retreat house. It was a splendid country house built just before the 1914 war, and gifted to the diocese by the family after the death of their only son in that war.

The house, a large comfortable country house, shabbily furnished by donations on a room-by-room basis by the Mothers' Union, was located in a fairly isolated valley served by an unreliable railway. The station, a good twenty minutes' walk away, provided the nearest point of access by public transport.

For David the drive over from Manchester had been without incident, although it was clear to him that the Mini, which he had bought for a few hundred pounds would soon need some major repairs. The engine kept cutting out at crossroads and junctions, usually, and most infuriatingly, when he was about to pull away at traffic lights which made it look as though he had stalled the car.

The trip to Manchester had gone well and his mother had been delighted to see him. His father, less expressive had taken him to the club and bought him a pint. It was clear to David that they were both delighted by his success at escaping their background, but at the same puzzled and sad at losing him. His father in particular seemed confused, wanting at the same time as boasting at his achievement, wanting also to criticise him for 'turning his back on his own'. David found himself insisting that they should come to Drissburgh for a holiday. However, he secretly hoped that the excuses they offered were real enough to keep them from naming an actual date.

His father's last words when he was leaving made it clear, 'We'll see you then lad, next time you're over this way'.

The estate where his parents lived was close to the city centre. One day he retraced his steps to the building on Whitworth Street where he had been to school. It was a red brick memorial, offering only unhappy memories of wasted days, bullying teachers like Mr. Rourke, who had once beaten him savagely around the head, for singing out of tune or key, or both. This was during a practice of the school song for speech day. And, of course, there were bullying children. These were not David's happiest days, and as he walked on into the city centre to find a present for his mother, he reflected on how much he had changed, and how the expectations of his teachers had been turned on their heads by his vocation. It began with night school and theological college, to ordination and a career with prospects. No one can stop me from singing now he thought, even if it's still out of tune, and out of key.

His only remaining friend from those days had remained in Manchester and was now a police constable, working in the area where they had both grown up. He'd not planned to look Pete up on this visit but had stumbled into him almost by accident one evening in the club. The night had drifted on into the early hours, as they swapped pints and stories. Pete was annoyed that David's ordination had gone unacknowledged, and that no-one had made the journey to support him at what should have been a time for recognising his achievement. 'I'm surprised that Mr. Hamer didn't mention it, I saw him a few weeks ago but he never said anything about it.'

'No', said David, 'I'm not surprised really, I think he's got mixed feelings about it. I saw him yesterday and I think in some ways he regrets encouraging me.'

'Why', asked Pete.

'Because I think he's a bit disillusioned by the system. But, like I told him, I've got no expectations, so I can't be disappointed really. In fact I'll probably end up being a disappointment to the system in the end'.

'I'll drink to that', said Pete, raising his glass to drain

it as he saw the barman coming over to clear the tables at the end of the night.

Now, driving down the narrow lane that led to Worlby Grange, David thought about the evening with his father, and with Pete, and realised how much he'd changed. But he also realised that it was only enough to ensure that he had a passport out of Manchester and his old life. It was not enough to give him a passport into his new life; not in the fullest sense of being accepted by the diocese as represented by the chaplain, and anything approaching a friendship with any of the people he would be sharing the next few days with.

Having parked his car and found his room, David went off in search of whoever was around and the possibility of a coffee in the Kitchen. Mrs Bailey, the warden of Worlby Grange was a remarkable, fiercely independent person who ran the house with singular authority. She was not normally given to making particular friendships with her visitors and certainly not with the junior clergy. David sensed that she had made an exception in his case, and whilst nothing was scheduled until lunch, he felt fairly confident that he would find a much welcome cup of coffee waiting for him if he made his arrival known.

It was whilst he was in the kitchen, chatting to Mrs Bailey as she took advantage of the interruption to sip a cup of coffee with him, that the chaplain entered. Hardly able to keep his disapproval to himself, he consulted with Mrs Bailey over the numbers expected for lunch, and the arrangements for the bishop's visit on Thursday, all the while eyeing David with suspicion.

'We are waiting for you in the common room, David', he said as he left the kitchen.

'But I thought we didn't meet till lunch', David replied.

'That's true, but the early arrivals are chatting in the common room', this last comment over his shoulder as he left.

Mrs Bailey smiled. 'What he means, David', she said, 'is that you shouldn't be in the kitchen with the staff, you should be upstairs with the gentlemen'.

David grimaced. 'Watch him', she replied, to his unspoken criticism, 'he's dangerous that one, and you're not his most popular person either, I can tell.'

After lunch, during the first session, which was spent in pairs, sharing some of their discoveries about themselves, their strengths and weaknesses, in their first months in their parishes, the chaplain made his feelings clear.

'David' he opined, 'brought a particular contribution to his ministry. It was clear that his talent for getting alongside ordinary people might qualify him for a specialised ministry. Had he thought about industrial chaplaincy for instance. It was the kind of thing that people like him could undertake successfully, even if they found that they weren't called to parish ministry'.

It was toward the end of the week before David finally cracked. They were expecting the bishop that afternoon, and the chaplain had been leading a session on working with young people in the parish.

In fact, in Drissburgh, EBG had accepted David's view that youth work was a specialised activity and not one for the faint hearted. EBG encouraged him to become qualified as a youth worker, and because of this he was not sure he needed the chaplain's instant training session, and it showed on his face.

The session consisted of a role play, in which David was cast as a troublemaker who had turned up at the youth club and had to be turned away by the leader. That role was assumed by the chaplain himself.

The session started amicably enough, and as David arrived at the supposed reception area of the supposed youth club and asked to be allowed in, the chaplain refused. Very quickly the stakes were raised and suddenly David realised that what was being said was not a role play at all. Some of the points about his background, disruptive behaviour, surliness, lack of co-operation and the unsuitability of his appearance, were Sadler Lane's own very real opinions of David. The chaplain didn't want him out of his imaginary youth club, he wanted him out of the diocese.

David grew increasingly belligerent until, in what he knew was an all too real case of art imitating life, he decided to push past the chaplain into the club itself. The Chaplain tried to stop him, but David pushed him to one side and then involuntarily ducked as the chair that the chaplain had aimed at his head, swung by and crashed to the floor, coming to rest against his leg.

There was a silence in the room disturbed only by the chaplain's rough, panicky breathing as, red faced and obviously out of control, he fought with himself to bring his emotions back under control.

In the feedback on the session, the chaplain, who had

taken a five minute break at the end of the role play, when he had finally trusted himself to speak. He turned on David, accusing him of being out of control, clearly unfit to be allowed anywhere near young people, or anyone who was working with them. It was a matter he fully intended to bring up with EBG who he referred to as 'your vicar'.

David, who had found the session totally unreal to this point, finally exploded. To the embarrassment of the other course members, he turned on the chaplain before broadening his attack to include them all. 'You know', he stammered, beside himself with anger, and now genuinely out of control, 'I have no problem, communicating with people in the parish, my problem is other clergymen. You're shits, all of you, absolute fucking shits'.

The silence was powerful and went on for longer than anyone in the room was comfortable with, finally the chaplain spoke.

'Well, David, the bishop will be here this afternoon, and unless you can promise to control yourself better than you have done this morning I must ask you not to come to the session. I will not have language like that in front of the bishop and certainly not from one of his clergy'.

David smiled 'I won't swear as long as you don't throw chairs' he said, rising to leave the room.

It seemed to David as he walked around the garden that afternoon, that he needed to do something to sort out the situation that was rapidly building to a major confrontation. It was a confrontation that he couldn't possibly win because the chaplain had all the cards. He knew that a report would go to EBG about the course, and decided he needed to see EBG the minute he got back to Drissburgh. To see him for no other reason than he knew that if anyone would take his side it was the man who was rapidly becoming his only real friend in the diocese as well as being his vicar and his boss.

During the session with the bishop, David remained silent, only answering the Bishop's direct question to him, as simply as he could. He had no wish at this stage to get into some complex dialogue with authority. He knew that his outburst earlier would have been reported, and he had no wish to make matters worse. The Bishop was really concerned to hear the stories of those he was already identifying as the rising stars amongst the new intake of deacons. The chaplain appeared surprisingly nervous at the presence of the bishop and was taking every opportunity to ingratiate himself. So, David's silence went largely unnoticed.

As he said goodbye to Mrs Bailey, and headed the car toward Drissburgh, David began to think again about Gilly. Her story, her physical presence, the feel of her cheek brushing his face like a petal falling. He realised how much he had missed her over the two weeks that he'd been away, and how much he was looking forward to seeing her again.

And deep in the distance he heard an alarm bell ring, and dismissed it as his imagination.

The road to Drissburgh passed through Worsby before heading down the narrow country lane that ended in the centre of the village. At the junction where the two roads headed separately, one to the deserted quayside, and the other up past the church to the headland.

David parked the mini next to his cottage and let himself in. Shuddering at the untidiness, and his lifestyle, he attempted to tidy away some of the clothes and clutter that were scattered around the small living room. Realising no-one was likely to visit, he let them drop and went into the kitchen to put the kettle on to make himself a cup of tea. Whilst the kettle was boiling he telephoned the vicarage to let EBG know of his return but there was no answer. After letting the telephone ring for a while he replaced the receiver, poured the boiling water onto a tea bag, and sorted through his post.

Amongst the usual junk mail and circular letters was a letter addressed in small, precise handwriting which he didn't recognise.

Inside there was a letter from Gilly asking if they might meet on his return, as she wanted to discuss something important with him. Something that was really, fairly urgent, and asking him to telephone her.

Dialling her number he knew that what he was feeling was something more than would be associated with a vicar telephoning one of his parishioners to make an appointment for a pastoral visit. When she answered, he felt the urgency in his voice, as he introduced himself, and suggested that, in response to her letter, that he might visit that afternoon. Gilly thought that as the kids would be around then that it might be better if he came later that evening, and they arranged the time for 8:30 pm.

As he was looking through his diary and wondering what he might do next, the telephone rang. This time he was altogether more businesslike, almost to the point of brusqueness, as he recognised Sadler Lane's voice.

'David' he began, 'I felt it necessary to appraise the bishop of your outburst, and naturally enough he was distressed. He wonders if you have given sufficient consideration to your going forward to Priesting, and wonders if it might be better to postpone things, say, for a year to give you time to work your future out'.

David was not sure how to respond, he was amazed at the audacity of the man, and annoyed with himself that he had given him the ammunition he needed to block his career.

'Look', he began, 'I'm sorry about that. I was wrong, and I'm sorry. It's just that I get angry, and confused and then say stupid thing. But it hasn't happened in the parish, and it wouldn't. Ask EBG, ask anyone, they will tell you. My ordination is too important to postpone, so much depends on it, you know that. It would mean that I've let everyone down, that I've let myself down, and I can't do that, you can't do that, the bishop can't do that'.

He realised as he spoke that he was losing something important. The chaplain paused before speaking. 'Well, David', he said, 'you must understand that we simply can't, won't put up with such appalling behaviour from junior clergy. From any clergyman who holds the bishop's licence for that matter. If you are to remain in this diocese you will, from now on, control that temper of yours. Consider this a warning. I will tell the bishop that we have spoken, and that you are remorseful and that we will be meeting regularly to monitor progress. Goodbye then,

I'll be calling over to Drissburgh in a week or two and perhaps we can meet then.'

David replaced the receiver without answering. He knew well enough that the chaplain was giving him due warning and there was little he could say.

The rest of the morning was spent without settling to any particular job. He tried to read, to write some letters, to think about a sermon for the coming Sunday, to plan some visits, but nothing held his attention. As he was beginning to think about lunch, a knock at the door announced the unexpected arrival of Bobby Edwards, who having accepted his offer of tea, lit a cigarette and settled down in the only remotely comfortable chair. He began, in his excitable way to tell David about the developments in St. Agatha's during his time away.

It seemed that there had been something of a scandal, and that Gilly had been at the centre of it. That EBG had been involved and Bobby thought that at one time the police had been called in to intervene.

It seemed that Gilly's husband had come over to Drissburgh to see the children and to talk to Gilly about the future. When he arrived she had been in the shower, or bath, and one of the children had opened the door, or maybe he'd let himself in, after all he would have a key to his own house wouldn't he. Anyway he'd spoken to Gilly through the bathroom door, which was locked and she had told him that she didn't want to see him and for him to go. The neighbours had said that her language was shocking.

What happened next would keep Drissburgh's

thriving gossip industry in business for years to come. Apparently, the husband had said that if he was going, then he was taking the children with him and proceeded to put them in the car. At this point Gilly had stormed out of the bathroom totally naked and begun to harangue her husband from the top of the stairs. The children began to scream, and hearing them, she'd come out of the house just as she was, and dragged the kids back out of the car.

Someone called the police who persuaded her to wrap a blanket round herself, but only after she'd made them promise that the children would stay.

David, who was at first amused, then outraged, and scandalised by Bobby's story, and just a little affected by the thought that everyone in Drissburgh had seen Gilly naked, could see that Bobby was clearly moved by the story he was telling.

According to Bobby, Gilly had not been seen much since the event, which had happened early in David's first week away, and had missed church last Sunday.

David was just a little suspicious. Bobby's visit was unusual, and he sensed that there was more to it than a desire to relate the latest village scandal.

'How's EBG', David asked. It appeared he was fine. 'Who was in church on Sunday?' Should he be planning to visit anyone? Bobby seemed to think that everyone who needed accounting for was there, or the reason for their missing church was known.

Lighting a second cigarette, Bobby asked David what he knew about Parkinson's disease. David admitted that he knew very little, apart from what he'd gleaned from the medical reports in his newspaper. It was a debilitating and incurable disease and that sufferers often had to undergo lots of tests and had to resign themselves to taking medication throughout their lives.

David decided that he ought to be more direct, and asked Bobby why he was interested. Bobby smiled sheepishly 'oh', he muttered 'I've got to go to hospital for some tests, but I don't think I'll go. I can't see what good it'll do'.

David sensed that he was not being told the whole truth, that Bobby was keeping something back.

'Have you told Hilda about this', he asked.

'No', Bobby replied 'I don't want to bother her', David was amazed. people and their relationships he thought, I'll never understand.

What David sensed however was that Bobby was afraid of something that he thought he had, or might have Parkinson's and at first David thought maybe it was fear of the illness that he sensed in Bobby. The longer they talked he wondered if what he was hearing was another fear altogether, but what it was, he didn't know.

Bobby showed no sense of wanting to leave, and as David was beginning to feel hungry, he suggested that he make some lunch. After consulting the empty pantry he suggested soup and a steak pie cooked from the tin in which it was purchased. This was washed down with a couple of mugs of tea.

Over lunch Bobby talked about his son Peter and his worries for the future. Of his concern for the boy, and what would happen to him after he and Hilda were gone.

David thought maybe there were some good places. Places locally, homes and sheltered accommodation where Peter would be well looked after. He could see in Bobby's face and general demeanour the storm clouds gathering.

Bobby was someone whose hold on his life was suddenly beginning to slip, and his visit here this morning was connected to the fact that what he wanted from David was something that EBG would never give.

When finally, Bobby left, David set out to walk up to the headland. Passing the church he saw the door open and walking up the path he literally bumped into EBG, changing the notices in the porch. Greeting his curate, he announced that some of the notices had been there since before he was vicar, and that it would give the congregation something to talk about before the service on Sunday. David smiled.

'How did the course go?' EBG frowned as he heard about the role play and David's outburst,

'You are a bloody fool; you know that don't you. You've got so much to offer. Not to the church, that doesn't count, but to people. You give them such warm encouragement; you help them believe in themselves. That's why Sadler Lane and his ilk will always have it in for you. Because you are what they claim to be, and you show them up. For God's sake David, you're on the verge of a worthwhile career, don't give Sadler Lane the excuse he's looking for to take it away from you.

'Where are you going now?' David told him. 'Well, call in at the Vicarage on your way back and we'll have tea'.

Leaving the church David turned and headed up the road to the turning circle. Pausing, he climbed the wall and headed across the rough tussocky grass. To his left the ocean raged at the rocks below, surf crashing itself onto the jagged rocks and then retracting, drawing back torn and bleeding into the boiling ocean.

As he walked, the constant roar from the buffeting wind acted as a powerful cleansing agent, scouring the thoughts from his mind and the words from his lips.

He struggled to hold onto the conflicting sentiments he had. His puzzlement about the chaplain, his vocation, the bishop, the parish and above all, Gilly.

He was torn between his genuine pastoral impulse to reach out to someone who was hurting, to offer the loving support that was the currency of his vocation, and the need to satisfy his own need for emotional and sexual nourishment which recognised Gilly as someone who was capable of giving that to him.

As he wrestled with these conflicts he walked quickly and purposefully toward Swanborough reaching the river sooner than on any previous occasion.

The river was high but passable with effort. Removing his clothes, which he bundled into two roughly even parcels and threw across to the far bank, he set off to wade the stream. In the middle of the river, with the water deepening with each cautious step, he pushed against the flowing water, gasping at the cold which took his breath away. Kicking for the opposite bank he scrambled ashore, and rubbing himself down with a tee shirt, dressed, and headed down toward Swanborough.

According to EBG, at one time there had been a bridge at the crossing point, known as The Monks Bridge. Named after the monastery at Swanborough, it was still shown on the Ordnance Survey Maps, but apart from some large stones in the centre of the river and scattered along both banks there was no evidence of the bridge remaining.

The walk to Swanborough was, for this reason, regarded as something of a challenge by people in Drissburgh and each year the two villages participated in the Drissburgh Challenge. Each village fielding a team, to race from Drissburgh to Swanshurst culminating in the winning team downing a pint each in the Swan.

Honours were roughly even, and taken with the challenge, David had entered for the next race in exchange for sponsorship towards new choir robes for the choir at St. Agatha's.

When he returned to Drissburgh David called into the Vicarage. Bobby who was just leaving shot him a warning glance, clearly David was not to mention their earlier conversation.

After Bobby had gone EBG seemed reluctant to return to their earlier subject, and David who had no great desire to be told again what a fool he was, was happy enough to allow EBG to steer the conversation along the safer routes of trivial matters relating to parish administration.

His preaching schedule and Sunday services drifted into a conversation about confirmation classes, before EBG remarked on the time and suggested that they ate together, and as he had an evening meeting to get to in

Worsby that they ought to set out now.

For some reason, David seemed happier keeping the information about his evening commitment to himself.

Ringing the doorbell, he stood back and noticed the curtain in an upstairs room rise briefly and fall again. Then, hearing footsteps, the door opened.

Gilly stood back to let him in and, after a slightly uncomfortable moment's pause, she ushered him into the sitting room. Motioning him toward the settee, and seeing him comfortably settled, she sat down on the floor, by his feet.

Looking around the small cottage he noticed the tasteful furnishings and decoration, complimented by the subtle lighting. In the fireplace he noticed a colourful display of dried flowers and driftwood which he admired. Gilly smiled with pleasure, which he assumed arose because she was responsible for the arrangement.

She offered him coffee, which he declined and then for some while they sat in silence. He noticed her legs, which were slim, and brown from the sunbathing. She must sunbathe a lot he thought, and remembering her body in bra and panties, lying on the concrete of the fort and then realised with embarrassment that more than his imagination was being stimulated.

She was kneeling, half sitting at his feet and swaying slightly then as though absently mindedly picking something from the floor. She leant forward, intentionally or not he would never be sure, but as she did the front of her sweatshirt opened revealing her breasts. Small, braless and evenly tanned. Looking up, he saw her watching him, observing his reaction to this teasing display before reaching up and in a single fluid movement, she removed the sweatshirt and leaned back, displaying herself to him to perfect advantage.

He knew immediately that it was all over. She had won and he could only surrender, reaching forward he pulled her gently toward him and kissed her mouth. Brushing his lips against hers before moving from her lips to her neck, tracing a line along her cheek, kissing and sucking her flesh in little bites, from her neck he reached down to take her nipple into his mouth and caressing its erectness with his tongue, he gently rolled her nipple between his teeth. All the while teasing her with threatened bites which caused her to involuntarily pull away, then return for more.

When she finally spoke she said, 'I don't know whether to be pleased or disappointed that you're so obviously experienced. My fantasy was seducing a virgin'.

He smiled and pulled her into himself. Holding her tightly he felt her push against him and realised she was easing herself out of the rest of her clothes. When she was completely naked, she stood, taking an obvious pleasure in his enjoyment of her, before taking his hand and leading him upstairs to the bedroom. It had obviously been prepared for the seduction judging by the bottle of red wine and the two glasses on the bedside table.

She was completely at ease with her nakedness, and was clearly enjoying the sight reflected in the wardrobe mirror of her own nudity, which contrasted with his own stiffly suited figure with dog collar, and his bulging trousers.

She pressed herself against him and then reaching up took his collar in her teeth and pulled it slowly from its fastenings under his shirt.

Then pushing him back on the bed she unbuckled and unzipped his trousers and taking his enlarged cock in her hands, she slowly traced her tongue from the tip to the base and down, taking each of his balls in turn into her mouth. She sucked until they ached with an excruciating pleasure that he wished would go on forever.

Naked, finally he slid into her and they made love again, and again. In between she took him again in her mouth, and as he came she pulled him so that he spilled into her and she drank him greedily.

The second time they made love, as he came she whispered into his ear that from now on she would call him her second coming.

For David, this sex was a miracle. He knew now that there was a good deal of confusion around, she was clearly no innocent whose trust he had betrayed, and he knew that his vocation as a man transcended his other vocation.

He also knew, or at least suspected, that she had been less than honest with him and that, if she had taken lovers at her husband's suggestion, she was probably a more than willing partner.

But she moved around the bedroom, graceful and confident in her nudity, as she sipped wine from his mouth. As she snuggled down under the duvet, skin on skin, sang the body electric, and this whole experience was an erotic poem. They were the stanzas, verses, metre and rhyme.

He examined her closely, as a blind man with eyes closed he breathed deeply of her scents. Sweat and perfume, sex and semen, rich scents that he tasted and breathed, and kissed her head to toe and back, licking her breasts and nipples, sucking toes and kissing her vagina. Dripping wine into the cup of her stomach and drinking noisily and greedily, spilling and staining the sheets.

He saw the small blemishes on her skin, the bruises fading and the wounds that she had sustained in the battle of the sexes. At the place of each bruise, each scar, each small stretch mark he placed a kiss and claimed it as his own.

Later they talked, about how he had become a clergyman, about EBG and St. Agatha's. Then about her and her marriage, about her husband and his passions. For David sex was important when he didn't have it, but to her husband it was almost a sacramental thing, to be taken, broken and shared. It was true what she had told David on the headland, but that was years before and that was the first time. Since then she had, at her husband's suggestion taken lovers, had encouraged him to watch as she had made love to them. She had performed, shown off and relished the moment when beside himself, he would take her and make love to her, both of them oblivious to the young man she had brought home for their mutual pleasure.

But it was also true, she said, that she realised how driven she had become. She had left her husband, who had taken another lover, because what he demanded from her was becoming more insatiable, and she was frightened to think where it might end.

What she tried to make David see was that she had come to the stage where unless they had become lovers, she would never be able to receive the help he could give her. Help which she desperately needed.

David was, he knew, confused. He needed to have someone in his life with whom he could sustain an intimate and sexual relationship. He was too much a child of his times to be worried about the niceties of marriage, whatever the Church might teach. But there was something about what was going on here that bothered him.

What he was being offered distorted already stretched values. For Gilly he was someone who would counsel and support her.

But to get to the stage where what he was offering and what she wanted from him, could be given and received, it had to be mediated through a transaction that was about as honest as two people had to be when they had stripped away all the pretences.

David wasn't sure that he was ready for sex as therapy. He still believed in old fashioned love and commitment.

They sat in bed content to see and be seen. They drank their wine and fed each other savoury biscuits in a ceremony that troubled and delighted David. Then they made love again, slowly and gently. David held back until Gilly reached her own climax, crying out, small cries of delight, fear and triumph.

When it was time to go she showed him to the door, and he set out to walk back through the village to his cottage with its view of the sea. The moon tracked a path across the water, looking as though he had left a light on. It was the moon's reflection on his window.

He was tired and at the same time elated. He knew that he would find it hard settling to sleep; the memories of that night would remain with him for some time yet.

When he got to his door he decided to walk a little way up the road, and past the church yard. He imagined it would be too dark to risk walking out over the headland itself, but the moonlight was bright and before long he found himself at the fort, sheltering against one of the concrete pillars that imitated as a medieval arch. Staring out over the ocean, noticing for the first time the slight phosphorescence that cast an eerie glow on the water's surface.

The next day, scarcely able to believe what had happened, David decided to go into Worsby, thinking that a trip to the supermarket for some essentials, and a visit to Shore's the Bookseller, was as good a way of celebrating the remarkable events of the night before as any. Especially so if he combined it with a visit to the Red Lion coffee shop for a doughnut breakfast.

As he pulled out of Drissburgh he passed Hilda, Bobby's wife and the redoubtable treasurer and secretary of the PCC, standing at the bus stop. Pulling up, he asked her if he could offer her a lift. As luck would have it and to his surprise, she was waiting for the Worsby bus.

Climbing into the Mini she settled herself into the seat with her shopping bag on her lap.

At first they drove along in silence, but eventually David mentioned Bobby, asking in passing how he was. Hilda, who was not given much to small talk, seemed glad of the opportunity to share her own worries.

It seemed that Bobby had as long as she had known him, been afraid of Doctors. Not in themselves, he'd encouraged her to see the doctor when she was ill. He was happy enough visiting in hospital, or wherever, if someone was ill or in for treatment. But for himself, to the best of her knowledge, and she'd known Bobby for fifty years, he had never visited the doctor until recently. The doctor had visited, and noticed that Bobby's hand was shaking and had asked to see him. He'd gone along but was clearly unhappy. And now the doctor was talking about this Parkinson's disease and about taking Bobby into hospital for tests.

She thought he wouldn't go, that in the end he would simply refuse but she was also worried that if he didn't, he would become so ill that it would disable him.

As they drove along, she spoke about Bobby as though he was already out of her life, as though he might already have died, and David challenged her about this. She paused, in an almost embarrassed way, before remarking that as far as she knew or dare admit to herself, she'd always known that Bobby would go at the first obstacle. That he had neither the willpower nor the determination for a real fight. She'd seen once on a TV programme about some black men in Australia, who would lie down and die if someone put a curse on them. She knew, as soon as the doctors got their hands on Bobby that's exactly what he would do.

David was amazed. There was, he knew, a powerful mix of wisdom and folklore in what Hilda was saying.

It was also from a Christian point of view, completely unacceptable, and at odds with Christian doctrine. It was a kind of northern voodoo, as though once anointed with the blood of the headless chicken, Bobby was cursed and would lay down to die.

He tried to argue his case with Hilda, but she was implacable. She was, he could tell, deeply troubled about this man to whom she had promised for better or worse. But for two people who claimed to be Christian, who attended church weekly, and who were as deeply involved as Bobby and Hilda were with the life of the local church, the fatalism that she was representing was simply unacceptable. But it was also, he knew, unanswerable.

This was the ideal pastoral opportunity. One that his pastoral studies' tutor at college would have seen as quite literally heaven sent. Here they were in his car, driving for forty minutes with an opportunity for a meaningful and uninterrupted conversation. He knew that he should somehow, offer the moment to God who would use him as the instrument of wise counsel and pastoral intervention.

But all he could think to say was a suggestion that maybe if Bobby could see the doctor at home, in familiar surroundings, then he would be reassured that there was nothing to fear from what were routine tests after all. They might even look back on the episode as a quite unnecessary worry about nothing.

Hilda, he could see, was unimpressed, and as they pulled into Worsby he realised that the opportunity had passed. He parked the car, and refusing his offer of a lift back to Drissburgh, Hilda set off in the direction of the small market where she did her regular weekly shop. David turned and headed for the Red Lion where he knew from a previous visit he would find excellent homemade doughnuts and good strong coffee.

Soon he was settled in a corner of the bar with cake and coffee to hand, and a copy of the local paper to read. In this way he passed an exceptionally pleasant forty minutes before venturing out to Shore's the Bookseller, where he found a tattered copy of *Sex, Love and Marriage* by Roland H. Bainton, published as a Fontana paperback in 1958.

Catching his eye on the shelf, the title had struck him as entirely appropriate given the situation into which he was becoming embroiled. Flipping through the pages, he could see that as the blurb suggested, maybe his own situation was really only the same as that faced by St. Augustine. Wasn't he the saint whose prayer had been the constant comfort of sinners down the years, 'Lord, make me good, but not yet'.

Clutching his book and a few essential items from the supermarket David returned to the Mini and headed out of Worsby for home.

On the journey back he began to think about his sermon for the coming Sunday. EBG had asked him to preach at the evening service, and as far as he knew, the chaplain was planning to be there to assess him for the preaching element of his diaconal assessment.

He knew that if he was to impress the chaplain he would have to work hard at getting the sermon right, and as he thought about it he began to think that it might be a good occasion to say something about himself and his own understanding of vocation, and the role of calling in relation to the job of being a clergyman.

If he was to find himself in the position of privilege, six foot above contradiction, then he might as well use it.

That Sunday the chaplain preceded him into the Sanctuary and David, as the Preacher walked in the procession side by side with EBG.

Sitting in the curate's pew he looked down at the congregation. The first person he saw was Gilly with her two daughters sitting in the first pew. When their eyes met she smiled at him -- the sweet innocence of her smile belied by the knowing wink that accompanied it. David felt a reddening in his cheeks, and a stirring which made him glad he was wearing a Cassock and Surplice. During the confession he made an extra effort, and as he ascended the pulpit stairs he tried to avoid catching her eye.

David was aware that both Gilly, who he wished to impress, and the Chaplain who he knew could affect his future career in ways that were less than helpful, were both going to be in the congregation when he preached his sermon. For that reason he decided that he would base the sermon on a particular text. It was an old fashioned but useful way of grounding the sermon.

He decided to preach on verses 46 and 49 from Chapter 10 of St John's Gospel. "Nathaniel said to Philip, 'can anything good come out of Nazareth?' Philip responded, 'Come and see.' When Nathaniel had met Jesus he said to him, 'Rabbi', you are the Son of God! You are the King of Israel."

David hoped that as Nathaniel was convinced, so he

might convince both his supporter and his doubter.

David went on to expound his text.

'As you heard in the second lesson this evening, Philip, having been called by Jesus saw Nathaniel sitting beneath a fig tree and went to tell him about Jesus. At first Nathaniel was reluctant to meet Jesus, but he was persuaded by Philip and went with him. Upon meeting Jesus his mood changed, almost immediately.

'To see that this is so, compare the almost cynical nature of, "Can anything good come out of Nazareth?" with the awe-filled, "Rabbi, you are the Son of God, You are the King of Israel".

'What a difference there is between the mood of these two sentences. Scepticism transformed into adoration, doubt into belief. Yet it is only right that such a difference should exist, for between these two sentences being spoken, Nathaniel encountered the greatest life changing force the world has ever known.

'Jesus Christ, the man in whom the truth of His divinity was so compellingly apparent that no one could resist Him.

'Nathaniel need not have come to Jesus, he could have refused Philip's invitation, but he didn't, he came.

'Perhaps his interest was aroused by Philip's enthusiasm. Perhaps he came out of mere curiosity, whichever it was, and we will never know, the point remains, he came. And it was this one simple act of coming to see for himself, that changed his whole life.

'Even though Nathaniel does not appear to have been chosen by Jesus as a disciple, in the way that the other disciples were chosen, it remains that having come to see for himself, from that moment on his life was changed.

'He became what we might call a new man. He would remain in his ordinary job, but now he would do that job "in Christ".

'Some of us, for reasons that must vary a good deal from person to person, are called to live a special kind of life. And we are not, it seems, always the Nathaniel; pleasant, peaceable men, able to work out our salvation by living ordinary, if Christ-centered lives.

'There are figures in the New Testament, and amongst the disciples, from amongst whom we might take our models. Mine is Peter, or Simon as he was before he met Christ.

'When I read about this fisherman, I imagine him casting his huge, heavy nets, trawling for fish, handling the great baskets full of slippery silver damp fish.

'I see him as a big man with his rough, calloused, workaday hands and strong fingers. Uncouth, not at all the refined cultured or educated man that has long been the image in this country of the clergyman.

'For me, Peter is Peter the Rock, a tempestuous man, blustering and blundering, clumsy and impulsive.

'He is not young anymore, which means that he will be stubborn and set in his ways, with just too many hard-to-change ideas.

'Yes, he is a rough man, a man who has lived a rough life. He is easily provoked, this Peter of my imagination, and at times his choice of language might be frowned upon.

'Yet when he came to Jesus, as a simple enquirer, for he too came to see, Jesus chose him. Chose him to follow, to serve, to be with Him, and in due course he sent him, along with the other disciples, out preaching and healing.

'Peter became a disciple along with the others who were chosen by Jesus, because he came and saw, was chosen and obeyed.

'In the three years that they were with Jesus, something happened to these men. Silent and unnoticed Jesus, by word and by example, created all the possibilities for change. In the heart of each disciple was planted a seed. It was a seed that would need time to germinate. In time, of course, it did, and they preached the Gospel, the Good News and at great personal cost.

'When we look at the fearlessness, even the arrogance and the confidence of the disciples we meet in the Book of Acts, and compare them with the weak, insufficient and oh! so human men of the Gospels, we can begin to understand what is meant by the outpouring of the Spirit.

'It was not the men, with their failings and their humanity that Jesus chose. It was their possibilities in the spirit which only he could see.

'And today the world continues to be filled with the Nathaniels and Peters of our own time -- men who must be prepared to come, see and to obey the will of the Lord as you and I must, whatever it may mean for us too, in our lives.

'You may be a Nathaniel, or a Philip, a James an Andrew, or like me a Peter, whichever, you can be sure that if you come to see Jesus this Christmas, you will be chosen, perhaps to continue living in the world in a new, and fuller understanding of Christ, Saviour and King. Or, like Peter, challenged to leave all in a peculiar relationship with God and the World.

'Whichever it is to be, we must first 'Come and See', and then obey in the knowledge that whatever our inadequacies, which are probably many, they will be reduced to nothing by the power of the Spirit working in and through us.

'Come, see, obey.

'These are the three key words about the relationship of man to Christ. These three words provide me with what I need to answer to those who ask me the only too common question of the new curate, "Why did you want to be ordained?"

'The simple, almost trite answer is, I don't *want* to be ordained, I have no alternative.

'In recent months the church has made much of the fact that the numbers of those offering themselves for the ministry have been steadily decreasing, and the church has tried in a number of ways to get men looking at the question of vocation and asking, is this the life for me?

'Well!

'I think such an approach is far too simple. No one can answer that question, not even especially the person asking it. Imagine if Peter had asked that question of himself. Think of some of his experiences.

'Think of "get thee behind me Satan". Think of denying Christ three times. Think of that awful time between Good Friday and Easter when Peter's world lay shattered at his feet.

'The answer to Peter's doubts lay not in his own assessment of his possibilities but in his simple faith in Jesus, whom he knew, and was prepared to obey.

'There are many times in my own life when I feel that I am being presumptuous in seeking ordination. I am uncertain whether I will fulfil the demands that will be made on me, but I know I must try because I came to Jesus, saw and am trying to obey.

'And it is in this obeying, that faced with the question about what is there that is good that can come from Nazareth, I know where I must look to find Him. He who was manifested in the body, vindicated in the spirit, seen by the angels, who was proclaimed among the nations, believed in throughout the world and glorified in high heaven.

'Whom we must see and Obey.'

David finished his sermon and returned to his seat. After a while he looked across at EBG who motioned his head in the chaplain's direction as their eyes met. The Chaplain smiled in an encouraging sort of way.

It was only later, after the service, that the chaplain whispered to David that he thought the sermon was fine. It was, he said, the kerygma, which EBG later translated as a compliment, meaning the heart of the gospel message.

The only other feedback came from Gilly's daughter some days later. She told him that from time to time when he was thinking, his eyes rolled up and you could only see the white bits. Amid a good deal of laughter David blushed.

As a precaution David had decided that they needed a cover story to justify their frequent meetings and to her secret amusement Gilly had agreed.

Between them they had decided that they would need to meet regularly in order to plan a special service for the children to mark the new year, a service to which the whole parish, not just the regular churchgoers, would be invited, the service would involve some participation from the children in the form of tableaux and maybe some of the older children would be invited to come and demonstrate their Christmas toys.

So far their meetings had involved a good deal of physical activity and little talking, and in particular no discussion of the forthcoming service.

They met at strange times. and following a chance encounter in the newsagents, Gilly had accepted an invitation for lunch which they had eaten in bed, where they were now lying, David stroking the small of her back with one hand the other being cupped around her breast which he was gently squeezing.

They lay together. forgetting both the time and all the plans with which they had begun the day. Gilly in particular had arranged to see a solicitor to discuss her legal position in the likely event of divorce proceedings. and David had intended to visit Bobby before making a couple of funeral visits in the later part of the afternoon.

As they lay there lost in the sensual, physical presence of each other, the telephone began to ring. Given the mechanical nature of a telephone, it ought properly to give exactly the same ring on each occasion that a call is received. But, like all mechanical objects it has a life of its own, and as far as David was concerned there was on this occasion something about the telephone and the urgency of its ringing that caused him to take more notice than he might otherwise have done.

As he rushed for the instrument he slipped on the wooden floor and his foot caught in the rug so that when he picked the phone up he was a little out of breath, 'Hello', he answered, 'David Saxon, who is this?'

'David, this is the Vicar. I thought I should warn you that the chaplain is on his way round. He's been here for lunch and wants to talk to you about your sermon, you know he was impressed. Well, he wants to enter it, or you, anyway, in a competition run by the Church Times. So he's on his way round, he should be with you any minute. Forewarned is forearmed as they say.'

David was in a flat panic, he scrambled into his own clothes practically screaming at Gilly to dress and leave, whilst she was lying in his bed not attempting to get up, get dressed or leave.

'Oh Gilly', please it's my career',

'But David, she laughed, even if I were to stay here he's not going to come into the bedroom is he? And as soon as you're talking I can just leave quietly, you can say I'm the cleaning lady or something'.

'Gilly, please *get dressed!* And please let's at least pretend to be planning the service, it is the cover story we agreed on'.

Just as she fastened the last button on her blouse and was zipping her skirt, the doorbell rang, opening the door,

David ushered the chaplain into the small sitting room and motioned him to sit.

'This is Gilly, from the young wives, we're planning a children's service for the New Year'.

'Well', said the chaplain, 'I must say, David, things are looking better all the time', then turning to Gilly. 'I'm so sorry to interrupt your conversation, but David and I have one or two matters of importance to discuss, I'm sure you understand'.

'That's okay', Gilly replied, 'I was leaving, and I'm sure that David and I can come together another day'.

David, in his hurry to usher her out corrected her, unnecessarily drawing attention to her *double entendre*. 'Bye, see you soon then Gilly, bye'.

Offering the chaplain tea, David steered him into the kitchen and away from the bedroom and the unmistakeable smell of bedclothes, which he was convinced were exuding their certain scents into the hall and living room.

Feeling more comfortable at the kitchen table they waded through the tiresome but necessary small talk. The chaplain clearly at ease with himself and his charge.

'Well, David, let me say right away, how impressed I was with that sermon the other evening. It was far and away the best of the sermons I've heard from your P.O.T. group, and I have no hesitation in recommending it to the Bishop.

David smiled, he felt somewhat foolish, and decided that it was best to say nothing.

Undeterred the chaplain carried on with an erudite and accomplished review of the sermon, commenting on some of the finer theological points, and clearly not unaware of the dramatic quality of the presentation. David, who when he did arrive at a moment of theological clarity, did so by accident rather than by design, began to feel uncomfortable. It would have been better all round he thought, if his sermon had failed.

At least The Chaplain who was expecting a disaster wouldn't have been disappointed, and this visit could have been avoided, thank goodness, he thought that EBG had thought to telephone a warning, imagine if The Chaplain had rang the doorbell whilst he and Gilly had been in bed, he'd have certainly recommended that one to the Bishop and the Bishop wouldn't have been amused that's for sure.

The Chaplain who had begun to gain the impression that for the past ten minutes he'd been talking mainly to himself, turned the conversation into a more direct question and answer session, but David, still rattled by the almost discovery, wasn't really up to the tutorial, and finally with a half apology, confessed that to the best of his knowledge the sermon had been written without reference to books, on the drive back from Worsby and written down quickly on the Saturday night before it was preached, the draft which he still had was in fact in pencil.

The Chaplain then mentioned the competition, which, because he had an advance warning, David was able to anticipate and to his surprise head off, the conversation between the two men then drifted into niceties, about the parish, the cottage David lived in and finally EBG, about whom The Chaplain was less than complimentary, suggesting that the future of the Church lay more with men like himself and he implied as long as he shaped up, possibly David.

Letting him out of the door, David turned back inside and began to shake, the emotion of the almost discovery and the fact of spending the last twenty minutes in polite conversation with someone he so thoroughly detested and whose company he would normally avoid at all costs, was too much to bear, sitting in his living room staring out at the sea he suddenly saw Gilly approaching the house and then cross the road to knock at his door.

As the door shut after her letting her into the cottage they both began to laugh and Gilly who had a mimic's gift for ridicule mimicked The Chaplain as he had sat there discussing the weather before suggesting she leave so that they could get on with the real business man to man.

'Well David', she mimicked, 'and what were you doing with that nice young lady'.

'Oh', she went on to ridicule David, 'We were fucking your honour'.

'That's nice David, do you fuck all your parishioners?'

'Only the pretty ones, your honour'.

'Well I'm glad to hear it, keep it up'.

'Yes sir, your honour sir', and in her own voice and with a decidedly sharper tone, 'Arse lick, arse lick'.

David blushed and they both burst into uncontrollable laughter at his embarrassment and her complete lack of concern, 'but supposing EBG hadn't rung and that awful man had found us in bed'.

'Well', Gilly replied briskly, 'He did, and he didn't, so good on EBG and down with The Chaplain and all who sail in him, I bet he's queer'.

'Oh come on', said David, 'he's married'.

'So what', said Gilly, 'most of them are, but I can tell'.

'How?' asked David somewhat naively.

'Not how', she replied sweetly, 'When, when I'm in bed with two men who are more interested in each other than me, then I know'.

At that point David gave up, partly because he thought she was pulling his leg and partly because he feared she might not be.

Retreat

We retire to the place, governed by
A 12 hour clock of time and tide
Arrive on time or prepare to be left on the far side
The shapely curve of the dunes
Leads us to a timeless place
Where we wrestle with cross and crossing
Words spoken in haste can't be withdrawn
After reading the news
Crosswords, help us to keep
A certain perspective
Five down, for fellow
Employee put, workmate
Rather than none
And evasion for the dodging
Of responsibility as my enemies
Plot against me I am thrown back on who I am
Repeating with every step along the strand
I am who I am not what I am
To recover, rediscover
That sense of being

That sense of purpose
Exploring new words
As two down, to carry out
To execute, to stand on the stones
The spirit here of saints
Who have stood on these same stones
Heard the same words
Broken the same bread
And spilt this self same wine
The crucial clue
that becomes the crux
of the word puzzle
How to reinvent self
How to find a way
Of being who rather than what you are

EBG

Headings

The crisis at the Edwards' house was deepening. Bobby had been sinking deeper and deeper into a depression that was becoming clinically concerning. The Doctor had been called, but this served only to deepen Bobby's depression, adding even more concern to the worries of those who cared for him. The dilemma was a simple one. No doctor meant there was no care, and nothing being attempted to halt Bobby's steady decline. The presence of the doctor on the other hand meant that Bobby's depression steadily worsened.

The doctor, who travelled from Worsby to maintain a small surgery in Drissburgh, and whose practice was growing sufficiently for him to begin to think in terms of extending the partnership and to acquire permanent premises in Drissburgh, was clearly mystified by Bobby's decline.

As he repeatedly told Hilda, 'there is in fact nothing wrong with him. He's remarkably healthy for his age, I suggested the tests so that we could keep an eye on that slight shakiness. I had absolutely no idea that it would cause this, and to be absolutely honest, no real idea of what to do about it'.

David began to visit regularly, partly because he was genuinely concerned about the crotchety old couple, who had made him welcome in Drissburgh, preparing the ground for his general acceptance. And partly because he knew that EBG was nearly as afraid of things medical as Bobby was. It would help EBG if he could avoid going because his curate was visiting already. David became a go between, carrying messages from EBG to Hilda and back again.

Sitting at the bedside of a man who was withdrawing from the world around him by degrees, was a strange and sad experience. The two of them would sit in silence, Bobby lying flat on his back. He would stare at the ceiling, or helped into a chair by David, would sit with a cigarette in his mouth dropping ash onto his trousers.

Very occasionally, if David made a joke or witty comment, Bobby could be seen to smile, but the smile was clearly meant to be a private affair as though the joke was for him alone and not aimed at any one else or to be shared.

On rare occasions, David got through the defences. Once, when he was bringing Communion to Bobby, David was struck a by bizarre thought which followed on from a previous conversation he'd had with Bobby. It was about the disposal of some old communion materials from the church, including a small, portable altar that was infested with woodworm. It had been dumped in a shed at the rear of the church where the gardening tools and mower were stored.

Eventually, Bobby had insisted that everything that had been used for, or had come into contact with, communion activity should be disposed of properly; which meant that it should be burned.

During the communion the Edwards' dog, a small,

smelly, white poodle had come into the room and was watching the proceedings with what David felt amounted to disdain. Halfway through the service David, who was holding a book in one hand and the paten in the other, reached to turn a page, fumbled and dropped the bread. The dog darted forward but David was quicker, and retrieved the bread from the floor before the dog could snaffle it.

'Well', he remarked without thinking, 'that was a lucky escape for you dog, if you'd eaten that, you'd have had to be burned'.

Bobby who had watched all of this fandango with complete disinterest suddenly laughed and said quite sharply, 'he's right laddy, we'd have had to burn you, for eating religious things, it's the only way, to dispose of things properly, decently'. Turning to David, he said in a self-pitying tone, 'and how will you dispose of me? Properly too, I hope'.

David, not certain of how to respond had muttered, 'not yet Bobby, it's much too soon to think of morbid things like that'.

But Bobby made no response, and the communion finished. David went down to the kitchen to drink a cup of tea with Hilda. He'd never found her easy to talk to, but because of worries about Bobby and their son, whose illness had long been a source of concern to both Hilda and Bobby, she was coming to value talking to the young man. His particular gift it was to balance a genuine ordinariness, with the vocation he pursued, which had the effect of setting him apart from ordinary people.

Spending longer than he planned over the cup of tea and needing to get home to meet Gilly, with whom he planned to walk out over the headland that afternoon, David finally excused himself promising to return the next day.

As he turned the key in the lock and opened his front door, a sixth sense alerted him to the presence of someone in his house. A cursory check revealed that the kitchen and living room were empty, so he opened the bedroom door to see Gilly with a welcoming smile on her lips, sit up in his bed and hold out her arms invitingly.

Needing no second invitation, David quickly divested himself and climbed into the narrow single bed feeling the electric shock as his skin touched hers and they snuggled down together.

Lunch, which they ate in bed, consisted of bread and some cheese rescued from the back of the fridge. He'd had to cut away the mould, and then it was washed down with communion wine from the bottle that David had used for the service at Bobby's.

With Gilly lying on her stomach David had poured the wine into the basin formed from the hollow in the small of her back and drank from it greedily. When she turned to face him he kissed her. Her mouth, neck, breasts and stomach were sticky from the wine. They laughed at his retelling of the story of Bobby's dog, and she asked if he should burn her as well, maybe she was a witch.

'No', David whispered, 'not a witch, you are a chalice from which I drink deeply'. They laughed again at the tackiness of the remark.

It was a remarkable relationship that developed in full view of the parish, of EBG and of Gilly's husband who would occasionally visit for a weekend. As Gilly explained, he clearly relished hearing of her affair with a mystery lover whose identity she wouldn't reveal. But the details of their lovemaking she shared with her husband, who she thought, assumed that some of their activities were at the least exaggerated in the telling. They weren't.

> *'...you are here to kneel*
> *where prayer has been valid.*
> *And prayer is more*
> *Than an order of words,*
> *the conscious occupation*
> *Of the praying mind,*
> *or the sound of the voice praying'*

TS Eliot *Little Gidding*

The House Martins
Are building again
Their nests of mud thatched
into the under eaves of the house
This constant attention
To the detail of the task
Finds echoes in the birdsong, bee drone
Of this English summer day
Natures tapestry
Weaves its pattern, Eliot's
Voluptuary sweetness
Erupts around us
In profusions
Luxuriant green
Intoxicating scents
Deep rose embers
Of the fire which once
burned in the bud
And we are here for prayer
To dip into the deep
Flowing stream of prayer which
Across time has acquired its own validity
The precious sentimentality
Of the scraps of memory
Thought and unfulfilled aspiration

Are pieced together
In a patchwork design
We throw over our bed
And as we sleep
Embraced in its warmth
Our dreams help us make sense
Of what was, what is
And what is yet to be

EBG

Confession

Crossing the hedge through a gap worn by the passage of time, and secured as a right of way by a numberless procession of villagers, courting couples, weekend walkers and the occasional choirman late for the service, David turned to follow the coastal path to the headland.

It was clear to him that his problems, compounded by his own stupidity and sense of panic at what was now unfolding, would soon overtake him. His priesting was a month away, and he knew that on the night before his Ordination after the week of retreat he would be required to make his confession to the Bishop's Chaplain as spiritual director of the junior clergy.

What would he say? How could he admit that in a moment of foolishness, delight, pleasure, mutual gratification, grace, openness to the other, sweat, arousal and finally, spent passion, he had abused the trust that had been placed in him. He had taken advantage both of his pastoral relationship, and the vulnerability of someone whose hurts and wounds he would, he knew, eventually rub salt into, even if it was the salt of his own tears.

He passed up the lane following the road to the turning circle and on across the rough grass to the bay on the far side of the headland. It had become his own private place for communing, with the experience that others called, but he could no longer refer to as God.

Finding some shelter behind a stretch of broken wall

he sat. Below him the sea rolled endlessly into the bay, two sounds mingled, with the call of the gulls and the dull whistle of the wind in this exposed place. From one side of the headland the surging sound of surf, a deep growling roar, sucking the pebbles on the beach backwards and forwards in a perpetual, eternal motion of water, and the oily detritus of civilization which was washed up there, polluting the bay and making it unsuitable as a place for children to play.

On the other side of the headland, on the rocks that ringed the cliff was the crashing sound of splintering and breaking under the relentless battering of the sea. It seemed determined to find a way through the land itself in a cosmic game of hard and soft, out of which soft would finally and inevitably carve its victory.

In the distance, Whale Rock maintained its lonely vigil protesting against the aggression of this wild ocean's constant battering.

The roaring silence raged around him as he sat hunched and defiant.

Standing he hurled his bitter resentment into the wind, which tore it from his lips and jeeringly broadcast it aloud to the gulls and the distant horizon. PISS; SHIT; FUCK; FUCK; FUCK; FUCK; he screamed spitting the cleansing words out of his mouth, purifying the blood.

Images of her body. Nakedness. The signs of childbearing, the small blemishes on the skin, downy hair on nipples and upper lips. Casting the images out to sea, out over the headland to crash to the rocks below.

The utter unbearable, unrealisable, pain of it; the pain

of relationship. Burying himself in the flesh of another. Coming up for air. Becoming one flesh with someone whose one fleshness was already consummated with not just another, but with others plural. .

Kissing and gently licking the raw, red weals and bruises inflicted on her as punishment by another, despite his constantly pushing her out into the disillusioning, hopelessness of her infidelity. Yet she was faithful too, to both husband and lover. She was the victim, bearing in her own flesh the stigmata of love.

The ordination retreat was held in the same diocesan conference centre as David's last confrontation with the Bishop's Chaplain. David again lingered in the kitchen as his fellow ordinands gathered in the common room one floor up. Eventually he went up to join the group and to get ready for the retreat to begin. Before the traditional silence there was an opportunity to reflect on the highs and lows of their year as deacons. David told a story about the time he had tried to talk to the children in the local primary school. On the face of it the lesson had been on the history of Drissburgh and its sea-fairing past, but it had all got mixed up with his vocation and the fact that he was about to stop being a deacon and become a priest.

One of the children had been writing about what happened when viking invaders came in olden times. He had written that the villagers rushed out and set fire to the deacons, as a warning of imminent disaster.

Even the chaplain had managed to smile and had thought to himself that just maybe his plan for David might work, after all he was clearly more relaxed and more prepared to co-operate than had seemed possible a year earlier.

Introducing the retreat the chaplain made mention that he was available by appointment to hear confessions, and that a timetable was on the board if any of the deacons wished to prepare themselves for their priesting by letting go of things that they wanted to leave in the past.

The silence began after supper, and the Chaplain on his way to his room after the meal stopped to check the board. To his amazement he saw David's name written on the list to make his confession the following day. The Chaplain really could not believe his good fortune, what a success story, the most unlikely and unpromising of last year's intake suddenly turning the corner. He must make absolutely sure that he was the one to take full advantage of this conversion.

It comes to this, a box, a shape, an imposed structure, a confessional. As that which has gone before, and that which comes after, is joined at a point in time, a moment when everything that is said and everything that takes place must serve this discipline of truth.

Kneeling in the deep silence, in the semi-darkness, as a visitor, a stranger, an observer at his own wake, he heard his low murmuring voice.

'Father, forgive me for I have sinned. It is some time, a year, since my last confession.' He listed the sins of omission and commission, pride, greed, sloth, his anger too frequently directed at those who had no part in causing his regular loss of self-control and, finally in this place that demanded truth he had to speak the words that he would rather keep unsaid.

'I have betrayed a trust, Father, a great trust', (now it was out and he was heading down a dead end street at ninety miles an hour, feeling scared and at the same time spiritually reckless). 'I have entered into a relationship with a person , a married person, a member of our young wives group at St. Agatha's, a parishioner'.

There it was out, in the open, or at least the semi -ark mystery of the confessional.

There was a silence, during which nothing was said. The silence was overpowering and across the distance he could hear the chapel clock ticking, slowly measuring out his future like grains of sand dropping one by one through the measure.

When he finally spoke the Chaplain's question surprised him.

'Is it known? Do the parishioners know of your... affair', nearly choking on the word, 'does the person's husband know?'

He answered carefully. No, he thought it was a well-kept secret, and really there was no reason for anyone to know and the husband well, yes, the husband did know and in a strange way, approved, such was the nature of their relationship.

The confessional for the priest is an enormous privilege and responsibility. To be given this information, this power, in the context of confession, spiritual counsel, rather than by way of one of the awful development of ministry sessions that the diocese increasingly preferred, was clearly going to be difficult for the Bishop's Chaplain.

That much was clear. Should he tell the Bishop? Would three Hail Mary's and a Rosary recitation be an adequate act of contrition? It was agony for the Chaplain and in a perverse way David enjoyed seeing him struggle with his conscience.

Of course if he was challenged outside the confessional he would know the source of the leak, but which was the greater sin?

Adultery, or failing to honour the privacy of the confessional, and in the event the Bishop would only have to imply that the information had come from the parish and, at that first hint that the affair had become public knowledge he was acting with pastoral expediency to avoid a public scandal.

For both The Chaplain and by implication the Bishop there was the certainty that they were acting with the best interests of the church and the parish in mind, that whatever they did, however wrong it might be, they could be certain that what David had done was more wrong still.

In reality, however, there was no intention to deal with the situation pastorally. There was a hasty panic-stricken endeavour to avoid a public scandal. Newspapers, television, reporters, all that, and in avoiding the interest it would create and pretending that all was well when all was clearly not well. The two clergyman were prepared to ride roughshod over the feelings of those people, sad, confused, disturbed who were caught up in the situation.

It was a measure of the church's inability to deal in any serious way with the issues of human sexuality and human emotions.

The Chaplain went through a check list of what should be avoided and what might happen next.

Embarrassment is the first thing to avoid, so no public scandal. In fact, if the situation could be presented in such a way that the Bishop could present it as a humorous anecdote in his club or at General Synod or in the House of Lords, or as an entertainment for his cronies, then it could be passed off reasonably easily.

Creating an advantage was the thing to aim for if the chaplain could find a way of using this extraordinary confession as a lever. Then he could perhaps exercise some control over this unruly, and essentially disruptive young man who was about to become a priest.

Clearly they might have to buy off the woman in question, or her husband, but their silence could be bought fairly cheaply if what David had confessed was true. Then he could even be presented as an innocent victim of an attempt to discredit the church.

Given the discretion of the confessional and the need to be silent, even the Bishop would not necessarily expect his Chaplain to break a solemn vow, except under a similarly binding 'confession'. So, he calculated, there was advantage to be gained and very little to lose and therefore he concluded maybe I need to stick with my plan.

As David knelt in the confessional he had little or no idea what was going through the Chaplain's mind, but somehow the reaction he was getting was not at all what he expected.

Rather than a hysterical outburst such as he had experienced on a previous occasion, there was a restrained and measured silence as the Chaplain listened to what was being said. He asked one or two questions, more of a general nature, and as though he was an animal sniffing out just how dangerous this territory really was. The Chaplain offered David the forgiveness which belonged to his office in the traditional words, and then said as a penance, you should avoid seeing this person, but if you must, buy her a small silver cross and ask her to wear it whenever you might meet, then when temptation threatens to overwhelm you focus on the cross at her neck, and remind yourself that your first love is the Christ who was crucified for the world's sin.

And with that David was free to leave the dimly lit chapel and in the silence, continue to reflect on what he had done, and await the repercussions which would surely follow.

Getting on with it

My faltering, dog-eared dreams
My heartaches, plans and schemes
Are all rolled up and counted in
Here's hoping the good outweighs the sin
I fly the kites of constant hopes
Continually bouncing off the ropes
But for all my constant battling
Success remains just staying in the ring
Don't claim too much for me
There's no real clarity I'm all at sea
The comings and goings, ins and outs
Getting on with it despite the doubts
So how do you rate success
Keeping straight avoiding the mess
Life is simply not well planned
So let us publish and be damned

EBG

Aubade for Bobby

David's youth was both a solace and a challenge at the bedside of the dying. Amazed, that despite his confession his ordination had gone ahead, and realising that whatever the diocesan authorities made of his confession, that could mean that he still had both an important job to do and a ministry to exercise. He headed from the meeting directly to Bobby and Hilda Edward's house. He realised that what was happening here was in itself a tragedy that would unfold with all the inevitability of a car crash.

Bobby Edwards was afraid, and he was dying of fear. The fear made him grey, and the greyness spread like a dismal blanket across his face and into his eyes, but as David realised, there was no way that he or anyone else was going to be able to exorcise that fear.

Opening the small garden gate he approached the door, and as he raised his hand to knock, the door opened and the doctor stepped out. Eyeing David with a faintly veiled look of contempt that seemed to David to say, as science leaves superstition arrives. The doctor turned to Hilda, and to David's acute embarrassment announced that unless he pulled himself together and stopped behaving like a damned fool, Bobby would be dead before they could get him into the hospital.

David was appalled by the doctor's attitude and it was immediately obvious, as soon as he entered Bobby's room, that it was the fear of the hospital that was killing him, not the illness itself which, according to the Doctor, was perfectly treatable. The fear of entering the place of no return, the sterile, clinical corridors, offered no comfort but were themselves a place of terror for Bobby. He now lay, resolutely still, refusing to communicate and his eyes stayed fixed on a dark stain above the fireplace in the small bedroom, the sheets pulled high up under his chin.

The doctor, who had examined him as thoroughly as he was able, given the complete lack of co-operation he received from the patient, was simply a number on his records. Bobby had never visited the surgery throughout the whole of his adult life, could find nothing of consequence the matter with him and said so. Nevertheless, because Bobby had collapsed so dramatically, and remained unconscious for as long as he had, the doctor had thought it wise to refer his patient to the hospital for tests, and it was this that had affected Bobby so dramatically and left him lying wrapped in a bed sheet, his lifeless eyes staring at the ceiling and the slow creeping, grey pallor, invading his face and hands.

Entering the room David whispered to Hilda that she should feel free to take a break, that he was prepared to stay for a while, so that she could pop out to the shops or next door for a chat with the neighbour. The neighbour's concern was evident in the way they had enquired how Bobby was, as his mysterious illness appeared to grow worse.

David took Hilda's place on the chair by the bed and sat quietly.

As he waited, he noticed the deterioration that was taking place before his eyes. A greyness had invaded the skin of the man lying in front of him, and as he lay there Bobby laboured with each painful breath.

It appeared to David that the man was racked by pain, and David realised that he was standing guard over the drama of death, as this human being, this man, who was a father, a husband, a church member and, in his own idiosyncratic way, a generous and caring person, simply died from his fear.

It was tragic and irrational, and David, holding his grey, cold hand knew that only a miracle would save him and that the age of miracles had long passed.

David also knew that this death, to which he was witness was in no way redeemed by the dignity that the Bishop's Chaplain had spoken of in his post-ordination course. This was dying without purpose or reason, and in its own way it represented a shabby tragedy. Here was a man who professed faith in God but who had no faith whatsoever. A man whose tragedy was that his faith had no sustaining quality at all. It could not cast out fear but only surrender to it, it was a faith that shunned the light and embraced the darkness of death, hiding there from its fear.

Looking down on Bobby's still form, which appeared to be shrinking before his eyes, David felt not pity but scorn and he knew that what had happened to him, this love he felt as a gift, dangerous and yet so worthwhile, the sudden breaking into his life of light and hope and purpose was what was real, not this false, hopeless faith that shrank in fear at the first test.

And what the church represented and preached, was summed up for him by the Bishop's Chaplain, whose narrow minded ideology, which was what passed for a faith was no faith at all. It had sought to condemn and dismiss his feelings -- but the condemnation somehow he knew missed the mark, because what he knew and what he felt was what was authentic, a whole unfolding possibility calling him into the adventure which was living on the edge of risk.

For now, however, all he could do was sit and wait, helpless in the face of what he did not understand, as death's drama unfolded to its mysterious conclusion.

Between them, he and Hilda sat up most of the night, at one point sensing the discomfort being experienced by the dying man between them they lifted him, working together in silence, the soon-to-be discredited clergyman and the soon to be widowed woman. They attended in intimate detail to the needs of a man dying in the darkness of his fear.

There was the waiting. And as he waited David offered prayers, which were as much for himself and what was to become of him, as for Bobby. And there was the light, returning to make the bitter sweet, displacing the darkness, renewing hope, sunshine streaming across the ocean, and flooding in through the open curtains heralding a new day, and new possibilities. Bobby slipped from this life because he was afraid to risk and to face the challenge of his illness, and as his days ended a new day dawned. Rising, David turned away from the past, from death, from the night and from yesterday, to the things he could see, feel, taste and know.

Leaving the inner sanctuary of the courts of death, he turned greedily to embrace life, and deep in his heart the question turned and turned and made itself known as he headed out across the cliff path away from the village and into the light.

Yesterday he had struggled with the possibility of sacrifice and vocation. He had contemplated the possibility of sacrificing his love for Gilly and following the dictates of the Bishop and his Chaplain, avoiding the public scandal, putting her, in the expression they had used so quaintly, quietly away. But now he knew without a doubt that such a course of action was simply not possible.

At four in the morning Bobby died. David had been half asleep when he heard the death rattle and from Hilda a sharp intake of breath followed by a muted sob.

Together they said a short prayer, and sat quietly holding hands. Hilda then went to call the doctor and the undertaker, to set the arrangements for Bobby's funeral in motion.

David realised that distressing as the situation was, Hilda needed to be alone, and so he made to leave, pausing for a moment. She asked quietly, 'you will take the funeral won't you?'

In agreeing, David felt a silent shift in his awareness of the challenge of vocation. Maybe, he thought, this reality is the one I need to hold onto, and turning to Hilda he said 'yes, of course, it would be a privilege'.

Leaving the house he headed out on the headland. He stood looking out to sea, the light glinting on the water, sea birds fishing, and in the distance as he watched, a seal swam inquisitively close, rising and falling with the steady rhythm of the ocean swell, proud possessor of his ocean domain. As he stood transfixed by the steady rise and fall of the water's rhythmic heartbeat, he saw himself as the watcher, but also the watched.

Someone no longer alone he was, he finally knew, loved in a way that was real, warm and reciprocated. Turning, he walked towards the light.

Ordained priest in the church of God, against all possible odds, David knew that there would be a price to pay, and the Chaplain who now had power over him would certainly extract the full value in whatever currency he chose.

Moving On

Struggling to hold on to the past
He loosed his hand to reach out
Slipped and was swept away by the blast
So he goes accelerating back to the future
Empty kitchen
Unmade bed Silence where the music
Echoed through his head
It came to this
Finally he notes
A relationship ended signalled
By a rash of post-it-notes
Now from the future he looks back
To count the losses and the gains
His life if slightly used is still serviceable
Apart from the insistent pain

Moves Afoot

The letter, when it came, was in the most impressive envelope, which bore the post mark of the Cathedral Office so clearly that whatever it contained, there was no great desire on the part of the sender to make a secret of it.

David had little or no desire to read the contents and so left it unopened on the hall table.

Following the retreat and his ordination, David had expected some fall out from his confession, but there was nothing but silence.

Bobby's funeral had gone as well as these occasions do, and David had both conducted the service and preached. EBG had robed and led the procession, and said the prayers, leaving everything else to his curate.

David had kept an eye on Hilda, who had borne it well given the strain she was under, and she seemed pleased to have his regular visits.

The congregation had turned out in force for the ordination, and there were no empty seats. Even EBG had robed and processed with the diocesan clergy. He had also participated in the strange ritual where the clergy join the Bishop in putting hands on the young priestly head, as each is ordained in turn.

David had bought, as instructed, a small silver cross which he had presented to Gilly, explaining that unless they could find some way of being together permanently it might be better to cool things -- at least for now.

If she was disappointed Gilly did not show it. She said that whilst she understood, at that time her husband would not consider anything as radical as a divorce, but, if it was okay, she would like to see David from time to time, socially.

He had hoped for more but realised that whilst love might in a theological sense be redemptive, in practice even Heloise and Abelard had not been able to convince the authorities that their affair was anything other than straightforward old fashioned lust. David had no desire to be castrated for his affair with Ginny.

At the ordination retreat, which had once again been a silent affair, there had been little opportunity for discussion, but David had managed a brief conversation with Neil who told him that he had received another nocturnal visit from his young tormentor.

It seemed that on this occasion he had retreated behind his own locked door and, as David had insisted, telephoned the police. They had arrived fairly quickly and found the young man still on the premises ransacking the parish office. Neil had heard the noise from his flat and had been quite alarmed, but the presence of the police had reassured him, and it wasn't long before the young man was led away.

It turned out that he was well known to the police, and had been for some time. The police had reassured Neil that he would be dealt with and that the vicar had already agreed to press charges, not so much for the impact on Neil's sense of wellbeing and safety, as for the damage to the parish property.

The lad's name was Keith. He was one of six children, and had four older brothers and a sister. The family were well known in the area and Keith's brothers, uncles and father had all spent time in jail, where it seemed Keith was about to follow them.

Neil, for whom this was such a new experience and one of which he had no knowledge, and for which he was completely unprepared, decided that as part of his own preparation for the life ahead he should at least attend the trial.

The magistrates' court was a bustling hive of activity with smart-suited solicitors, bored policemen shuffling their papers, popping outside for a smoke on the steps, or inside looking for their clients, and, if the scheduled appearance was due, looking anxiously at their watches whilst scanning the crowded lobby for sight of a face they might recognise.

The magistrates, all volunteers, were a peculiar mix of the pompous and the self-serving. They sat on a raised bench which gave them an overview of the court, and as they recognised various of the solicitors and policeman, a greeting would be exchanged. The courtroom itself was presided over by the magistrate's clerk, whose job it was to maintain order and advise the magistrates on the finer points of the law and what their powers allowed... in particular when having found a defendant guilty they had to decide what sentence to impose. They had power to sentence up to two years in custody, and if they felt that the case merited a more serious sentence they would then refer the matter to the county court.

When Neil arrived he recognised Keith almost immediately standing with two women. The older, obviously his mother, still a young woman but tired and worn out with the effort of trying to manage her large and unruly family, and keep the household together. The other younger girl was, Neil assumed Keith's sister.

Neil was uncertain what to do, and what he thought might happen. Keith swore at him and demanded to know whether he was there to gloat when he was sent down.

Neil stuttered and stammered, he admitted to David that he was more nervous about the magistrates' court, fearing that any minute there would be a case of mistaken identity and that he would find himself in the dock being interrogated for a crime of which he had no memory.

David smiled, remembering the time that he had accompanied a friend of his who had managed to get into some kind of trouble, involving as he recalled, a bicycle that had an enforced change of ownership and kitchen re-spray. Before appearing again at the youth club with its new owner, unfortunately the entrepreneur who had seen an opportunity to earn some easy money had left the front cycle lamp unchanged, simply removing and replacing it without checking to see the previous owner's initials and address painted on the bottom of the lamp. David's experience of the magistrates court had made him nervous too.

Neil went on to describe the scene as Keith entered the dock, to an overture of weeping and wailing from the women in his life. The magistrate, who had whispered to her fellow magistrates and leaned forward to the justice's clerk, admonished Keith to remove his hands from his pockets, which Keith managed with the utmost reluctance.

The case was clear enough, open and shut. Neil suggested that the charges were being pressed by the vicar, who was not in court, although the subtlety was clearly lost on Keith who shot Neil an extremely dirty look.

Eventually the case was over, judgment was passed, the sentence pronounced and Keith was sent down for eighteen months.

David's reaction was to express a view that at least Neil would not be bothered for at least a year. Neil blushed, causing David to look more closely. It appeared that after the sentence had been passed, Neil left the court when with same young girl who he had, mistakenly as it appeared, thought was Keith's sister.

She was banging on the side of the van as it pulled out of the court, protesting as she did so just how much she loved Keith, and would be sure to wait for him until he returned.

Seeing Neil she screamed at him, causing him to respond with a look of shock. He assured her that it was not him who had pressed the charges but his boss, and the confused and hysterical conversation had resulted in him promising to visit Keith, and that is what he had done.

David shook his head, 'there really is no hope for you, is there?' he asked.

Neil wanted to tell David about his experiences but David cut him short. Another time he'd be more interested, but at that precise moment the Chaplain had come out of his room and set off to the chapel where the next session was due to begin.

David certainly enjoyed his job a good deal more now that he was a priest, and had, in a sense, both the power to say yes and no to the questions that were raised. He also felt that he needed to defer less to EBG when people wanted to know about the church and its rules. He was also more confident when approached by funeral directors and other clergy asking if he could take a service or offer Sunday cover.

This morning, with the letter from the diocese still on the mantelpiece of his cottage, David had spent time doing some follow-up visiting and had attended a meeting of local clergy. This had involved a lot of routine business about how the parishes locally could co-operate, alongside a discussion of a fairly technical passage from the New Testament. David was now heading back for lunch, and his unopened letter.

The letter came as both a shock and a puzzle to David when he opened it. His first thought was to examine the signature, which was, as he had suspected, the Chaplain's.

The opening was a surprise insofar as it began with a most cordial greeting. Having read it twice David turned it over to be sure that there was nothing on the other side to contradict the words he had been reading.

In essence the Chaplain, having given careful thought to David's situation, had realised that the diocese was in danger of making a mistake over someone. Someone who whilst not the easiest of characters, had much to offer the church and whose intelligence and ability needed a more supportive context than Drissburgh. For that reason, even though it was a little unorthodox given that Neil had only recently been priested, the decision had been made with the full support of the Bishop and the Dean, that David should be transferred with immediate effect to the currently vacant senior curacy at the Cathedral.

David was shocked and had to sit down. He wasn't sure what to do or what to think.

It was obvious that this was a way of keeping a closer eye on him. Better, as he had heard it put, to have the Indian on the inside of the tepee pissing out, than on the outside pissing in. But this was a prestigious appointment that had been discussed at the ordination retreat ,and in the clergy meeting that he had just attended. So why give it to someone who was already in the middle of a scandal and who by all accounts was seen as a troublemaker.

David reached for the telephone and rang the vicarage. EBG answered at the third ring,

'So the letter has come has it' was his opening comment.

David breathed a sigh of anger and relief, 'you knew, why didn't you say?'

'Because it wasn't for me to say.' I was asked, said I'd be sorry to lose you, but wouldn't stand in your way.

'But I don't want to go, I'm quite happy here and would rather see out my first curacy with you.' David was sure that he really meant the words as he spoke them, but at the same time he knew deep down that this offer was too good to be true, particularly following the confession that he had made before his ordination.

'Why not let's meet for lunch at The Mermaid, we can

talk things over?' EBG's offer was made straightforwardly and David accepted.

EBG was already standing at the bar when David arrived. He ordered a pint and scanned the menu before ordering his usual. David said that he would have the same, and they sat in a quiet corner of the pub.

'What's going on do you think?' David asked. He was uncertain as to how to take the letter, as it certainly was not a reward for good behaviour and, given his difficult relationship with the Chaplain, had come as a complete surprise.

EBG looked thoughtful.

'There are a number of things going on,' he said, 'first, I think that they are quite genuinely straining for new clergy. The general view is that the current intake of new curates is not going to set the church on fire. Too many have come straight from school via college without any real experience. Most of my generation had their education interrupted by National Service, and we had a bit more life experience, as you have. Second, I think that the Dean needs someone to help with the congregation. The Canons don't see themselves that way, too busy writing their books and attending meetings and planning their next trip away. Thirdly, I still think that you need to be careful, the Chaplain is playing games and setting you up to fail, that way he wins, you lose and they can say that you were not the right material.'

'So should I accept?' asked David.

'I don't see why not' EBG replied, 'the thing is you are unusual, you have wisdom, experience and frankly you can do better than Drissburgh. Second, you will get on well with the folk at the Cathedral, the congregation is made up of some good people and the staff team is okay.'

David grimaced, remembering his run in with the verger, although to be fair, at his priesting the verger in question appeared to have forgotten the incident and had been reasonably friendly.

EBG continued, 'the thing is, whatever happens, you won't fail, because whatever the Diocese seems to think, you do have a good way with people. Once you deal with that chip on your shoulder and let them get to know the real you, they'll respond well. There's not many newly-ordained curates that could have handled that difficult visit you had to deal with in your first few weeks here.'

David looked surprised, 'You knew about that?'

'Of course' his Vicar replied, smiling, 'it's my job to know.'

They finished their lunch and EBG looked at his watch before offering his apologies for, unusually, being in a rush and rose to leave. David thanked him and said that he would let him know his decision once it was made.

After lunch a long walk seemed the best. It was the only way to make a decision, and so David set out for the headland and the cliff path. As he walked he turned over in his mind the pluses and minuses of moving at this early stage. There were the benefits of moving into the city, the demands of the job he was being offered, and the many opportunities it would offer.

His walk took him by way of a long detour back to his cottage and arriving home he sat down with a mug of tea and the letter, eventually he reached for a pen and some paper and began to write. After the usual number of false starts and misspellings the letter took shape.

Satisfied with his reply and clear that acceptance was the only possible response, David sealed the letter into an envelope and put it to one side while he wrote a second letter to EBG. He thanked him for the opportunity he had been given, the support, and expressing the hope that their friendship would continue when he was at the Cathedral.

He popped to the post office and posted both letters, wondering what response there would be both from his friends and parishioners in Drissburgh, and from the Chaplain and the Dean.

From posting the letters, to the first response, was in David's experience a record. At 8:00 the next morning his phone rang just as he got into the house from the early service. EBG simply noted the reply and suggested saying nothing until a date had been agreed. As he explained to David, the protocol was for the announcement to be made on the same Sunday at each church, which meant that he had to liaise with the Dean. The Diocese would then formally announce the appointment through the Diocesan Communications officer who was himself a Canon at the Cathedral. The phone rang again. Answering it he heard the Chaplain congratulating him, and saying that they should meet fairly soon in order to hammer out all the details of the appointment. Discuss any improvements that were needed in the house, which was in The Close alongside the other Cathedral clergy houses, when David would start, and when any announcements should be made. The Chaplain's final words gave David a sudden shock.

'We all look forward to welcoming you as a neighbour'.

David replaced the receiver.

'What the hell is going on?' he wondered aloud. 'This is really crazy; they are all stark staring mad.'

Before he could wonder any further the phone rang again. The earpiece was still warm when David answered, and immediately the dark, honeyed tones of the Dean were whispering into his ear.

'David, I am so delighted that you will be joining us, I have heard so much about you from the Bishop's Chaplain, you come strongly recommended and I do so look forward to meeting you. Have you got your diary, let's fix a time now.'

Between the first formal letter to David's acceptance and the meetings with the Dean, the canons, at least those who were available, and the Chaplain, just under a week had elapsed and already the announcement was being planned for the following Sunday.

David was shown a lovely house in the corner of the Cathedral Close. It was small and had been used for various staff before being formally adopted as The Curatage, as the Dean referred to it,

'Now is it to your liking David?' he asked, 'we can decorate, we can improve the kitchen, whatever you need just ask the clerk of works, this is a Cathedral House not a Diocesan one and we do want you to be comfortable so anything you need, within reason, we will try to make sure that it is done. You will discover as you move on that the only time to get things right is before you move in. Once you are in they think that you will put up with any inconvenience, just because you didn't mention it at first.'

So there it was. David Saxon, the Cathedral curate, was now part of that close harmony he had wanted when he had first arrived at the Cathedral for his ordination just over a year ago.

When he met with the Chaplain they discussed his new role, and how the city would be so different from the village of Drissburgh. Greater opportunities as the Chaplain had put it, without changing his expression, for social intercourse, opportunities for art, culture, music, and, of course, an important ministry to support the Cathedral congregation.

There had been no mention at all of his confession. There was no reference to Gilly, and no reference to any of the difficulties that he had experienced with the Chaplain during his training sessions. Indeed, at one point, somewhat incredulously he had heard the Chaplain talking about the next Training Conference for New Clergy course and discussing what might happen, and how David could take more responsibility for helping run the course, 'Now that we are, so to say, colleagues'.

During this visit to the city David had again called in on Neil and they had spent part of an afternoon catching up on their news and that of the other curates.

Neil was clearly impressed by the change in David's circumstances, and certainly gave the impression that he was delighted that David's false start had been reversed. It was no small achievement as he expressed it, to become curate at the Cathedral within less than 18 months of arriving in the Diocese. There was no knowing where David's career would take him next and at what speed.

Neil was also keen to tell David about visiting the prison to see Keith. He was obviously impressed that Keith seemed a changed person and apologised for the trouble that he had caused Neil. He had apparently been attending the bible study put on the by the prison Chaplain, and was keen to show off his knowledge. Keith looked better physically too, and was taking a couple of education classes including an adult learn to read course.

David expressed his delight to hear all this, but warned Neil that Keith was essentially a con man who would use what opportunity he could to get on, and stay on the right side of anyone who was in a position to help him. Whilst he was in prison he was getting better rest in a bed of his own, he was exercising regularly, and he was off drugs. But once he was released it was very likely that he would revert to his old ways and if he couldn't get what he wanted by persuasion he would simply take it.

David tried to explain to Neil that people like Keith could function in prison rather better than in society at large, and it was that manageable environment that was suiting Keith but that underneath he was just the same person.

Neil was undeterred because he had in his own way found a direction for his work. As he explained to David, it might be possible for him to develop this side of ministry by working as a Chaplain in a prison, now that he was priested. It would only be another year before he could apply. He had seen the adverts in the *Church Times* and it looked like something that could well suit him after his first curacy.

The Poem Must be Spoken

Each day we plan careful progress
Some days are faster
Most are less
But now flowers grow where once there were none
A signature has
Replaced anon
In our garden we plant radish beds
The leaves come first
And then the heads
Each day we attend the newly planted garden
But after rain and sun
The ground begins to harden
But still the miracle is renewed
A delicate tracery
Of roots and stalks force through
The ground is hard and must be broken
As the poem, to be heard
Must first be spoken

EBG

The Move

On the Sunday, the announcement was made by EBG from the pulpit. There was little reaction from the congregation, who were aware that the curate was very much a trainee and would move sooner or later to a new job. After the service one or two of the congregation thanked him for his support and occasionally went so far as to wish him well. Hilda gave his hand a quiet squeeze and said nothing.

It was assumed that his leaving Drissburgh meant that he was no longer required to do any work, and his days grew longer, with much more freedom. He found himself travelling up to the city more frequently, looking in on the house where he would now be living. He had to buy furniture, given that the Drissburgh house was rented, and partially furnished. This was a new experience. David had not had to buy furniture before, and it came as a pleasant surprise to hear from Gilly who offered any help he might need with the move. She sensed an opportunity to bring flair and a much needed sensibility, in order to cope better with the salesman's pressure, into his furniture shopping. David asked Gilly if she was free to come into the city with him.

Gilly, describing herself as an interior design consultant, leapt at the opportunity, and so a date was set and they drove into the city together.

Without thinking, David drove into the Cathedral

Close and parked outside his soon-to-be-new home. Gilly seemed to be impressed. As they passed the front door, she saw that there were workmen inside, and taking full advantage of the opportunity, suggested to David that it would help her give much better advice if she could see the size and shape of the rooms where the where the furniture was to be placed.

Gilly was both attractive, and flirtatious, and knew how to persuade men to give her what she wanted. Much against his own better judgement, David agreed and they went into the house. The workmen were putting the finishing touches to the kitchen, which David had asked to be finished in a contemporary style. The men smiled when they saw him with Gilly and proceeded to pull his leg, 'Brought the wife for her approval sir?' David blushed.

'No this is Gilly, a friend, I needed some advice on furnishing'.

'Well said the foreman, help yourself sir, it's soon to be yours'.

David showed Gilly the lounge and study, and started to move back to the front door, but Gilly asked about upstairs.

'Let's see the bedrooms, how many, you'll need a bed, wardrobe, chest, and if you have visitors, what about a spare room?'

Reluctantly David followed her upstairs, with Gilly exuding coquettishness. leading the way.

'So which is your room?' she asked.

'This way', said David noticing that she wasn't wearing her silver cross, and regretting that he had embarked on this exercise. In the bedroom they suddenly became aware of each other, David could smell her scent and before he could stop himself, he reached out and they embraced and kissed. Gilly couldn't resist commenting that it was a shame that there was no bed or carpet because... as the thought hung in the air between them, becoming more intense, David heard footsteps on the stairs.

As they broke apart, there was a knock on the door and in stepped the Dean. David was sure that the look on his face gave the game away, and that the Dean would know immediately not only what was happening, but exactly who Gilly was. Surely the Chaplain would have made that clear.

'David, I saw your car outside and wanted to say, if there's anything ... oh my', he said, noticing Gilly.

'My dear, are you helping our new curate with his interior decorating? I am sure that he needs a woman's touch to make this place feel like home'.

Gilly, quite unfazed, smiled.

'Thank you, yes. David is our curate in Drissburgh, you know he lives in a rented place? Well, I offered to give him a hand choosing furniture, and just needed to see where the various pieces I have in mind, would fit'.

The Dean was obviously very taken by Gilly and began to chatter away.

'Look' he said, 'my next meeting is not for half an hour, why don't you both come across to The Deanery for coffee, that would be lovely and you can meet my wife'.

With David bringing up the rear, they began a stately procession across the Close, the Dean with an arm almost around, but not quite touching, Gilly's shoulder.

David heard him saying something about a woman's touch, wife, marriage and Gilly half turned and shot him a meaningful glance.

In The Deanery, the Dean's wife rose elegantly to the occasion as she doubtless did on any number of unscheduled occasions. She and David sipped their coffee while Gilly and the Dean chattered away as though they had been lifelong friends.

The half hour slipped by and a ring at the door bell called The Dean back to his routine. His wife, without being asked, answered the door and returned with the first arrival for the meeting, to David's horror it was the Bishop's Chaplain.

By now David was utterly bemused, he returned the Chaplain's greeting but before he could explain Gilly's presence The Dean had introduced her as though she was an old friend.

'Don't you think David is fortunate to have someone to help, that's the problem with being a bachelor, don't you think? The woman's touch, that's what a home needs. If David can't find his own we may well have to find him a wife. I'm sure there are some eligible young ladies amongst the cathedral congregation, that is, of course,' here he turned to Gilly, 'if I am not speaking out of turn?'

Gilly smiled and shook her head.

'We must get on with our shopping', she said, 'don't you think so, David?'

As they left The Close to head into the City, Gilly was full of teasing chatter, she challenged David.

'How on earth will you put up with such awful people? You really need to be sure that this is right, David, otherwise it will drive you mad. The Dean is empty headed but well meaning, and that Chaplain strikes me as a nasty piece of work, you need to watch out for him'.

Soon they were fully immersed in their shopping and having chosen sofas and chairs and tables they made their way to the bedroom department.

They pressed and prodded the mattresses until the salesman came across.

'You have to try' he said, 'it's the only way to be sure', and so in the finest department store in the city, laughing like teenagers, Gilly and David found themselves in bed with each other again.

The day had sped past. The house had Gilly's full approval, as did the furniture they had purchased, the Dean and the Chaplain fared less well in Gilly's assessment and over drinks in a city centre hotel they fell into a sense of companionship and pleasure in each other's company. David was reminded of what it had been that had drawn him to Gilly.

When Gilly returned from a visit to the powder room and placed a hotel key on the table between them, David realised that he cared less about the consequences of his actions over the next few hours than he did about the need he had to demonstrate the real affection he felt for this woman. This was even though he knew that the relationship would never be allowed to develop into the long-term, loving partnership he needed.

The next morning David remembered his car, still

parked in the Cathedral Close. He watched Gilly as she stepped out of the shower, he needed an explanation, one that would stand up to close examination. Seeing the panic on his face Gilly asked what the problem was, and as David tried to explain she laughed at his naivety and innocence.

'We had a drink in town to celebrate, and went back on the train', she said.

'It was quicker anyway, and you had to come back today'. David relaxed visibly.

'You are amazing,' he said, 'I commit a pretty major sin and instead of being censured I find myself on the moral high ground for not committing a minor one'.

Gilly smiled, 'experience', she said, 'now let's have breakfast, I'm starving'.

The furniture was ordered and the delivery arrangements made. The work on the house was finished and all too soon it was time for David to move.

His final service and farewell party at Drissburgh took place, there were good wishes from many people that had, over the short time, become friends, and he was handed a gift from the parish.

EBG had tried to get the parish to give something practical. The travelling communion set was ruled out, as was the Cope, because the Cathedral had its own, probably more than one. EBG had suggested carpets, which were ruled out because the parish didn't want people walking over their gift with muddy boots, and anyway, once down carpets couldn't be taken with you to the next house. Finally, a decision was made and David was presented with a very handsome desk, just the thing for the Cathedral curate on which to write his sermons, keep his diary and write letters to parishioners old and new.

As was often the case David then had almost a month between leaving one job and starting the next. EBG explained that Drissburgh would pay him for the first two weeks and the Cathedral for the final two weeks, and he would be expected to be in residence and ready to start work on the morning after his welcome service.

He arrived in the Cathedral Close to an invitation to lunch at the Deanery, and here he was introduced to the three Canons and their wives.

'What a pity', remarked the Dean, 'that your young lady friend couldn't make it, perhaps on another occasion?'

The lunch went well, and again the Chaplain continued his charm offensive. David was by now completely confused He had as good as told the man that he had been having an affair with a parishioner, and that she was married. He had been given advice, a penance and …nothing.

The anticipated explosion had simply not happened. It appeared that the Chaplain had kept the information to himself, as the rule of the confessional required, but which David had not expected.

Whilst the chapter, as the group of senior clergy at the Cathedral were called, were all, each in his own way charming and highly intelligent, they were also people who under normal circumstances, David would never have met, and with whom he had little or nothing in common. One was a son of a senior clergyman, a former

Archdeacon whose curate the Dean had been Another was the son of an ambassador and who had attended the same school as the Dean, and the third Canon shared a name with another clergyman in his previous Diocese, and rumour had it that there had been an administrative confusion and the letter from the Bishop had been sent to the wrong person. Once it had been accepted, the job was his. The Chaplain was there as the Bishop's nominee.

The clergy in The Close maintained a system known as residence, which meant that of the four, at any one time three were away. The Dean was, generally around, but for the month in residence, the Canon whose turn it was, Canon Buggins, was responsible for the worship and keeping the Cathedral wheels turning. As Curate, or minor canon, David was effectively the Revd. Dogsbody, as one canon put it over lunch to a ripple of polite laughter. Births, marriages and deaths, dear boy, and evensong on Fridays and Saturdays.

David had planned to spend some of his time off at home, at least back in his old home. However, his room had been let as his mother needed a little extra money, and a lodger was a good way of raising money without too much work. So, with the prospect of an uncomfortable night on the settee, he had set off with a heavy heart, aware that even in the two years since his ordination, he had drifted even further from his family and friends.

As he was drawing out of The Close he met the Chaplain who pulled over.

'David, the welcome service is on the first Sunday of next month. If you want to choose any favourite hymns do let the Master of Music know, so that the choir can practice them. And, of course, we will reserve places for your family and friends. At least this time your Vicar has motivated his congregation, and I gather that a group will be coming from Drissburgh.'

David thanked him and said that as he was away for a few days he would either phone the office or pop a letter in the post.

The Chaplain smiled, and then almost as an afterthought, asked after Gilly.

'Was she the young lady we have spoken about?'

David nodded, wondering what came next, but the only response from the Chaplain was a thoughtful look.

'David' he continued, 'I'd like to get to know you better, once you are installed and have started your work, maybe we could find time, we need to put the past behind us. I know that we can become friends given time, and I can help you, would like to help you, you know that'.

The last words were accompanied by a firm nod as though he was trying to convince David to say yes.

Just then another car came into the Close and the Chaplain had to pull forward, his last words were, 'don't forget the hymns. Then he was gone and David drove away thoughtfully.

Manchester in the early 70's was a grey, damp place. The next few years would see the emergence of a number of groups whose music would spill over onto the national scene. They put Manchester, or Madchester as it became known, at the centre of things musically, as once it had been a centre for engineering.

David's father had been an operative in a factory amongst other low-paid jobs and now as the industrial era was drawing to a close he was unemployed.

David's mother and older sister worked in low paid jobs in local factories, but his younger sister had a better job in a store in town. The hours were long and the pay was relatively low but at least she could dress well and stay clean during the day.

As usual his family were pleased to see him, but preoccupied with work and their own lives. His mother had made some effort and there was a steak pudding for tea, and he was relieved to hear that his sisters had agreed to share a room to allow him to have a bed for the duration of his stay.

After tea his father switched on the TV and the family settled down for an evening devoid of conversation, to watch Coronation Street and whatever followed. The only interruption came if there was any show of intimacy on the screen, when his mother, with a sharply indrawn breath would signal to his father to get up and switch channels, or if there was no alternative, to switch off completely.

Unemployment meant that father had to turn to hobbies to occupy his time and his latest was brewing his own beer. It meant that he had no need to spend money down at the local and could sit in his arm chair and drink to his heart's content.

He managed to work out that the finer points of brewing, the decanting and bottling were completely unnecessary as long as you didn't mind the beer being cloudy in the glass. So, the old man would sit with the dustbin, in which the beer was brewed, next to his chair, with a pint mug which he then dipped regularly into the dustbin until it was time for bed, or more often, he fell asleep in his chair.

David had brought a bottle of whiskey for his father and together they began to drink their way through the bottle, assisted by a regularly replenished pint glass of home brew.

As the evening wore on his father, who was by nature a taciturn man, began to share with David his untutored and bitter views about the church and its clergy. His view was that all clergy were, as he put it queer, some married as a way of putting people off the scent but most were as queer as a nine bob note. He was amazed that a son of his had gone into the church and he could only assume that David was that way inclined. Although he was sure that it was nothing he had done.

Clearly the whiskey and strong beer chasers had loosened his tongue, and he was giving vent to views that were extremely prejudiced, and came from somewhere deep down, from a place that usually remained well hidden.

David knew from experience that there was nothing to be gained from arguing with his father, and so he sat in an uncharacteristic silence and listened to the abuse until eventually the bottle was as empty as the dustbin. They both then made their way upstairs.

David was awakened in the early hours by sounds from the landing and realised that it was his father being sick into the toilet. Despite the fact that he was holding tightly to his sister's bed to stop it spinning, David smiled, you might think I've gone queer on you, he thought, but I can still drink you under the table.

The next day David called on Pete and together they hatched a plan to spend a couple of days walking in the Lake District. Pete was due a few days leave and so they packed boots and waterproofs and set off.

The journey went well and they found bed and breakfast in a pub near Ambleside. From there they planned to walk The Langdales the next day, weather permitting.

Sitting in the bar Pete asked how things were going. As David outlined the strange turn of events, his friend expressed a mixture of surprise and real pleasure that his old friend had managed, it seemed against all the odds, to make his mark in an alien environment.

After supper in the bar, and a relaxing cigarette, Pete raised the question of David's love life, almost but not quite reflecting his father's prejudice. Pete asked if David was still interested in women or was he, 'playing for the other side now?'

David was amazed just how deep-seated the prejudice was amongst people he had grown up with.

But he couldn't afford to alienate his oldest friend and before he could stop he found himself telling Pete about Gilly.

Pete became thoughtful as it became clear just how compromised David was, 'I hope she's worth it' was all he said.

'What do you mean?' David asked 'Well you could lose your job over a thing like this and what the hell will you do then, all that training, all that work will have gone to waste, over what…' he left his views hanging in the air.

For David the next couple of days passed in a daze as he tried to get his feelings under control. Somehow he had to find a way to make this relationship work or he had to end it now.

He had to confront Gilly's husband, find out what he wanted from their marriage, if anything, and then persuade her that her future lay with him. He also knew, in his heart, that that his job and the new opportunities offered by the Cathedral meant everything to him.

This was both a moral dilemma and a real challenge to his powers of persuasion. But if he could pull it off then not only would he find happiness in his new relationship, but his future would look and feel even more positive. Ending the relationship was not a choice, but things couldn't continue as they were. He needed to get things out and into the open without destroying his life into the bargain.

His visit home had been as expected, and as he was leaving, his mother explained that she wouldn't be at the church for his first service. She would have liked to come but his father had set his mind against it, and so David set off back to a new job, a new life and new challenges.

A Fragment

Footsteps outside the
Window, the tread of
Feet on gravel, the
Visitors who pause
And go their way
Their unanswered knock
Echoing in the empty hall
Way of our hearts.
Left alone
We measure distance
Casting the stone
Into the heart's well
And counting the moments
Until the distant echo tells
How far we are apart
How lonely passions
Separate us.
This continuing
Drama of our love

EBG

Close Harmony

David was welcomed to the Cathedral at a service which had obviously been planned with great care. As the Dean explained, 'it's what we do David, and we try to be good at it. After all, it's what the Bishop expects, and you will find as you settle into your new life that we don't have to look for it. People come to us, they expect us to provide worship which celebrates and expresses their thanks for the past and hopes for the future'.

As EBG had warned, the next day he started work. The Cathedral day began with a service at 7:00 am followed by a Communion. Breakfast was a great event shared with the homeless. As David quickly realised this meant raising money, organizing volunteers, screening the trouble makers, liaising with social services, police and probation, and it was his responsibility. No-one, of course, had thought to mention it, it was just the case.

By the time the volunteers had washed up, and cleaned down the hall, it was time for a series of meetings which lasted until the mid-day service, which was actually held at 1:50 pm.

The meetings varied between internal meetings, diary meetings, planning meetings, the Women's Fellowship, the Children's Committee, school visits. The whole sea of Cathedral life floated on a tide of coffee.

Afternoons were for visiting, and soon the little mini, which had shown signs of needing to be replaced began to flag as the mileage built up. The Cathedral congregation came from all over the city, mainly folk who had fallen out with their local vicar and gravitated inwards in a kind of reverse gravitational pull, until there was nowhere else to go.

Visits could take the form of a purely social call, a sick visit, a hospital visit or bringing the sacraments to someone unable to attend on Sunday. David quickly discovered that this was the best part of the day. Always, something new or unexpected would come up in conversation, and because people sensed his genuine interest in them, they tended to open to him and share their inner feelings.

At the end of the afternoon he would return to the Close, where there would be a service, or if he was in time, he could pop into choir practice to tease the youngsters and steal a cup of tea in the Cathedral kitchen with one or other of the choir mums.

The evening usually consisted of more meetings, home groups and if he was lucky, some free time for a concert or the cinema.

The days started to pass quickly and David realised that he was enjoying his time and beginning to get a real feel for the pastoral side of the job. He managed to maintain a separation from the other residents of the Close and to avoid being drawn into their petty feuds and squabbles.

He wasn't asked to preach very often, which disappointed him, as this was a part of the job that he particularly enjoyed. It appealed as it did partly to his ego, but also to a real sense of wanting to share something of the knowledge he had gained, as well as of the opinions he had formed.

The Cathedral was in the centre of the town, which meant that there was always a string of people passing through. People on their way into and out of the City Centre, shoppers and business people, tourists coming to look at the architecture. There was also a small museum of silverware, which the current Dean had assembled and placed in an underground room which had been artfully aged and renamed the Treasury. David thought that it had once been a small workshop or storeroom for the Vergers to keep the various bits and pieces needed for the smooth running of the Cathedral. Renaming it the Treasury had given it a dignity far beyond its original purpose and function.

Other visitors to The Close included parties of schoolchildren who came down to take part in the Cathedral's Education Days. This was another initiative of The Dean, who was clearly, David realised, only one part pastor, the other parts seemed to consist of market trader, showman, mountebank and holy fool.

Occasionally in the early morning The Close would fill with expensive motor cars and a Verger would be brought in especially for Car Park duty. These were the attendees at the Dean's breakfasts, when the local great and the good came to hear an inspirational speaker, eat bacon sandwiches and, as the Dean put, network.

As David settled into his new role he realised that the pattern of work was both the same as and different from that of a parish church. As the Dean said, at a Cathedral people come to you and there was never a quiet moment. Neither was there anywhere to hide. It seemed to David that you were always on show, coming and going from his small cottage, crossing the green to the Cathedral and the Vergers, and especially the older verger who remembered David from his ordination and seemed to relish the opportunity David's new role provided. He would treat him like the Revd. Dogsbody he was, until eventually David, having realised what was happening began to develop his own survival strategy.

Like many clergy do, he found it easier and less troublesome to say yes, agree to every request and then forget the bulk of them, only transferring a small proportion into his diary, and then pleading overwork and a 'memory like a sieve, I'm afraid, you should have reminded me'.

One morning after he had been at the Cathedral for some months David came out from a lunch-time service to walk across to his house, when a familiar figure, apparently admiring a small section of newly-dressed stone that had been artfully inserted into the Cathedral's west end, above the door.

Surprised and delighted he called out to Fr Hamer, the former curate from his parish back home.

'How are you Father?' he asked.

'David, do please call me Howard, after all it seems you're much the more senior of us now.'

David blushed, 'No, still only a curate'.

'Not so, after all, surely the Cathedral curate is a minor canon?'

David grinned, pleased to see his old mentor, who had played as important a part in his being ordained as

EBG, and who had obviously left home at some unearthly hour to make the journey across the Pennines to see his former ordinand in his new setting as Minor Canon of the Cathedral.

'Let's have some lunch', suggested David, and stopping at his house to drop off his bag, they set off to The Mitre.

After a couple of false starts in which David referred to his visitor as Father and had to be corrected by Fr Hamer, whose first name, David realised, he had never known, they settled into a comfortable conversation. David knew that Howard was, in fact, not that much older than he was himself. Mentioning this seemed somewhat rude, but as if guessing what was going through his mind, Howard said, 'Yes, that's right I was 23 when I was ordained and I imagine that we are not that far apart. I'm 29 now and you must be what 25? I must say' he continued, 'that it is good to see you doing well. The Diocese must think highly of you to place you here, it's a very high-profile role and a good chance to make the right contacts. You realise that it justifies my conviction that I was right to encourage you. No-one else supported me, the Vicar, who, as you realise now, was my boss, told me not to waste my time, but he didn't see what I saw, and I am very proud of what you have achieved'.

Just at that point, when David hadn't known quite what to say, a figure loomed over their table. Looking up David recognised the Chaplain.

'David, good to see you, are you going to introduce me to your guest?' David slightly rose, although why, he would never know, as the Chaplain proceeded to sit down. 'Hazel's away' he said, 'so I thought that I would lunch here today'. Turning to Howard and taking his cue from the clerical collar which signaled high rather than low church, he asked, 'that's if you don't mind, Father …?'

'Not at all', Howard replied graciously, 'David and I are old friends, I was curate in his sponsoring parish and wanted to congratulate him in person on his preferment'.

The Chaplain realised that here was an opportunity to build a much better profile of his protégé than David had been willing so far to afford him, and so put on his most charmingly oily persona for the occasion.

'Yes', he continued, 'we are all delighted to have winkled David out from that dead end parish. Now we can concentrate on developing his undoubted talent'. Then turning to David in an almost sinister observation, continued, 'who knows where it might end?'

The rest of the lunch passed without incident. After a while, David offered to walk with Howard through town to the railway station, Howard having admitted that he still rode a scooter because he had failed his driving test six times.

Over a coffee in the railway station buffet, Howard offered to look the Chaplain up in Crockford's to see if they might know anyone in common that he could check up and advise David. His final comment was uncharacteristically negative.

'Be careful David, there's something about that chap. I wouldn't trust him, there's something about the man I really don't like. But I know you,' and he smiled as if remembering something from the past, 'you can look after yourself, as I have reason to be grateful for'.

Returning to the Cathedral, David found himself passing Neil's front door and he stopped to call on his friend. Answering the door Neil looked pleased to see him and David brought him up to date with all the news at the Cathedral, before moving on to his lunch with Howard and the Chaplain. Neil's eyes narrowed and almost before he could stop himself he mentioned to David that he had applied to the Home Office to be considered for appointment as a Prison Chaplain. He had been for an interview in London, and afterwards, knowing it had been more successful than he hoped, he was leaving in three months to start his Prison Chaplain's training. He said the job was challenging, and that had attracted him, but it was a way out of an awful parish and an insufferably snobbish vicar without causing any trouble, and the job was much better paid.

'But', said Neil, 'that's not the point of what I want to tell you.' Returning to his theme, he told David that whilst he had been in London he had stayed with an old college friend. The friend was now a curate in the Southwark Diocese and was, as Neil put it, more attracted to boys than girls. 'Yes', he agreed in answer to David's straight question, 'Homosexual'.

Ignoring David's interruptions Neil went on to describe how they had been in the bar of a theatre, near Leicester Square when who should come in but the Bishop's Chaplain. Neil started to attract his attention when his friend grabbed his arm, and collecting their drinks, moved fairly swiftly out of the room and into the next bar which was quieter.

Neil expressed surprise, to which the friend responded.

'He's well known in my circles. He's predatory, and last week I made the mistake of agreeing to go to bed with him, not a pleasant experience I can tell you. I've still got the scars to prove it. Apparently he's high up in a Diocese up north and I suppose he thinks he's anonymous in London. He certainly didn't know that I was a clergyman, and he mustn't find out'.

David whistled under his breath.

'Well, well, the things you find out'. He decided that he needed to tell someone his secret and, as Neil was leaving, he was a good candidate. David told him about Gilly and then went on to describe his decision to make his confession before his priesting. How he had expected not to be ordained, how in fact nothing had happened, other than being offered the Cathedral curacy and how amazed he had been, of course, as he agreed with Neil this information shed a quite different light on everything.

David spent the next few months observing the Chaplain as he moved between the Cathedral and the Bishop's house, his sermon's, when he preached, his behaviour at meetings and his frequent visits to London. He thought of some of the ordinands and staff at his college, and recalled asking on one occasion of a junior member of staff about his interest in girls and the strange secret smile on his face as he agreed that no he was not really interested in girls; the fact that he was interested in boys was left unsaid.

So the Chaplain has a double life, thought David.

Marriage is a cover story. Obviously he had worked out that if he was to have a career in the church, then he had to fulfill not only the job description but the personal specification as well. He had not only to be heterosexual, but he also had to be seen to be heterosexual. Poor Hazel, thought David, I wonder if she knows, or if she knows, whether she cares.

Occasionally Gilly came into the city and they might meet. If she stayed it was always in a different hotel, and David knew that even in a city the risk of being recognised, as the Chaplain had been in London, was very real. When they couldn't meet they would speak on the telephone. Her moods were variable and he was never certain what reception he might get. It was clear that having seen his new life, and home in the city, and having a hand in ensuring that he was comfortable in it, Gilly was feeling dissatisfied with her old life in Drissburgh. He asked about the children, and her husband, and sometimes she would have a lot to say but at other times however she would remain silent.

Over the days and weeks David tried to make his feelings clear, and to press her, cautiously, so that she wouldn't simply put the telephone down. Occasionally she did put the phone down when she felt that he was being too pressing. Attempting to persuade her that if she could leave her husband and sue for divorce, then whilst the church wouldn't formally bless their marriage, if they married in a registry office then after a time people would accept them as man and wife. In due course, when he had a parish of his own they would arrive as the vicar and his wife and no-one would ever know, to which Gilly would simply say, 'David you are such a romantic, of course they will'.

Finally he could stand it no longer and after a particularly long and difficult telephone call he managed to persuade Gilly that they should take a holiday. His one surprise with the job he had taken on was that it was financially so well rewarded. His mother and both his sisters worked longer hours for less money. The various perks that came with the job, from expenses to free meals to the house and council tax all paid for, and with a low-interest loan for his new car meant that he had been saving and so could afford not just a holiday but a holiday abroad.

So with her full agreement he went ahead and booked it, using one of the bigger travel agents in town. He knew that eyebrows were raised by the different names and the implicit *scandal* but he was an anonymous member of the public going on holiday with a friend.

Requiem

The surreal quality of the light
the air, sounds of the night echo in the square
The complex history of shadows
interplay of earth and blood a winter sun
The promenade fills the busy
streets with crowds
In our attics high above the pigeons bring
Messages with greetings
From the ones we love

EBG

A Good Break

For their holiday they had chosen the anonymity of a city on the Mediterranean. In part to avoid the possibility of being seen together in one of the holiday destinations which were becoming more popular as people's incomes increased, and partly to disappear into the anonymous crowd. Despite Gilly's refusal to take his concerns seriously, or even to care, David had insisted that the possibility of bumping into someone they knew, or who knew them, was a real one.

They had also taken the further precaution of avoiding hotels, by booking an anonymous apartment in the city. The attic apartment was, however, charming and well equipped. The receptionist had demonstrated the override on the lift which gave them access over the other apartments to the private roof terrace. Here, they enjoyed the first of the morning sun, which last all day into the evening, privacy, and views across the city to the port and beyond to the Mediterranean.

Each day followed a typical holiday pattern. They rose when the sun poured into their bedroom window. The rich, Mediterranean sun was warm from the early morning, and a typical day began lazily with breakfast on the terrace. For David, the cold and damp of his northern city seemed unimaginable, and the contrast with the noisy, jostling, edginess of the homeless breakfast couldn't have been greater.

From the rear of the terrace, just a stone's throw across the rooftops, crowded with washing lines, aerials, pigeons, and sun loungers. These indicated the rented holiday apartments, then there were tables and chairs on the local Spanish roof terraces. A view of the church of Santa Maria was prominent, and its bells rang the quarter hours throughout the day, bringing a reminder of David's home in the Cathedral Close.

Following a leisurely breakfast they both dressed and, leaving the apartment, spent the morning wandering the narrow streets and passageways of the old city. There was so much to see and it was all so different in sight, sound, sense, and smell to the England they knew.

David could not understand how it was possible for each small independent store, often selling just one line, to survive. One store which fascinated Gilly was a jewellery shop selling brooches and necklaces, hand made on the premises by the young proprietor in a leather apron. Another shop selling just handbags, another, speciality tea and coffee. How did they all make a living? In England the supermarkets were beginning to flex their corporate and financial muscles and small businesses were beginning to feel the pressure as profit margins had to be reduced in order to compete with strong commercial pressure.

Each day Gilly fell in love with a piece of jewellery, a bag, or purse, or dress, blouse, or skirt, but the tight budget meant that most mornings were spent window shopping.

They found a small coffee shop in the square by the church and it became their regular calling point for morning coffee and pastry. David had been shocked by the fresh, bitter, tanginess of real coffee. Having only ever drunk instant coffee at college, and before that a peculiar drink which his mother had called coffee which came from a bottle with a picture of an army officer sitting outside a tent with Indian bearers in attendance. Called Camp Coffee it was made with sterilised milk.

The coffee in Spain was a revelation to David's palate, jaded by the blandness of post war British austerity.

Lunch was taken later than in England and so they would while away more time, before finding a small restaurant where they would order the daily set menu. As the holiday passed their lunches became longer and more relaxed. Gilly in particular enjoyed the private conceit of pretending that, as long as she didn't speak, local people would take her for a local, as she blended in so well with local people, in her fashionable outfits.

Once she had mastered the art of using the local telephones she managed to phone home. She spoke with her mother, who was looking after her children in Drissburgh. She greeted the children, who reported that her husband had put in an appearance and was staying over with the children, who seemed pleased to have their father back.

After lunch they would find a quiet space in the local park, or join the general excursion along the sea front. David remembered the idea of a promenade from childhood visits to Blackpool and Scarborough, resorts on the north west and east coasts of England. It was true, he remembered, that people walked up and down, but in

England a Promenade was spelled with a capital P, whereas here, on the Mediterranean coast, a promenade was literally a walk. It was, as his infant teacher had drummed into his young head, a doing word.

Evening at this time of year was a little cooler, and usually they would sit inside a local restaurant enjoying the many small individual dishes that the Spanish call tapas. For their very British palates, there were some unusual tastes and flavours, which gave their meals an exotic quality. This was enhanced by the cheap wine which they tended to drink by the glass, unaware that a flask, or bottle, could be had so much more cheaply.

They were an unusual mixture, this young Anglican curate and his lover. Relatively adventurous and sophisticated, having broken free of their working class backgrounds, and even now pushing the boundaries of what was possible in Britain. Continental holidays were still relatively uncommon, and most people who could afford the price would choose a package holiday in a resort where the hotels served English food. But, they were also naïve in their experimentation, and in their seeking to pretend to be choosing a more unconventional life for themselves, whilst risking everything that they had achieved in their lives.

David had risked everything by his confession before his ordination as Priest. If the Chaplain ever discovered, or it became common knowledge that his adulterous relationship had extended as far as spending ten days living as man and wife with his lover, then clearly his career in the church would come to an abrupt end. He would be looking for another career, however, as EBG had once remarked quoting scripture, he was, 'too proud to beg and too weak to dig' and as he knew only too well he couldn't teach.

Gilly's life was even more of a mess than David's. Her husband lived a separate life, away from Drissburgh, where Gilly was left with their children, with little hope of escape. Her various dreams and hopes for a new life, would flare brilliantly for a brief moment and then she was back living in a quiet cul-de-sac of an English seaside town, with no promenade, and nothing but a past which had evaporated with recession and an economy that had stalled.

She lived in a house owned by her husband, on a similar grace and favour basis to David's housing arrangements in the curate's house in The Close. Her bizarre life style had left its mark on her relationships – not only in the past, but also, she increasingly suspected, in the future also.

The intensity of living for ten days in a small apartment, being forced into degrees of intimacy which David had never experienced before, also began to take its toll on their relationship. There were, what his mother might have called, words. There was no obvious point where it became clear, but as they each packed their suitcase on the final day and went downstairs for the last time to take their taxi to the airport, they both knew, in their hearts that, as much as they shared strong feelings for each other, which might even amount to love, that the relationship was at an end.

For David, the moment of truth had arrived as he was

sitting on the terrace of the apartment with a morning coffee as Gilly prepared herself for the day ahead. The bell from Santa Maria rang the quarter hour and his mind went back to the Cathedral and the life he had and the colleagues whose support he enjoyed in The Close.

At his ordination he had jeered inwardly when he noticed the sign stamped onto the chairs, 'Close Harmony'. He had rejected out of hand the idea that what he was seeing, in the relationships between Bishop, Dean and Chaplain were in any way close or harmonious. Now, however, after time spent, as The Dean had put it, as a member of the team, having sat in on staff meetings, observed the sharp theological mind of one colleague, the administrative skills and experience of another and the commitment of the canon whose main responsibilities lay in his work for the Diocese as what was called Missioner.

David realised that having such a strong team at the heart of the Diocese, and more importantly being part of it, was of value not only to the city but to the Diocese as a whole. The team of which he was part, exercised a sophisticated ribaldry, a gentle puncturing of egos, a quietly pulling down a peg or two here and there between the clergy. This was also reflected in the relationships between the wives, who exercised their own shadow roles, quietly but effectively. The Dean's wife was clearly first among equals, in a team where one of the wives supported David in his sick visiting responsibility, and in taking communion to those unable to make the Sunday service. Another led the Sunday school and yet another, who worked as a teacher in a city school, assisted David with the bible study groups.

Maybe there was less harmony and closeness than David would have liked, but there was professional respect and support, and having found himself part of this eccentric team, David realised that he had the choice of leaving his old life behind and moving forward. Not only in a professional career, which no-one in his family had ever managed before him, but also, and more importantly, in a job that he was beginning to love and which he experienced as a continually unfolding privilege. There were also the opportunities afforded by the trust people had in the collar he rarely wore. EBG was right in saying that it was a job that he was cut out for, and he couldn't, wouldn't ,shouldn't, throw it away for something he was not certain of, which was fraught with difficulties and which, if he was entirely honest with himself, he could see had no future.

Gilly also had reservations. She knew that unless David was prepared to give up his career in the church, their relationship had no future. Her husband would never give up, and he would always be her children's father. David was unaware that she had been to see EBG and had made her own confession, and that EBG, who obviously had his young colleague's interests close at heart, had nevertheless been open and even handed. His final words had stayed with her, 'your marriage vows were until death', he had said. 'That is not a statement of hope, it is a statement of fact. Even if you divorce and marry David, you will be stuck with the man who is the father of your children. He may have wronged you in so many ways, you may wish that you had met your second husband first, but you didn't, that may be your misfortune, but should it be David's as well'.

Gilly knew that if she became the cause of David's losing the job he clearly loved, and the opportunity for a career that he had worked so hard to achieve, even if David could live with that, she couldn't.

They had flown from Manchester, which David still thought of as Ringway, travelling separately. As the plane touched down they both knew that an important moment had arrived. They went through passport control, with a strange look from the officer, then through customs and into the arrival lounge.

Fortunately, Gilly's bag came through on the belt before David's and they agreed that she should go on ahead and meet in the coffee lounge outside. David then waited for his bag to arrive. As he followed Gilly into the lounge outside, he heard her name being called and looking up, saw her husband, with three excited children. Gilly glanced around wildly and then, ignoring David completely, went across to the small group and hugged each child in turn before handing her bag to her husband and taking his outstretched hand and walking to the exit.

David, with two days left before he was due back at the Cathedral decided to head home. A surprise visit, he thought, won't be welcomed, but his dad would enjoy sharing the Talisker, he had originally bought with EBG in mind.

These People

These people their quiet conceits
Their bitter pains, their birthing, marrying
Their dying is celebrated and mourned
Here the dead bury the dead
Here the lonely comfort the lonely
Here the stranger's sadness absorbs the sorrow
And here I intone the words
taken from the book, here
I light the candle, recite prayers
Did I choose this life, or choose
to remain a lightning strip
earthing a people's pain

EBG

Back to Work

On his return to The Close, David stepped directly into the busy flow of Cathedral life. Again, his daily routine became unrecognisable, either from his experience in Drissburgh, or the relaxed days of his recent holiday.

As Cathedral curate, David was there to act as the oil in the machine. Each of his colleagues had defined responsibilities which, following their early gathering as a chapter for daily prayers, they set about their daily tasks, often leaving the Close after breakfast and not being seen again until evening prayers. These were followed by meetings, dinner parties, drinks parties and a variety of semi-social, semi-business events.

For the Dean the job always came down to money. The Cathedral was a small business, funded by a cocktail of money. From the collections given by the Sunday morning congregation, visitors' donations, and what could be earned and raised to supplement the grant received from the Church Commissioners.

Two of the Canons had jobs related to the Cathedral, but neither of those were particularly demanding. The Canon Theologian explained to David early on in his time at the Cathedral that he expected to produce a book every three years, and that each new book should reflect how his thinking had developed over that time. As far as David could see, his daily pattern consisted of reading, writing and in the afternoons listening to the classical music that drifted through the open study window. Occasionally he disappeared to attend, read a paper at, or chair one of the theological conferences around the country that drew the interest of academics and theologians alike. On one occasion he became extremely excited and enthusiastic to be invited to chair a working party for the Church of England's newly formed Synod. For this he was given extended leave of absence because, as the Dean announced, it would bring great credit to the Cathedral, which was one of the newer parish church Cathedrals. It had been founded around a hundred years ago when the new Diocese came into existence and these new Cathedrals were looked own on by the more ancient ones.

The second of the two Cathedral canons was an elderly priest who had been made a canon following a long and illustrious ministry in one of the larger parish churches in the Diocese. It appeared that, largely because he kept his profile so low, everyone had forgotten about him and now, long after he should have retired, but relying on the rules which meant that he had a job for life, he would make his way slowly and painfully across the Close for the evening service, and, too infirm to join the procession, would be assisted by one of the vergers into his stall to wait for the service to begin.

He rarely preached, but insisted on reading the lessons which involved a long and perilous trek across the chancel from his stall to the lectern. This heroic effort so exhausted him that he would then spend the evening 'resting his eyes' in front of the old black and white television which he had rented from Radio Rentals, and which offered a view of the world through a fog of black and white mist, which, whilst restful, clouded his view of the world.

Throughout this compendious daily drama and indifference strode the figure of the Bishop's Chaplain. The Bishop himself was rarely seen, as the Chaplain explained to David, his day was divided into half hour slots, during which all those who needed to see him, would be welcomed, attended to courteously within their allotted time slot then equally courteously dismissed by a laconic comment or gesture. At this point the Chaplain would appear at the door smiling and show the supplicant out.

Obviously the bishop had other duties. There were civic occasions, visits to London and the mysterious office 'preparation'. Although again, much of that work, sermons, papers, speeches were the Chaplain's responsibility, and it was the Chaplain who maintained the diary, constantly negotiating between the two diary secretaries to protect the Bishop.

As far as David could see, however, the role of the Bishop was defined by his membership of an exclusive club, one which would serve to protect him throughout his working life and into retirement. Very much as EBG had warned, David could recognise deeply-seated corruption in the systems that were in place to govern the life of the church. He could also recognise that the Chaplain was caught up in the corruption, indeed sought to defend it, because he wanted to become part of the club in order to achieve all the personal benefits that it offered him.

David was attracted and repelled by the life he was

surrounded by. As curate he was required to spend time visiting the congregation. This was often a delightful and enjoyable duty. But two things disturbed him, the first was simply that his job was to ensure that the congregation was nurtured so that they would keep attending the Cathedral, usually in preference to their local parish church, and to keep contributing their donations each week. If ever he met local clergy whilst he was out visiting, as he had to, in 'their' parish, he was always made aware that he was trespassing, or even poaching, stealing 'their' game.

However, by far the worst thing, which David found most difficult to cope with, was to spend all his time listening to people telling him how wonderful the Dean was. Also how marvelous a certain Canon, usually long dead had been, without any acknowledgement that he was the one actually visiting them, and having to keep to himself the appallingly rude and indiscreet comments that the Dean had made when he heard who David was planning to visit. If the Dean's wife was in earshot she would reproach him, but her cautions were always laughed off.

So this was the pattern of David's first few months in his new job. If he saw the Chaplain at a distance he would find an opportunity to avoid a face-to-face meeting, but that was not always possible.

His first long conversation took place one morning after the homeless breakfast. David and a few volunteers had washed up, wiped down and put away the tables and were lingering over a final cup of coffee. David was aware that retaining these volunteers was crucial to the continuing success of the breakfast, and was a responsibility he had been given by the Dean. So he was happy to give them the time, even if it was biting into other commitments he had made.

There had been an incident that morning when a young man, who was a regular at the breakfast and a known drug user, had come in with his girlfriend. She was a young, middle-class girl, who should quite clearly have been at school. Although David's enquiry had been brushed over, suddenly in the middle of everything, between the cornflakes and the bacon sandwiches, Vinny had drawn a knife and attacked an older man on another table. David had to intervene, and found himself between Vinny, holding a large and fierce looking kitchen knife with a razor sharp serrated edge, and the older man, a Glaswegian called Charley. Vinny, realizing that Charley was obscured by David's bulk between them, and that he might end up stabbing the wrong man, hesitated long enough for David to hold out his hand and what he hoped was a reasonable voice asked Vinny to give him the knife.

This, Vinny refused to do, but said that if Charley apologised for insulting his girlfriend, that he would drop the matter this time. David then had the difficult job of persuading Charley to offer the apology which he was not ready to do. Thankfully Charley had slept off the effects of last night's drink, and was still only a little way into this morning's bottle, the effects of which had so far been absorbed by the bacon sandwiches. Vinny re-sheathed his knife and left with his girlfriend tottering behind. She had on too high heels, with too short a skirt and smudged eye make up, swearing loudly that Charley should watch out in future.

Charley returned to his bacon sandwich and his bottle. David, still feeling the effect of the adrenaline rush, was none the wiser about the insult or what had been said.

Sitting now and discussing the morning's events with his volunteers, David looked up to see the Chaplain.

'Aah, David' he began, 'pleased to catch you, how are you?'

David noticed the volunteers gather up their cups and start to leave. Somehow he thought that the Chaplain made them more nervous than Vinny and Charley together.

'Fine.' David's cautious reply was as neutral as he could manage, no hostility, but not welcoming either.

'There's something I need to discuss with you about the next training conference for the new clergy, it will be your last. I've managed to persuade the bishop to waive your third year, now that you are here in the Cathedral, and more in the centre of things. Much of what happens in the third year you'll already know, and what you don't you can always ask'.

David's finely judged silence, he hoped, indicated that he was content with the decision and interested in what came next.

Before the Chaplain continued, to David's dismay the volunteers called from the door, coats already buttoned up as they prepared to leave, offering their goodbyes and see-you-tomorrows. They left David and the Chaplain alone to continue their conversation.

'Coffee?' David offered. The Chaplain, to David's

growing dismay accepted and David escaped briefly into the kitchen to boil the kettle, returning with two cups, he again waited without saying anything.

'How are you liking the job?' the Chaplain enquired.

'Very much, interesting, varied, a lot more responsibility than I expected'

'Good that's good. Well, the training event next month, it's the meeting when this year's priests meet with the new deacons. You remember?'

David nodded.

'We think it's a good way to build relationships among the younger clergy who were made deacon when you were priested'.

Again David nodded, so far this had been a very one-sided conversation.

'What I thought David, was that we might lead it together'

David's face clearly registered the surprise he was feeling.

'The thing is you know the group and are well regarded. After all, your recent promotion has rather made you '*primus inter pares,* with your fellow curates'

David blinked and the Chaplain interpreted, 'first among equals?'

This time David made no response, there was something about the Chaplain which reminded him of Vinny as he had asked him to hand over the knife, cold, unfeeling, devious, and out for himself. David knew that he was being used and that there was nothing he could do about it.

'So I will draw up the programme and then we can decide who leads what part. There is one thing however, the course runs from Tuesday to Friday morning, and I have an important meeting with the bishop on Wednesday which I can't escape. So, Wednesday afternoon and Thursday morning will be yours to run as you choose. You could talk about your first few months at the Cathedral.' Finishing his coffee, and without waiting for a reply, the Chaplain left.

David was left sitting at the table dumbfounded.

Less than two years ago he had left theological college a young working class lad, who had broken through the barriers of class that had paralysed the Church of England for a thousand years. There was no tradition, as in the Catholic Church, where young working-class boys could enter a seven year training for the priesthood.

In the Church of England, theological college followed a University degree. That David had managed to avoid that route was of itself a minor miracle. At his selection conference in his home Diocese, he had been told that with his limited academic skills and poor background, he should choose a course that he had some hope of finishing successfully, rather than a degree course. So had been advised to seek a pre-theological course, followed by the basic level course leading to ordination, rather than a degree.

Now he was at the centre of diocesan business and intrigue, meeting senior staff on a daily, routine basis, offering his own views when invited and now being invited to act as a tutor on a course for his own contemporaries.

After all, he reasoned, these were people he had been ordained with, all still in their first parishes, whilst he had already moved on. Clearly there will be a script, he reasoned. He wasn't being asked to design the course. He was, at the end of the day, just a handy person, a person on hand, who could stand in for the Chaplain.

As he considered the implications it became clear to David that he was pleased to be asked, and confident that he could rise to the challenge. He certainly wouldn't be letting the Diocese or himself down, but still he had some anxiety, after all, how would the others react?

For some time David had planned a return visit to Drissburgh and with his day off due, he telephoned EBG who promptly invited him to lunch. On his way to the station David passed a quality wine and spirits shop and was delighted to find a bottle of Talisker to replace the one he had drunk with his father in yet another expensive failure at building a relationship. Shocked at the retail price compared to the duty-free shop at the airport, he nevertheless paid up and headed to the station. He caught the fast train to Drissburgh and arrived in time for lunch. As usual, lunch was at The Mermaid and he joined EBG in ordering the special of the day.

Having explained his predicament and his amazement at the Chaplain's request, which had come as more of an instruction, he waited for EBG's response. To his surprise his former vicar suggested that they walk back to the Rectory, explaining as they walked that even in Drissburgh things might be overheard and misunderstood, or understood only too well.

Once in the house EBG uncorked the Talisker, handed David a glass and then taking his own, sat back and asked, 'so how was the holiday?'

'Oh fine, great, enjoyed it,' David replied weakly.

'And Gilly,' EBG went on, 'did you enjoy her too?'

David could not help hearing the criticism implied in EBG's question, and realised with dismay that what he thought had been a discreet relationship was in fact an open secret. If only, he hoped, in Drissburgh.

'Oh, don't worry,' EBG continued as if reading his former curate's mind, 'she came to see me, we talked, it's over of course, you know that, but not because she doesn't love you. No, it's over because she loves you too much for your own good. You are a fool, David, but you are a lucky fool. I'm not bothered about the sex, or for that matter that you lied, oh alright' seeing David's pained reaction, 'you didn't lie, you just chose to say nothing, which amounts to the same thing'.

'Well' David interjected, 'I did say something, you see and that's the problem'.

He went on to tell EBG about the confession, how he had wanted to marry Gilly, how on holiday he had realised how much his job meant to him, and that in the end he had let her go knowing in his heart that she was the right person for him, but that they had met in the wrong circumstances, at the wrong time.

EBG was silent for a while, sipped his whiskey and reflected before he responded to David.

'What really bothers me is the confession, you have given that man ammunition which he can use against you.

You need to be prepared for that, because he will, because he can'.

'I know.' David acknowledged the truth of EBG's comment before going on to describe the conversation after the homeless breakfast session. EBG again took a moment to digest this information and was thoughtful. 'One thing,' he continued, 'and it works very much in your favour, he's not setting you up to fail, because you won't fail. Another is that if he's grooming you, again for what we don't know, how will he use the ammunition you have given him?'

It was David's turn to be thoughtful as he told EBG about Neil's conversation with his friend in London. EBG shifted in his chair, reaching for the bottle, poured himself another glass indicating to David that he should do the same.

'You know, David' he continued, 'I'd like to see that bastard found out before it's too late and he's dug himself in too deep. But now's not the time, now all we can do is wait for his next move.

Vocation

The steady ocean draws
itself onto the shore
sinking into the thirsty sand
My vocation comes to this
Constant drowning in a sea
of expectations, failure
They want more than I can give
more forgiveness, more reassurance
I become the means of their forgetting
I gather the burdens and carry them
far out into the ocean, they return
with the tide, a constant reminder
of our frailty, mine and theirs

EBG

Changing the Plan

As he made his way back to the station, feeling the effects of the Talisker, David caught sight of a young girl with her friends, who he recognised as Gilly's daughter. She waved and ran across to him, 'Have you come to see my Mum?' she asked.

'No,' David replied, 'I came to see the vicar, and now I have to get back home'.

'She'll be sad,' said the girl 'but I'll tell her that I saw you' with which she ran off to rejoin her friends, who, looking David, ran off together shrieking with laughter.

As the train neared the city, David thought that he might look in on Neil, who had now been accepted by the Home Office as a Prison Chaplain and would soon be leaving the parish after the next clergy training course.

Fortunately, Neil was at home, and David was invited in with a reminder that he didn't have long. There was an evening meeting that Neil was required to attend, but there was time for a cup of tea and, Neil thought, if there was enough bread, some cheese on toast.

As Neil was making the tea, David looked around the flat and realised that over the last two years he had come to value his friendship with Neil. He would miss him when he left for whichever prison he was to spend his first months as an assistant prison Chaplain.

'Durham,' Neil announced, reading David's mind, 'next month. I've told my boss here. He's not happy, he said that he had expected me to stay for at least three years. And that people were being promoted much earlier than in his day, doubtless an oblique reference to you, that people were missing out on the benefits of the acquired wisdom of the more experienced priest'.

'Like him?'

Neil laughed, 'Of course, just like him'.

David started to tell Neil about the events at the homeless breakfast, and the subsequent conversation with the Chaplain.

Neil laughed again, 'More ammunition for my vicar then, no doubt he's waiting for the call to act as tutor on the course. All that experience going to waste. He will be disappointed'.

David reflected on Neil's comment before asking 'How do you think the others will react?'

'They'll be OK' said Neil somewhat hesitantly, and hearing the kettle, he made to leave the room. 'Not very well, you mean', again David was thoughtful. Somehow he had to find a way of fulfilling the task he had been given, without it costing him the friendship and, more importantly, the co-operation, of the other young clergy in the group.

Neil came back with tea and the promised plate of cheese on toast. David laughed.

'You'll soon be dining on prison food, so tell me about Durham, when do you start, who is the Chaplain there?'

Neil began to explain about his new situation, his interest had started when his flat had been broken into and his visits to Keith in the remand centre. Those visits had given Neil an insight into the lives of these youngsters, and had visited him for the whole of his sentence. He had just been released, and Neil had seen some real positive changes in the lad, and in his attitudes.

Listening to Neil gave David the germ of an idea. Rather than him talking about his first months at the Cathedral, as the Chaplain had suggested, which was a suggestion that would not endear him to people he had been ordained with only a couple of years before. He knew they were, in many cases, better qualified and certainly more committed than he had been. It would be better to use the time to get them thinking, as Neil had, about the particular events and experiences in their first few months that they would wish to build on and carry forward into their future ministries.

'Make it about them, not me' thought David, and you have a group that should work quite well. Sharing his thoughts with Neil over tea and cheese on toast, it became more and more obvious that this was the way forward, and a way of avoiding the obvious trap that was being set for him.

Later that evening, David telephoned EBG with his half-formed plan. EBG's response was positive, and between them they took the plan a few steps further. The secret, David realised, was for it not to appear to be a plan at all. Much better if, once the Chaplain had left and David and the group had gathered for the session, for David, or better still Neil, to talk about his impending move to Durham, and why he had applied for Chaplaincy work in prison. The interview process that led to his appointment, and what he hoped to gain from his new role, that parish ministry wouldn't offer. That should be enough to get the others talking and David could then disappear into the background whilst the conversation flowed around him.

That way, EBG had advised, everyone in the group will be focused on themselves not you, and there will be little or no room for resentment to build.

The conference came round fairly quickly, and despite suggesting that there should be a planning meeting, David had not met the Chaplain, other than at the normal round of services at the Cathedral. Also, neither of them had mentioned the conference or the conversation they had about it.

The conference convened in the Diocesan Retreat House, a marvelous centre. Quite unlike other diocesan centres, this was set in the City, on one of the hills that surrounded the urban area. The house was nevertheless secluded by being set in its own grounds and approached by a long drive, leading to a patio area with a view across the city. As usual, the group, chatting animatedly began to gather in the Common Room, and also as usual David slipped into the kitchen for a coffee with the warden. Here he had his leg pulled about his rapid advancement.

'Careful,' the warden teased David as she joked with her staff, as though he couldn't hear what she was saying, 'here comes the new Canon, you'll have to watch your Ps and Qs or you'll find yourselves reported to the powers that be'.

David blushed, unused to this he attempted to offer reassurances. 'No, he replied, 'not Canon, I'm just the curate that's all. It's just a second curacy'.

The warden smiled. 'I'm not so sure about that' she said. 'I have a feeling that you are being set up for a fall. You need to be careful'

David's mystified look needed no other words, and so she pushed a conference programme across the table. There, the Chaplain's name as leader, was supported by his own as co-leader, prefaced by the title The Reverend, which he never normally used unless pressed, and certainly not with the members of the junior clergy group.

As he read through the programme he saw that on Wednesday night he had been given both a title for this session, 'The Cathedral at the Heart of the Diocese' and a new title for himself, The Reverend David Saxon, Minor Canon. He was speechless.

'Well Canon Saxon', said the Warden 'congratulations, I told you to watch out for that man, he's a sneaky one and he's up to something, I don't know what' but with him there's always something, I've never liked him since he arrived'.

As if on cue the kitchen door opened and the Chaplain entered, offering his greetings to the staff, he motioned to David that he was needed upstairs.

In the lead up to the conference, the Cathedral had been particularly busy, and David in particular had been caught up, with the Dean, in a number of events that had required planning meetings, with careful notes being taken and a draft service being agreed.

The Dean, who David, to his surprise and relief, had realised quite quickly was, at a personal level, a caring and engaging personality. He had said, 'the joy of serving in a Cathedral', was that people came to you. There were special services for a variety of organisations, some city based, some countywide and others linked to the Diocese. Very occasionally, an event would be requested that had national significance.

Given his busy schedule there had been very little time to think about the conference, and the Chaplain had used that to his advantage. It was clear that David had been set up. The co-leadership, the title, the programme, and the title for his Wednesday session had not been discussed or agreed with him except in the most general terms. David also noticed as he looked at the programme again, that he was named as President, and Preacher at the communion service on Thursday morning, even though at past conferences, the services were allocated in the first session and there had never before been a sermon slot. David knew that he had to think on his feet, and quickly if he was to retrieve the situation.

As usual, the conference started with lunch, before which the group gathered for a drink in the common room. When David entered one or two nodded a greeting, although he had a distinct feeling that others pointedly ignored him. The conference programme was on the table and its contents clearly read and noted. David smiled and nodded, returning people's greetings and joined Neil who was talking to one of the new deacons in front of the fire place. Neil's look made it clear that David had a problem.

This time however, unlike David's rescuing of Neil after the break-in, or his disarming of Vinny at the homeless breakfast, or rescuing a hapless youth who had been arrested for possession of drugs from the clutches of the local police, it was clearly suggested by Neil's warning glance, that it was David who was out of his depth on this occasion and Neil who could possibly rescue him.

As they filed into lunch the Chaplain indicated that he and David should share a table, ignoring the suggestion, David sat with Neil who immediately whispered, 'What's all this, I thought that we had agreed?'

'We had, but he put this out without discussing it with me, I'd never seen this until today'

It was clear that Neil was uncertain whether to believe him or not, 'He can't do that'.

'He did' David was emphatic, 'Well I plan to wait until he leaves on Wednesday, and then go back to our, your, first plan'.

'No', Neil's response was surprisingly firm for such a mild mannered person. 'That won't work because he's not leaving, the Bishop's diary has changed and he'll be here to sit in on the session'. He told us whilst you were in the kitchen. 'He says that he is looking forward to what you have to say.'

David could feel the noose tightening, he'd taken the Chaplain at face value and now here he was trussed up and laid out for the rest of the group. Feeling the panic rising, his first thought was what kind of family crisis could be invented to demand his instant departure for Manchester. He knew, however, that wouldn't work. One of the other clergy had been told before a previous conference that even the fact that his wife was having a baby was not a good enough reason to absent himself from the event, not if he wanted to be made priest. So births, marriages and deaths presumably would all have to be postponed for this conference.

So whatever underlay the Chaplain's devious plan, why he was being set up and for what, the trap had been well and truly set.

The first day passed without event. The group appeared as non-plussed as he was, and the session after supper gave various people an opportunity to talk about their parishes and the work they had been doing, the people they worked with, and the challenges they had faced.

Throughout the session the recurring theme was the same, 'nowt so queer as folk', a saying local to Yorkshire, which the Bishop had quoted in his charge to the young Deacons before their ordination.

To be a Deacon or Deaconess or a Priest in the Church of England was to engage in a strange occupation. The TV had it about right. Fey young men called Geoffrey struggling to cope with the strains and stresses of everyday living. Each of the group described the same experiences with people who appeared to be the same people in different parishes. It seemed to David that there were only so many types to go round, and that they were replicated in every parish across the country, which was why the clergy went around with a rictus-like grin permanently etched on their faces. Also why on their days off, they couldn't pass a hearse without a sudden anxiety attack, wondering if they had forgotten a funeral, and that at that precise moment, instead of relaxing or enjoying themselves they should be at a graveside or in a Crematorium Chapel.

He remembered EBG, whose own father had been a funeral director, telling him about a local curate who had forgotten a funeral. He had been reading, and was simply immersed in his book and had lost all sense of time. Later, when people found out he was criticised for his lapse because he didn't have a proper excuse such as being dead himself, he was 'only reading'.

Listening to his colleagues David realised that each and every parish had its Bobby, its Hilda, its Big Giver and its sermon critic. There were the ones elected and re-elected as Church Warden or Treasurer. Long-serving parish secretaries, the big giver had to be kept sweet although it was never clear whether the big referred to dress size or the size of their donation. And the sermon critic had to be humoured.

In every parish it seemed there was a constant demand for the basics of the faith to be explained, again and again. No one, it seemed, ever wanted to hear or know more than the basics, and the Church of England colluded with this 'hands together, eyes closed' understanding of religion, which was why adults who attended church had such a naive approach to their faith and children in their droves left Sunday school and the church itself at the great passing-out parade called confirmation, never to be seen again.

Yet as David knew, despite all this, good work was done, people were supported, there was value in the work he and the others had chosen and committed themselves to. And it was valued by those who benefited, which is why in his confrontation with Vinny, even though he had made himself vulnerable, Vinny had not attacked him and had allowed himself to be persuaded to step back from following through with his threats against Charley.

David, in his time in Drissburgh and now in the Cathedral, had often intrigued the non-believers that he met. 'How', they would ask, 'can anyone with any intelligence believe all this mumbo jumbo?'

As the conference progressed David's silence and non-participation became more and more noticeable, eventually in one particularly long and trying silence the Chaplain suddenly exploded.

'David what do you think? I can't bear your silence it's worse than your constantly interrupting.' This was a reference to the events at a previous training conference, when David's contribution had provoked an ironic and bitter riposte from the Chaplain in response to David's reference to the 'theology' of John Lennon's newly released solo records.

David knew that he had to take the first opportunity that came along, that this was probably it, and that if he didn't take it now, he would be left with a one-and-half-hour session with a meaningless title and little or nothing to say.

'I was thinking' he began, 'that we've started a really interesting discussion here. After all, we are all of us in the same situation really. It sounds as if all of us have the same group of parishioners, including some who appear to be the same people, just with different names, if you know what I mean. So there is a limit as to how far we can take this discussion about the parish and parish ministry. What would be really interesting for me, and I suspect for everyone else, but we can check that, is to hear why Neil has decided to specialise in Prison Chaplaincy. What motivated him It is after all a pretty radical decision, what do others think?'

The Chaplain looked both dumbfounded and furious, and his eyes seemed to signal David not to pursue the idea any further. Ignoring the warning David continued.

'I think as joint course leaders we can be pretty flexible. After all, we are leaders in the church, so I was thinking that my slot on Wednesday could be opened up. It would give us all an opportunity to hear from Neil and share our own experiences and think about how they are beginning to shape our future ministries, and where we might be used in the scheme of things'.

The Chaplain seemed to know when to admit defeat. After all, he had stated clearly that David was co-leading, so if the co-leader had proposed a shift in the direction the week would take, and it was his slot that he was forfeiting. The whole thought process was written on the Chaplain's face. Furrowed brow and twitching eye rows, everyone knew that they were witnessing a titanic clash, between two strong-minded individuals, but no one knew what it was about. Everyone in the room assumed that David had agreed the programme in advance and was happy with it.

Turning to Neil, the Chaplain suggested that if he was unhappy with such a radical change, and with no time to prepare, he could always say no. But Neil, who had already written his talk, said no he was happy to go along with the suggestion and that was that.

With Neil's agreement to the change in the programme there was little else the Chaplain could do and the session ended.

Under his breath David breathed a sigh of relief, hardly daring to believe that he had managed to turn things round without at least publicly having a major row with his co-leader. Over supper he thanked Neil for his support and asked what he would say. Neil's response was to outline a short presentation, beginning with his first meeting with Keith, but without mentioning David, then his subsequent visits to see him in prison. He thought he would describe the interview at the Home Office, where an innocent remark he had made started a row between the Senior Chaplain and Bishop for Prisons, which had to be refereed by the panel Chairman, a Civil Servant. This meant that the Chaplain had to apologise to the Bishop, the Bishop had responded tetchily that they had agreed not to be divided in their opinions in front of the candidates. Neil had thought it wisest to apologise to both of them.

David laughed at this. 'It's everywhere isn't it. Petty jealousy and disagreements. Anyway, at least this time we have won'.

Neil's response was more guarded, 'only this time' he said, 'it's far from over between you two'.

I come into
the presence

I come into the presence of
still Water
resting in the quiet pools
as the giddy water roars past
floating in the gentle eddy
in the quiet corner of the stream
as with Larkin's invented religion
dedicated and named after water
I come into the presence of
still water where I find my faith
in the gentle support of water
occasionally flicking a hand as the water bears my
weightless self
and the dappled trout nibble my toes

EBG

Further
Developments

The rest of the course passed without event. The Wednesday evening session went well, and the other members of the group were encouraged by Neil's enthusiasm for his new role. His ability to link it with his experience in the parish, together with his acknowledgement of how crucial David's intervention had been at the time, without appearing to criticise his vicar, encouraged other members of the group to open up and reflect something of their own experience.

This session it was the Chaplain who remained silent throughout, until the very end. After David had thanked Neil and summed up, when he offered his own thanks to David for his original idea, and to assure Neil of his good wishes for the future.

Back at the Cathedral David stepped straight into the preparations for what was an annual event in which he, as curate was heavily involved. The Cathedral Company of the Boys' Brigade was well established in that part of the city, offering a recreational Friday evening session with vaguely militaristic overtones in its leadership, structure and uniform.

Nearly all the boys who formed the Company came from the nearby estates, made up of medium rise blocks, some of which overlooked the Cathedral Close. The youngsters were typical inner-city kids who roamed the streets with confidence borne of familiarity. The annual camp was a highlight of their year, providing many of them with the only holiday they would have.

The camp traditionally took place in the Lake District and was in itself a remarkable logistical exercise. As the Dean observed to David when he gave him the responsibility for overseeing the Company, and the annual camp, 'just leave them to their own devices and you'll be amazed how these ordinary working-class chaps can organise the whole thing effectively, and without spending too much. You'll see, it's quite remarkable. Which David had to admit, it was. As the captain explained, neither the youngsters or their families could afford to spend a lot of money. Much of the cost of the camp was paid through money raised earlier in the year, mainly through jumble sales and collections.

Transport was provided in the form of a lorry provided free of charge by a local firm which one of the officers worked for. It was loaned on condition that he drove it, and that it was back clean and tidy, undamaged and ready to start work on the Monday. What that meant in practice was that the tents and equipment were loaded on the Friday night, delivered on the Saturday to the site, which was a field by Lake Windermere, and an advance party of older boys erected the camp ready for the company's arrival the next day.

The preparations had begun early this year because of events at last year's camp. There had been problems between the company and a scout troop from David's home town, and the owner of the site who had at first banned the Cathedral Company from ever returning. This edict had been relaxed only after the Company Captain had reassured him that there would be no repeat of the trouble.

The camp had been marred by a pitched battle between the Boys' Brigade youngsters and a Scout Troop sharing the same field. It had become a mini War of the Roses, and the first-aid tent had become a centre of operations, stemming bleeding noses and tending black eyes. Fortunately there had been no serious injuries but by the end of the battle, the Scout Leader and the Boys, Brigade Captain had themselves almost come to blows each defending his own boys' innocence and presenting them as victims of an unprovoked attack by the other group.

David had to attend a planning meeting which had, as its main agenda item, to ensure that there was no repeat of last year's pitched battle. Following an exchange of correspondence, the scouts had refused to book their camp a week later, and so hostilities were due to recommence.

The previous year the challenge to an inter-organisation football match had been the trigger. The two teams had assembled ready for the kick off and the Scout Troop had volunteered one of their leaders as referee. All had gone well until the first foul, which had left the Boys' Brigade centre forward lying face down in the mud clutching his leg and appeals for a penalty refused. The ball had been kicked into the lake, by whom, no-one was certain and before long a full pitched battle had broken out.

As David listened to the discussion it became clear that with the youngsters they had in the company, not to mention the officers, any inter organization games would have the same result. Complete separation of the two groups was the only effective way of ensuring there would be no repeat of last year's problems.

As the conversation went on, with various proposals being put forward and then withdrawn, David's mind began to wander. He found himself thinking about the young clergy group and the quite extraordinary degree of subterfuge and dishonesty the Bishop's Chaplain had used in order to create a rift between himself and the other clergy in the group. To pretend that he was away with the Bishop, only then be present at David's session, was that to catch him out in some way. David was uncertain as to the motivation behind such scheming, but the man was clearly not to be trusted, but what was he hoping to achieve? What was his aim in isolating David from his peer group.

As the camp planning meeting came to an end the inevitable conclusion was that there should be no contact at all between the two organisations, and that the Boys' Brigade officers, including David, would have to be extra vigilant when darkness fell.

The other officers, who were clearly fond, and not a little proud of their young charges, laughed when they were reminded of a story about an incident a few years before on another site. The company's older boys, most of whom had now left the company, had left their tents in the middle of the night and managed to collapse three of four of the scout tents before the alarm had been raised. They had managed to get back to their own tents, and the crime would not have been discovered but for a couple of them having stepped in cow pats which they then smeared on their sleeping bags, causing the other boys in their tents to complain long and loudly.

David left the meeting promising that he would be well prepared for the camp, and that not only would he lead the daily act of worship and the night prayers, but that he would participate in other activities as required. Arriving at the front door of his house he noticed that he'd had a visitor whilst he was out, and opening his front door, stopped to pick up the envelope which had dropped onto the mat. The note was from the Chaplain inviting him to supper on the following Friday evening. Added to the bottom of the note was a p.s. suggesting that he might like to bring the 'delightful young lady' who had assisted him in decorating his house.

David went into the kitchen to make himself a cup of coffee and while the kettle boiled he carefully studied the note again. Was the Chaplain simply being disingenuous, surely he had made the connection between the 'delightful young lady' and the subject of David's ill-advised confession, or possibly not?

David mused on the invitation as he got himself ready for an early night. His first instinct was to ring Gilly and invite her along. She would doubtless enjoy herself and would charm the other guests, but then she would not be able to get home to Drissburgh that night and she couldn't stay with him. No, he thought, that simply wouldn't work, and anyway he had promised EBG to take fewer risks. He then thought of inviting his sister but dismissed that idea immediately, realizing that she would find the company and setting strange and completely outside her experience. Even he, David realised, had changed a great deal in a short time. So much so that she might find him pretty strange. In the end he decided that he would attend the dinner alone. Who knows, the Chaplain might invite another guest, a blind date. David smiled at the thought of the Chaplain, with his own secret life, arranging a dinner party to introduce him to a woman.

The alarm raised him from a fitful sleep in which he had a number of strange dreams filled with bizarre characters, not the least, the Chaplain himself. David realised that since his ordination his dreams had begun to follow a regular pattern, usually consisting of a gathering, a meeting, or occasion, more often than not a service.

He would appear at the front of the church, or theatre, or meeting room and a crowd would be gathered. They would continue to talk animatedly and whatever he tried to attract their attention or bring them to some sort of order, he was ignored.

In this way the event, or the service, or whatever occasion it was, could never be properly started and David's frustration would increase until it spilled over into the here and now and he would awake.

Last night's dream had followed that pattern, with the Chaplain playing a key role. The Chaplain constantly diverted attention from David, who was increasingly ignored and isolated by the congregation. At one point, increasingly frustrated with being ignored, and by the role of the Chaplain, and in order to regain the initiative David had held out his hands in a formal liturgical greeting and used the opening words of the communion service, but to no avail.

Eventually he had turned on his heel to leave the Church, only to find his way blocked by a milling crowd of choristers who wouldn't allow him to pass. This led to him being surrounded on all sides by the congregation, led now by the Chaplain, pointing and laughing. Eventually the laughter had acquired a regular metallic tone and he had realised that it was the alarm clock and he was released from the nightmare.

Leaving the house in the false dawn of the lights from the City leaching into the Close, David was usually first in the crypt chapel where the Chapter met for prayers. As curate, it was his job to prepare the books, using coloured ribbons to mark the service, the psalms and readings of the day. As the clergy arrived they took their seats, conveying silent greetings to one another until the Canon in residence arrived and began the service.

David particularly enjoyed the atmosphere in the Cathedral at this early service. The lighting was just sufficient to guide people from the side entrance. That entrance was used until the verger opened the main doors at around nine to the crypt chapel. As he walked along the south transept, past the high altar, the early light would etch the windows, the grey industrial light of this northern city, filtering into dusty corners. Occasionally, on a brighter morning, the sun would reflect the colours from the east window with a wash of soft pastel greens and reds.

Alongside the light there was a rich depth of silence which seemed to echo, in their absence, the choir's singing, and underneath it all the murmured voices reciting the prayers. All those who had worshipped here, for over the thousand years the building had stood on the site, whilst the city, over that time had grown up around it.

The clergy arrived and usually left in silence. Occasionally an item of news of national, or international significance, was brought into the prayers and might occasion a whispered conversation. Mostly, people had to get back to their houses for breakfast and on to the meetings which filled their days.

It was, David reflected, a strange existence, this little group of houses set around a green space in the centre of a city. They were colleagues certainly, neighbours certainly, friends not necessarily, but always courteous to each other. They came and went, keeping their business to themselves unless required by the Dean to take part in some Cathedral activity. They also had to be on their guard much of the time because there were vulnerable, sometimes undesirable elements who would come into the Close. Security was a constant issue. Doors had to be locked, and there had been break ins, burglaries and even fights in the Close which was the old churchyard, long since closed for burials and maintained by the local authority.

David had discovered people sleeping out overnight, encouraged by the quietness. They were unlikely to be disturbed by a routine police patrol, and with the added advantage of being first in the queue for the homeless breakfast, which was David's first duty each working day, after the service had ended.

The Chaplain usually attended early prayers in the private chapel in the Bishop's House, although occasionally they would both appear at the Cathedral. David had noticed that there was little love lost between the Dean and the Bishop, they were both strong-minded, ambitious men who had as EBG would have said, climbed the greasy pole through a mixture of recognised ability and patronage. Now they were neighbours, and in the hierarchy of the Cathedral and Diocese the Dean was the Bishop's number two. However, the bishop attended the Cathedral by invitation, as the Dean would delight in making clear when he organised the procession on a Sunday, when the Bishop was there in his capacity as a member of chapter rather than as Diocesan Bishop.

The issue that divided them was the thorny issue of the ordination to the priesthood of women. The Bishop was in favour, because the Dean suggested his wife insisted on it. Whilst the Dean was very much against it, although David had noticed that in discussion he would change his views and would appear less opposed to the idea when he remembered that when the inevitable happened, he would be retired and largely unaffected.

Crossing the Close, David spotted the Chaplain. Under normal circumstances he would have taken avoiding action, but David needed to respond the invitation to supper that he had received.

'David' the Chaplain greeted him, 'I did think that the conference went well. Although I was sorry that you felt unable to talk about your life here at the Cathedral as I'd suggested. But in the event, nevertheless, I must say Neil was very good. He will be a loss to the Diocese and to Parish ministry, and your idea was a very good one, excellent, inspired and it did encourage the others to contribute which they don't always do'.

David nodded, 'I just wanted to thank you for invitation to supper, I'd pleased to accept, but on my own I'm afraid, my interior designer can't make it'.

'Sorry to hear that my wife will be disappointed, but don't worry there is someone else coming so you won't be the only singleton'

David must have looked suddenly more interested, but the Chaplain laughed, 'you'll find out soon enough, see you on Friday'.

David was beginning to find the relationship between himself and the Chaplain increasingly confusing. Clearly the man was deceitful. The underhand practices, the duplicity and dishonesty, made that clear, but they were accompanied, as this invitation to supper demonstrated with an expression of charm that implied openness and friendship. And then there was the warning from Neil that made it clear, that underlying the Chaplain's bizarre behaviour was something much more sinister.

From what he had gathered from EBG and from Neil, who were his two main sources of information, the Chaplain had arrived in the Diocese from a spell on the staff of a theological college in the south. He had been a curate in a south-coast parish where he had completed a PhD to add to his degree and his theological studies.

There was nothing in his career that had marked him until he had been identified by the Bishop. They had apparently met at a conference where the Bishop had been impressed by his contribution, and offered him the post of Chaplain which had just become vacant as a result of the preferment of the previous post holder.

In his role he acted as adviser to the Bishop, gate keeper and keeper of the Bishop's Diary. It was a key role if only because on a daily basis he would answer letters as though from the Bishop, so to all intents and purposes in the Diocese he and the Bishop were one and the same person speaking with one voice.

David was intrigued by the invitation and what it might mean or what might be revealed. Whilst the formal business of the Diocese and the Cathedral happened during normal office hours, from time to time, what the Dean referred to, with a twinkle in his eye, as the real business, would take place during the carefully orchestrated dinner parties that took place in the Close. Occasionally, as though vying with each other, the three Canon's houses would have their collection of cars parked outside signalling who had been the most successful at gathering an interesting and influential group around their dining table. Careers were not necessarily made or broken on these occasions, but often, patronage would be secured that would in the longer term carry significant influence in determining the career progression of this or that individual.

David had gained some insight from one of the cathedral congregation who he had taken to visiting regularly. The Claytons were a well-known industrial family in the City who had attended the cathedral for years. The husband had at one time acted as both High Sheriff of the County and Lord Lieutenant. They counted amongst their friends former clergy who had gone on to become Deans in other Cathedrals and at least two who had been made Bishop. Now in their eighties, they were both fairly indiscreet and it was from them that David began to understand how the church really functioned, and how its wheels were oiled.

A dinner party he knew was never really about the food served, some of which was very poor. The Deanery food was especially poor unless there was a semi-formal occasion when Dean could bring in some of the Cathedral's domestic staff who would cook and serve. There was a false modesty or an inverted snobbery by which the Dean, with a particular flourish would serve Shepherd's Pie at dinner, or at his invitation-only breakfasts, bacon sandwiches with brown sauce.

David continued to puzzle over the invitation to supper. There would be some underlying purpose to be served, but what it might be David had no idea. All he could do under the circumstances was to turn up with the obligatory bottle of wine, and as a special gesture suggested by EBG, flowers for the Chaplain's long-suffering and taken-for-granted wife. David had so far only seen her at a distance and who, in an odd way he was looking forward to meeting properly for the first time as a guest at her table.

The Fine Art of Skimming Stones

My best was
A twelver, twelve
Flat leaps of stones, skimming
Across mill pond water
Like twelve mill stones
Spinning on hot afternoons
Spent, searching for the
Ideal, flat, smooth, rounded
Pebbly stone, comfortable
Between thumb and forefinger
To throw, pulling back with five
Deft fingers, to fly, and spin
Across the water, fascinating children
With my childish skill

EBG

Dining
with the Enemy

Arriving at the door of the Chaplain's house David knocked. He had been uncertain as to how to dress or what to bring, but in the event had chosen jeans and his usual black polo neck. As he had originally imagined it, he brought a bottle of wine, and flowers. In answer to his knock the Chaplain threw the door open with a flourish,

'David there you are, do come in and meet the others'

Leading the way into the lounge David was introduced by his host. 'Everyone, this is David, a rising star in the Cathedral firmament. David, this is everyone, now introduce yourselves whilst I organise some drinks'.

For David this was a first. Such formal supper parties with people you had never met before were an alien experience. At home, the only socializing was reserved for holiday occasions such as Christmas, New Year or Easter, and then only at family parties where obviously everyone knew each other. At college, and in Drissburgh, there had only been informal gatherings with people bringing their own drinks and possibly some sandwiches and crisps on offer. Perhaps on special occasions a sausage roll to pad out the buffet. So this was the first supper party at the home of the enemy. He was on guard.

Taking the initiative the other male guest introduced himself as Jack Rogers, he was apparently a vicar in a London parish. His wife Suzie was introduced and she was, he explained American, although whether he was apologizing for this David was unclear. She was apparently the daughter, it was explained to David, as though this was a perfectly normal thing for someone to be, of a diplomat who had been stationed in London. There she and Jack had met at a drinks party at the embassy in Grosvenor Square. David nodded vaguely recalling a demonstration outside the Embassy a report of which had recently been on television.

When the family moved back to the States, Jack insisted on telling the whole story, she had stayed on. Suzie was a good head taller than Jack, who seemed to find it necessary to make up for his lack of stature by his pomposity. Already in the Chaplain's absence he had assumed command of the situation with an affected nonchalance which David recognised as masking his uncertainty and absolute lack of confidence.

Turning to the other guest, Jack introduced her as Madeleine, a Deaconess also from London. According to Jack, although David thought she looked perfectly capable of introducing herself, she was an important campaigner for the ordination of women. David must have appeared nonplussed because without giving either David or Madeleine a chance to speak, he launched into a monologue about an informal campaign which had been sparked by events in the States, where there was an increasing demand for women to be ordained. 'And remember, David, what happens in America today happens in Britain ten years later. So it is only a matter of time!'

David could feel his anger rising at this pompous little man who seemed to enjoy the sound of his own voice, and was about to cut him off when the Chaplain entered the room with a tray of glasses. 'Aah, Michael' Jack barely paused for breath, 'a libation, how gracious'.

David was uncertain that he had ever known the Chaplain's first name. 'Michael', he smiled to himself, wondering if maybe that was the name sewn into his underpants, St Michael no doubt, suits him perfectly.

'David, what are you smiling about? Let us into the secret'

'Oh, nothing Michael, nothing important' at the use of his first name, David thought that he noticed the Chaplain react sharply before realising that he had now changed the rules of the game that he and David had played. Maybe sensing a slightly awkward moment the chaplain's wife was next to speak.

'David, thank you so much for the flowers, they are lovely'

To complicate the evening still further it turned out that the Chaplain's wife was also called Suzie.

'Well let's make ourselves comfortable, supper isn't quite ready, no point in everyone standing around, now, David, where are you going to sit?

David took a chair near to where Madeleine was sitting on the sofa, with the American Suzie on her left.

David hoped that this would allow their conversation not to be interrupted by Jack, who was by now engaged in some sort of half-whispered, private exchange with the Chaplain.

'So you work here at the Cathedral with Michael?'

The conversation ran on in a slightly stilted fashion, touching on David's experiences at college, his home background, Madeleine's role as a Deaconess in a neighbouring parish, to the one where Jack was Vicar.

David struggled as he tried to avoid leading the conversation to the thorny subject of the church's ordaining women. Without fully understanding why, he thought he was vaguely against, and he realised, or at least imagined as the conversation continued that he and Madeleine had very little in common. He had to admit that she was attractive, again taller than Jack, with curly blond hair and an open and attractive smile.

'So where were you at school?' David turned as Jack repeated the question, which to David's ears and experience was a strangely worded question. David had attended a local secondary school and had left an academic failure, with the headmaster's words ringing in his ears. 'Saxon, it would benefit neither you nor the school for you to remain here a day longer than necessary'.

He certainly didn't think of himself as having been 'at school'. He was rescued here by the Chaplain, who chided Jack, reminding him that David was one of the new generation of working-class ordinands, who were bringing a new and altogether more authentic experience to the church's ministry, than their public school contemporaries ever could hope to do.

But Jack was not to be put off. For some reason, David realised that his very presence, or his height, somehow offended or challenged Jack's sensibilities and the evening would be a long and tedious one. It was an evening in which he would have to constantly bite his tongue out of respect for his hosts, but in particular

Michael's wife, Suzie.

Typical, David thought. He had struggled most of his schooldays with smaller people picking on him because of his height. Kids at school, and a particularly obnoxious and feisty kid who had waited for him outside school on a number of occasions to pick fights. Like a little Jack Russell he persisted until eventually David had returned the aggression. Literally picking the smaller boy up and throwing him to the ground. The boy had then returned to school in tears and David had been punished by the Head Teacher for his violent outburst.

'So you went to a CACTM selection conference, and then straight to theological college, and were ordained here, and before you know it you are at the Cathedral. Rapid promotion wouldn't you say, you must tell us your secret.' Again Jack's aggression was clearly showing through and once again David was rescued by the Chaplain.

'Leave him alone Jack. In this Diocese he's one of our stars, we've got high hopes for him'.

David saw a look pass between the two men, but what its significance was he had no idea. Ignoring Jack's question David responded instead to a more gentle question from Madeleine about his role in the Cathedral.

As he explained his role, and how his day varied, with the many and quite different meetings, the visiting, Madeleine asked what part of the job gave him the greatest satisfaction. David spoke at length about his pastoral role in general terms, but Madeleine was insistent. Moving the conversation nearer to where she wanted it, ordination of women. What had it meant, priesthood? Did it bring satisfaction to be able to celebrate the communion, baptise or marry people? David tried to appear non-committal but knew that his answers revealed the simple truth that she was right. His role was deeply satisfying in its completeness.

Madeleine was at pains to reassure him that she accepted that in the present climate in the church, where even a union with the Methodist Church had recently failed to gain the necessary support, the ordination of women to the priesthood was still a long way in the future. She was convinced not only that it would happen, but that it would happen in time for her. David and she began to warm to each other, and as she described her own background and training David realised that she was in many ways well-qualified to undertake the role. He found himself thinking of the women he knew at theological college, almost camp followers, who had attached themselves to students in order to become the next best thing to a vicar, a vicar's wife. As the conversation progressed Madeleine agreed that this happened, but that she was determined to express herself through ministry until her vocation was formally recognised.

David was, he realised, being challenged by the conversation, which was unlike any previous conversation, when his reflections were again rudely interrupted by Jack's insistence.

'Come on Maddy, stop hogging the Cathedral curate'.

David was sensitive enough, perhaps too much so, to hear the sneer in the use of the title 'curate'.

Jack continued in his strange, hectoring style. 'I'm

interested to know a few things, what was your degree in David?'

David reacted sharply and before he could control himself he turned the question back onto the questioner.

'So Jack, were you at Oxford or Cambridge?'

He surprised himself, but the aggression of the smaller man had begun to get under his skin, become an irritation, and was in itself a discourtesy not only to David, which hardly mattered, but also to his hosts which mattered more. After all, he thought to himself, he hadn't done or said anything to deserve such an unprovoked interrogation or such a display of aggression from the smaller man, which was why he knew he was feeling so annoyed.

Again the Chaplain came to the rescue, almost like the referee in a football match between two ill-matched teams.

'Supper's ready.' And with that he started to usher his guests into the dining room, sitting David next to Madeleine and opposite Suzie, reserving the top seat for himself. He put Jack to his left and Madeleine to his right. David noticed that the chair nearest to the kitchen was reserved for the other Suzie.

More wine was poured, starters served and grace was said, before the conversation was once again started by Jack. It appeared he had a headful of opinions on any given subject, and an apparent belief that people were keen to learn what those opinions were.

Again he appeared to delight in needling David, although by now his very presence was enough to achieve that if he only would have enough sense to realise it. This time he accused David of being against the ordination of women. However on this occasion before David could reply, both Suzie and Madeleine, almost in unison, declared his comments to be unfair.

'You have no idea what David thinks,' his wife retorted, and anyway it will be years before the Church of England comes anywhere near agreeing. In the states things are different – there are some angry women there, and they won't be put off. And as it becomes easier to cross the Atlantic, if a woman priest comes to the UK she will expect to be given the courtesy of an Altar'.

Madeleine agreed, and mentioned two women that she had met at a conference the year before, neither name meaning anything to David. He didn't speak, and on balance he thought the wisest course. As his mother always advised, 'least said soonest mended'. Whilst he would have been happy to take Jack on, he knew that would also mean taking on both Suzie and Madeleine as well and for the moment he thought that wasn't such a good idea. He realised that he was just a little intrigued by her and her views, which whilst they were unorthodox, were also stimulating.

If the Chaplain, Michael, thought that he was match-making, then in David's opinion, he could have done worse than a woman who at least shared some of David's own views, and whose opinions were well thought out, and expressed. David had to admit that Jack had guessed right, insofar that he was not sold on the idea of women being ordained, although he also recognised that it was not something to which he had given very much thought.

Having been headed off in his first attack on David, Jack was determined to get a response and again launched an unprovoked attack on clergy without degrees. How could they lead their people, he demanded to know. How could their sermons be understood or even be worth hearing at all, if all they could do was rehash second rate material from *The Church Times*?

Again the Chaplain came to David's rescue. He answered Jack's question by describing the impact of David's sermon in Drissburgh, and the power not only of the words, but of David's delivery which had given them both the authority and authenticity of kerygma. This support seemed to stop Jack in his tracks, and again David was aware of an exchange of looks between the two men. Suzie, Michaels wife, cleared away the first course, declining David's offer of help and returned with a strange dish which she announced was a Lasagne. It came with a salad and yet another bottle of red wine. It tasted increasingly sour, and left David with a feeling that he could do with a pint of beer to wash away the taste.

As the main course was being served and the glasses refilled the Chaplain asked David if he was aware of the history of The Cathedral Close. David had to admit that he knew very little about it.

'Well, of course' Michael continued, 'the houses are relatively new, and before The Close was built, the Canons all lived out of town in a posh suburb. There was no community at all and getting into services was difficult. All the newer Cathedrals, and certainly the former parish churches had a similar problem. Fortunately, the churchyard here had not been built on, and so a scheme was planned, money was raised and the houses were built on the old graveyard. All apart from yours David, which was the former lodge right by the gate, where the verger lived. The Bishop's house and offices and this house were developed out of the old vicarage, parish rooms and clergy house'.

Jack was obviously desperate to interrupt. He hadn't heard his own voice in a while now, but again Michael gave him a look full of meaning and continued.

'There's a lovely story about the new houses. After the chapter were all installed, the Dean's wife decided that there should be more neighbourly activity in The Close, and so she planned a Safari Supper'. Noticing David's puzzled look he explained that it meant the diners travelled around with a different course served in each house'.

Surprisingly, this gained a positive reaction from Suzie, who apparently thought that it was a lovely idea. 'We should reinstate it', she suggested, but Michael was by now in full flight and not to be diverted.

'Well,' he continued, 'the thing is that the Dean's wife had so planned it that they came to the Deanery last. This was because she wanted to show off her walled garden, a feature that she had insisted on for security, but also as an amenity to replace the garden she had lost in the previous house. The garden had its own lighting, switched on from the dining room which had French windows onto a patio, and a small lawn which had been recently turfed. So, marching everyone into the dining room, where there was cheese and biscuits and port, she switched on the outside lights to a stunned silence. You wouldn't believe it, but there on the grass was a couple having sex. Both starkers, apparently they had climbed over the wall for privacy. Well, Mrs Dean was horrified and called out in a shrill voice, that became ever shriller, Dean, Dean, don't just stand there do something. The couple, of course, just leapt up, grabbing their clothes and ran out of the gate. Hopefully they got dressed before they ran out of the Close itself'.

Amidst gales of laughter form his guests and by now in full flight, he went on to describe the reaction from the Dean's wife the next day at a coffee morning. She recounted the story and apparently told her listeners that the chap was a gentlemen really, because as she explained he had 'folded his clothes into a neat pile' whilst she was a slattern. 'Her clothes were scattered all over the grass, and some she even left behind, but she didn't say which.'

David found the story hard to credit, but was, she reassured him, that it was true, and part of cathedral folklore that he had not heard until now.

Eventually the conversation meandered, largely as a result of the wine, until it ran into a *cul de sac* immediately after pudding, and just before coffee. Even Jack had gone off the boil, partly, thought David because the Chaplain, who David was seeing in a completely different light this evening, seemed to have the better stories.

David had thought it wisest to keep his thoughts to himself, knowing that stories about working-class life in post-war Manchester couldn't compare with life at school or university. Eventually, judging the time to be right, he excused himself, offering thanks to the two Suzies and Madeleine, and choosing to ignore Jack altogether. At the door the Chaplain thanked him for the flowers and then said, 'I wanted you to meet Jack, he's definitely on the way up, and being married to an ambassador's daughter won't harm his career prospects. But that's not the reason I wanted you to meet him. He's chairing a conference on this business about women in the church. He's keen on it because Suzie is, and there's a speaker from the States. Madeleine is speaking, and I have been invited to attend as a theological consultant. I've been asked to nominate someone from this diocese and if you'd like to come I can nominate you'.

David thanked him, pleading that he was too busy at the Cathedral to spare the time, but the Chaplain was not that easily dissuaded.

'Don't worry, I'll fix it with the Dean. You'll enjoy it and it won't do your prospects any harm. You'll make some good contacts and the subject matter is important, it's the future and you can't fight it'.

Walking back to his own house David thought about the evening,. The strange conversations, the different faces of the Chaplain, or Michael as he must now call him. He also thought about Madeleine and her role at the conference. After all, David reflected, she may be a Deaconess who wants to be a priest, but she is still a woman and she seemed to show some interest in him and his opinions. As he arrived at his own front door it seemed more than ever to be a curious development. The Chaplain, with different faces for different occasions and different people. Suzie's nervousness at any remark aimed in her direction from her husband, as though she was afraid. Shutting the door behind him, David couldn't help feeling that there was yet more to this than met the eye.

It was apparent that the Chaplain's guests were staying overnight, and so David had arranged that the next morning he would meet Madeleine and show her something of the City. On Saturday the chapter didn't meet for prayers, but some of David's homeless breakfast volunteers, and occasionally one or other of the clients would meet for prayers at eight o'clock and this was followed by a simple social breakfast that allowed the team to catch up on news. Here they would share their thoughts and enjoy each other's company without the normal pressures associated with preparing, cooking, serving and cleaning up after sixty or so, noisy, argumentative clients.

Madeleine arrived as promised, and with her fine features, height and curly blonde hair, attracted appreciative comments, all loudly whispered to David, in the full knowledge that she could hear everything that was said. Used to the earthiness of northern humour and the affectionate banter that accompanied anything that was new or unusual, David simply smiled, 'just ignore them' he said, 'they'll soon lose interest'.

After breakfast, as he wandered around the market with his companion, David recognised that whilst he had not planned it that way, his split with Gilly was now complete. That he had in a very real sense committed himself to this strange life, despite still being a fish out of water, and that a long distance friendship with someone who at least understood what he was experiencing might just be what he needed.

He mentioned to Madeleine the possibility that he might be at the conference and that he knew that she was speaking.

'It would be great if you could be there,' she replied with what seemed to be genuine enthusiasm, 'we need all the support we can muster, it's going to be a long haul'.

The Fulmar

The Fulmar feeds and flies.
In the gale's bitter teeth.
Strong winds chill the bones.
This land of Saints and tides.
In the Island church prayers for the dead and dying.
Memory imprinted in the genetic blueprint of a people.
Not the Saints' imprint but the unsanctified.
Across hostile waters that will win in the end.
Swamp these lands and wash out the memory
Unsettle the settlements and turn the village to raw
Earth and sand dunes.
Scatter the sheep.
Unfold the lambs.
Listen carefully to the caterwauling wind
This thin place between heaven and earth
This place of quiet death.
Of wailing birth

EBG

Figures in
their Landscape

The landscape of the Church of England in the early 1970s was one of change. In most aspects of its life, the Church was in a state of flux, as the old conservative agenda gave way to a new, more liberal hegemony.

In worship for example, most of the old service books had been abandoned in favour of a series of booklets, pamphlets and cyclo-styled sheets. Series One rapidly gave way to Series Two and then Series Three, each published in a different, non-descript shade of pastel. The booklets seemed to sum up the indecision of an institution that had set sail into uncharted waters, whilst seeking to clarify, modernise and make its public worship relevant.

In the Cathedral the Dean had despaired. Partly this was because the booklets which replaced the traditional Book of Common Prayer rapidly became dog eared and had to be replaced at not inconsiderable expense. Also, because the more traditional members of the congregation, who given that this was the Cathedral, were in the majority, complained bitterly about the loss of service, which the exasperated Dean complained bitterly had been introduced three hundred years earlier. This service, which in any case was not the original service as devised by Cranmer, as they thought. It was a more recent, and in some ways much more confused version, which tried to look in two directions at once. It had been introduced in 1928, despite having been voted in by

General Synod's predecessor body, vetoed by Parliament but then introduced any way.

This era of confusion affected everybody. In his first weeks as a newly ordained Deacon David had accompanied EBG to the Cathedral for a debate, in which he had to cast his vote for or against the Church of England uniting with the Methodist Church (he had voted against). David new little or nothing about Methodism, despite in his younger days attending a Methodist Sunday school where he won a prize in a scripture examination. But in the youth fellowship, which was part of the Methodist church's scheme for engaging with the youth of his neighbourhood, he had been out-pointed in the boxing by a larger stronger boy, who, he vaguely recalled, boxed him into a corner, keeping him there until the bell rang.

Uncertain about its liturgy and confused about its ecumenical relationships the Church of England was also unclear about aspects of its ministry. There were rumblings in the church about women, and whether they should or could be ordained as Priests. There was a view that homosexuality, which was barely mentioned or understood, was not to be tolerated.

David had heard rumours from his old theological college that the principal had not been offered the Bishop's job he had hoped for, but had been made a Residentiary Canon of a Cathedral because of a scandal linking him with a young chorister in the Choir school. He had, apparently, developed a fondness for the boy but found himself competing for his affections with another clergyman. Eventually, voices had been raised after Evensong at the back of the Cathedral, and the matter had been brought to the attention of the Bishop. He had long since realised that matters had gone far beyond an amusing anecdote to entertain his fellow Bishops over dinner in his club. Reluctantly he had to intervene, and had arranged for the offer of the Canonry, impressing on the Principal that it was not to be refused.

Whilst at college David had never deviated from his own fairly straightforward working class heterosexual world view. With no allusions or interest in the goings-on in the college, he had certainly never entertained, nor had he been propositioned with the idea that he should explore other sides of his sexuality. Nevertheless, he was aware that despite only being interested in the opposite sex, he had at times over a late night coffee or glass of wine in a fellow student's room been drawn into the fascinating and seductive world suggested by the attitudes and behaviour of both staff and fellow students.

On one occasion he had been called into the Principal's office to be carpeted, with another student with whom he had made an unofficial visit to London. He had wanted to see a concert and had persuaded a fellow student to join him. They had hitch-hiked to London and attended the concert in Hyde Park, then arrived back, utterly exhausted the next day, just in time for morning prayers. Their absence had been noticed and the Principal had been alerted, and had called them in to issue a verbal warning about their behaviour, which contravened the college rules.

Having issued the warning the college Principal dismissed them, then asked David to remain behind.

Once they were alone, the Principal had produced from his pocket a gaily coloured, patterned tie.

'I was in London myself yesterday' he said, 'in Carnaby Street, I saw this and bought it, it's for you'.

In his naivety David could only mutter a brief thank you. It did not occur to him that there could possibly be any other underlying motive. Needless to say he wore the tie on a number of occasions, explaining to those who asked, that it was a present from 'Harold'. That is until, on one occasion, he wore it at home for his parent's Wedding Anniversary. His Dad had become increasingly morose as the evening wore on, until his mother explained. His father was worried by the tie, which somehow suggested to his father that David was, as he put it, 'queer'. Once David removed the offending article all was well again.

On another occasion, it had been, as David recalled, an extremely warm evening, which a group of students had spent at the pub. David had been having a coffee with one of his fellow students, James Snowden in his rooms and they were disturbed by a knock on the door. The door opened and a head had popped round extending an invitation to them both to join a small group who were heading down to the local school, where they had permission to use the outdoor pool out of school hours.

Swept along, partly by the heat of the moment and the contagious enthusiasm of the other students and partly by the heat of the evening, David had gone along. Someone had produced a key for the gate and as though it was the most natural thing in the world David found himself swimming, completely naked with a group of laughing giggling men. He recalled some jokes being made and some affected appreciation of the physical attributes of the various members of the group, including his own. But whilst it was daring enough, and out of character for David, it had also been great fun and the cool water had been the perfect antidote to a hot and sticky evening.

The issue of sexuality, in particular amongst the single clergy was beginning to attract attention from the press. The Methodist Church had published a report about sexuality, and it was becoming clear that some clergy were being identified as somehow being on the edge of what was acceptable. Definitely not acceptable for people with their particular responsibilities, and their access to young people. One of David's contacts at college had been the victim of an assault by the guest master at a monastery where he had gone to be interviewed. He recalled the hot breath and stale sweatiness of his attacker as he was bear hugged into submission before being kissed forcibly on the mouth.

David had always maintained an open mind and had in his own way rather enjoyed the 'camp' atmosphere of the 'queers' in his circle at college. But he was, he felt, very clear about his own position. He had recently joked with his old school friend from Manchester, Pete, that his new job in the Cathedral was a 'missionary position' much to their mutual amusement.

Alongside liturgical change and the increased interest in sexuality, both generally in the wider society and in the church, the wind of change was also blowing both generally and more specifically amongst the clergy. This was over the business of women being ordained, and it was easy to see where, over time the fault lines would appear. The church divided along both liberal and conservative lines as well as the more traditional high church, low church divide.

It had never occurred to David during his time at college that such a possibility might be in the offing, and he had no particular view about it. Certainly he could see that a woman as committed as Madeleine would have strong views and that she might feel genuinely called to Priesthood. David, however, was realistic enough, having been well tutored by EBG, that the other significant change that was beginning to affect the Church was the idea that once ordained you had a job for life. Clearly, in the future, with an influx of women into ministry, many of the men who had been ordained would find themselves competing with women who might be better qualified, or prepared to work simply for the privilege of being a minister.

The disappearance of the job for life had affected his own family over generations. His family had been coalminers, and engineers, had worked in the mills, driven lorries, coaches and buses, but all these jobs had begun to disappear. So, it was no surprise to David listening to the gossip in gatherings of clergy to hear something of their fears.

As EBG had said more than once, his only security came from what was known as the parson's freehold. Take that away, as Bishops and Diocese were increasingly doing, and you took away the security. There would no longer be a job for life.

EBG had not developed his theme, but it was all too clear to David where the discussion was heading. If jobs were disappearing, security undermined, and then increased the workforce by ordaining women there would be problems. Some of those female ministers, because they had husbands in well paid jobs, may well be prepared to work without pay. Then, clearly, the whole nature of ministry would change.

As David saw it there were four main issues at stake. What would replace the Prayer Book? What about relationships with other denominations? And sexuality, and the ordination of women. None in themselves that significant or important, compared with say Northern Ireland, the future of Trade Unions, Cuba or the Cold War, or as much as pop music or football. However, get the right answers to wrong questions, or the wrong answers to the right questions, and his future, the future he had been given with his ordination, would be very different.

The conference papers, when they arrived, seemed to acknowledge that the conclusion David had arrived at for himself was the right one. He was unclear how to react to the agenda, but the last person he wanted to talk to was the Chaplain. He thought of ringing his former boss, whose views he respected ,and who always offered wise counsel, but in the end, he telephoned Madeleine. She seemed delighted to hear from him and they chatted amicably for some time until David mentioned the conference. Almost immediately he felt Madeleine's defences go up.

'Is there a problem?' she asked, 'what don't you agree with?'

David tried to explain. that he had no problem, that he agreed with almost everything, but that all the items to be discussed over the three whole days, with some fairly high powered and influential people, brought together at considerable expense, were almost, and before he could stop himself he heard the word as it came out of his mouth, 'irrelevant'.

Madeleine's silence was very powerful. She was clearly very unhappy and David feared that he was the direct cause of her unhappiness.

'So David, are you saying that the church's refusal to accept my vocation, its refusal to even consider that I as a woman, could be just as equally called to full-time ministry as, presumably, you feel yourself to be called, just because I am a woman is, irrelevant? Is that what you are saying David'?

He waited for the telephone to go dead, but it didn't, so there was hope, but the silence he could tell was deep and angry.

'No Madeleine, that's not what I am saying, not at all, and you know that. But this is not just about you or me. There are other issues at stake, the whole business of worship, all these silly booklets, we argue about, sexuality, ecumenism, what we do about Methodists all that, compared to what's going on around us. In Europe, the Cold War, strikes, unemployment, homelessness, these are big, important issues, affecting people. People who can't manage, people dying, for freedom, for I don't know what. This conference ignores the simple fact that there's a whole world out there, and it's hurting'.

'I know that David', she replied finally, 'but there's a whole world inside here, and it's hurting too'.

David knew that he was gaining a reputation for being impetuous, and that he could be quite hard hitting when he chose to be. Fortunately for him this was not one of those occasions, so he let it go.

'You're right, I'm sorry. Of course I do understand and I'm looking forward to hearing you speak, it will be great and if it's okay with you I thought that maybe afterward we could go out for a meal, a Chinese maybe?'

This time the silence was of a different order.

'That depends' she replied. 'The speakers are going for dinner on the first night, and I'm due to take the American visitor out for a meal sometime, and then there's the conference dinner. I'm sorry but I think we'll have to find another time'.

David realised that, for whatever reason, probably his own stupidity, he had thrown away any advantage he may have had. Madeleine had rejected his inept advances and quite clearly hadn't thought his opinions worth discussing. And, to cap it all, as he read the conference papers again he was going to have to spend even more time with the Chaplain's friend Jack, who as conference chair would have unlimited opportunity for sharing his wisdom with the delegates. Perhaps, he thought as he got himself ready for bed, he should just cancel.

At morning prayer the next day, as he was preparing the books and getting ready, Canon Phillips came in early. He greeted him almost affectionately.

'David, morning, hear you're off to this conference,

what's it called? 'How to be a Contemporary Church? Sounds like fun, three days up in town, gossiping with old chums, quite fancy it myself'.

David smiled to himself.

'Thanks Canon, you can have my place if you like, not sure what I can contribute'.

David went on to elaborate his reservations and mentioned how he had already offended one of the speakers. But Canon Philips wasn't to be bought off quite so cheaply.

'Thing is, dear boy, that this church of ours always thinks that its own affairs are more important. You're right of course, the world is going to hell in a hand cart and it might seem that we have no more than a passing interest in its affairs. That, however, is not our job. That's the job of economists and politicians and industrialists and academics of various disciplines. Our job is to uphold them with our prayers, and to date we have to get our prayers right. We have to be united because disunity is an offence to God. We have to be sure that people can manage their human affairs, and that's not just sex, mind you. We have to get the right people into ministry so that the ministers do their job right. Don't know about all these girls mind you. Still, it won't happen in my time, but it'll be a problem for your generation'

David acknowledged his advice. It was probably the longest conversation he had ever had with the old man, who was already on his knees in deep contemplation.

Reflecting on his senior colleague's words David realised that whilst he was right, it was possibly the case that he should be looking for some other outlet. If the cross had both upright and horizontal arms, maybe it was the open arms, rather than the relationship to heaven that was David's ultimate vocation to pursue. Oh well, he thought, nodding a greeting to each of the Canons, I may as well go to the conference and listen, it will do no harm. I might actually learn something and it will be good to catch up with Madeleine, as long as I don't put my foot in it again.

Suburbanisation

The brochure offers glimpses
of the future hints at the coming
suburbanisation of the landscape
Detached and semi
detached from the 'now'
hints at the developed 'then'
A year maybe two
ahead, the builders
pouring concrete
laying blocks
Installing roof trusses
slating and topping
out each new house
Soon these silent
crop-bearing fields
where barley grows
between the fallow years
will grow a place
where dinner parties
family rows

and children's tricks
or treats hold sway
And where, in each suburban
garden amongst the network
of drains and paths
and cul de sac
On verges and turfed lawns
barley will reappear
each tufted head a reminder
of what used to be before.

EBG

The Conference

The bus to London was almost full as David took his seat. The bus station had been almost empty, apart from a couple of regulars from the homeless breakfast who called out to him as he waited in the queue. Almost as soon as he returned their greetings he wished that he had ignored them. They came across to chat, as though they were old friends, which in a sense they were. This caused the other people in the queue to eye him with suspicion and move away slightly. Clearly they were suggesting by their body language, that he should have been keeping a better class of company.

The conversation was conducted in the usual loud voices, accompanied by a selection of harrumphs, snorts and expletives. The gist of it was they wanted to be reassured that his absence wouldn't mean the cancellation of the breakfast, and once reassured that their breakfast was quite safe and would be served promptly as usual. Much to David's relief, and without enquiring as to where he was heading or why, they drifted away from the bus station in the general direction of the Cathedral. Like two lost souls, apparently blown aimlessly, like the rubbish which had accumulated in the windy alleyways of the bus station, from last night's take away wrappers and fish and chip bags and trays.

Ignoring the disapproving glances from his fellow passengers, David handed over his bag to be stored in the luggage bay under the coach, found his seat and settled down with his book. He noticed to his relief, probably because of his earlier conversation, that most of the passengers gave him a wide berth. He had the seat to himself and because this was an express service it was likely that he would have it to himself for the whole journey through to London.

The bus pulled out and headed towards the motorway. Travelling south round the new one-way system which took it around the front of the Cathedral he saw his friends from the bus station, waving a fond farewell. The bus accelerated through the empty city streets. Another half an hour or so and the commuter traffic would have built up, but for now the driver was able to steer the bus through a series of green traffic lights and out onto the dual carriageway.

The bus had not been David's first choice of transport, but when he enquired, the Dean, who was normally fairly generous, made it clear that whilst he was prepared to allow David the time off to attend the conference, he could not pay expenses because it was not in reality cathedral business. David suspected that it was a combination of conflicting views relating to the conference theme. The Dean had already made it clear on a previous occasion that he was not entirely happy with the thought of women being ordained and seemed to share the general opinion of his generation that as long as it happened after he had retired it was really none of his business.

But David also recognised that any suggestion emanating from the Bishop's office was automatically viewed with suspicion in the Deanery. He couldn't really refuse to allow David the time off, the Chaplain would have seen through such a feeble excuse, but still there was no need, in the Dean's view to spend Cathedral money on funding the exercise. When David had explained this to the Chaplain, instead of offering to pay his travel expenses, as David had expected, the Chaplain had offered him a lift in his car. He was, he explained, travelling down a day early and staying with Jack and Suzie. They were entertaining the American speaker, and David was, at the end of the conference staying over again for an extra night to catch up with other friends.

The thought of being stuck in a car for four-and-a-half hours with the Chaplain, and then having to be subjected to Jack's condescension for a whole evening was too much for David to contemplate. So he had made the only sensible decision, which was to travel alone, at his own expense, using the cheapest route he could find.

The bus left at six in the morning and arrived in London at Victoria Coach Station at mid-day. It was a long journey, but preferable to the alternative and considerably cheaper than the train.

In the event, courtesy of his friends from the homeless breakfast, the journey was undisturbed and bearable, and they arrived at Victoria Bus Station on time. David was not used to London. It was, as a local Manchester-based television actor had once described it, 'like Manchester without the heart'. David noticed seemingly busy people pre-occupied with themselves, their work and the business of getting through the day as best they could.

Armed with his conference map, and an underground map, David set off to find the conference venue. The escalators, the noise of the trains, the swishing open and closing of the doors, he found confusing. Looking around he realized that no-one was exchanging eye contact, so he spent the journey checking the map above the window opposite and counting off the stations one by one.

Arriving at the reception he was greeted by a young, fresh-faced and charming nun who was acting as the receptionist for the conference. There was a pleasant exchange as he was asked where he had travelled from and whether he'd had a pleasant journey. He was allocated a room number and a key and told that he would be sharing a twin room with the Chaplain.

David's confusion must have shown on his face, and after he had asked if she could check again, the receptionist reassured him that she was quite sure. The Chaplain had booked the room himself, and that he had specifically asked for a twin room, and made it perfectly clear on his booking form that he would be sharing with the Reverend David Saxon. She reached into her file and showed David the copy of the booking form, 'that is you, isn't it?'

Finding his way to the room, David was dismayed to find a small twin-bedded room with only a bedside cabinet separating the two beds. There was a wash basin and a toilet and bathroom along the corridor, shared with five other rooms.

He unpacked with a heavy heart and a growing sense of unease. Fortunately, he had packed a tee-shirt and dressing gown, so if he had to get up in the night, he would at least be dressed for the trip along the corridor. But what game was being played here? If the Chaplain was staying with Jack, why did he need a room in the conference centre, and why share it with me. This was strange, and not a little unnerving given what David knew about the Chaplain and his anonymous life in London. Dismissing the thought David headed down to the conference hall where a number of delegates were beginning to gather in anticipation of the opening session, which was scheduled for four-thirty. Looking around the room he could see an odd collection of individuals. There were clergy in their collars, a couple of Franciscans in their brown habits, a couple of nuns in their black and white and one or two women without make up and the thin straggly, grey hair and clothes that David couldn't help thinking, exactly as his father might have said, were hippies. They obviously had no sense of having any interest in their appearance; doubtless, thought David, it's some kind of statement, or maybe they are just in a bit of a state.

A quick glance around the room produced no reaction from the other delegates. No smiles of welcome or any indication that his presence was of any interest at all to the other delegates. Realising that he had only eaten a couple of sandwiches on the bus, and that supper wasn't until seven that evening, he decided to pop out in search of a drink and hopefully some late lunch.

Outside it was a pleasant enough day, warmer than his northern city. Just along the street he found a pub with some outside tables. He ordered a pint and one of the pies the pub advertised itself as specialising in. Taking his lunch outside, he sat back to watch the hustle and bustle of the City as it passed by. People watching was a new experience, and certainly sitting mindlessly outside a pub at lunchtime. As he relaxed he thought how easy it would be to get used to a life like this, as so many of his homeless breakfast clients had.

As the early start took its effect under the warming sun, he sipped his beer, ate his late lunch, and reflected idly on his role at the Cathedral and the clients at his homeless breakfast. They had so obviously unsettled his fellow passengers, who were only too obviously relieved that his 'friends' had not been traveling on the bus with him.

He recalled early on in his time at the Cathedral an occasion when, in order to get to know his clients better, he had sat outside just like this, in a city centre car park. After an hour or two, almost without anyone noticing, he had been handed the bottle that was being shared around and some day-old bread that someone else had scrounged from a local bakery. He had found the experience strangely moving, and in a sermon he had preached a few weeks later, likened it to a form of communion. However rather than impressing his listeners, as it had impressed him, it had given rise to some hostile comments. Those directed toward him he had been able to deal with, but there were some to the Dean which had been reported back to him. He had a call from the Dean, which was not a reprimand exactly, but a reminder that he was, and should be on a different level to the congregation. All good Christian folk obviously, and it didn't do to liken them to the folk who attended the homeless breakfast. There was something said about the clients who couldn't help themselves and, those who obviously given their standing in the community, who not only could help themselves, but who, handled in the right way, could help others too.

David recognised that this was the nearest he had come to criticism of his work. It was a similar criticism to that offered more subtly by EBG. The Dean, obviously recognizing this, had offered it more as a piece of advice to his young colleague.

'We do our work, David, and we say our prayers. We're priests, not prophets, pastors and not politicians,' and that had been the end of it. As David mused on this he was awakened from his daydreaming by a voice he recognized, turning, he saw the Chaplain with Jack Rogers.

'David, I thought you'd be busy in the conference, getting to know people. It's a good opportunity to make contacts, network, you know it is important if you are going to make a sensible contribution later'.

David's response to the effect that he had a long journey and that this was effectively his lunch, albeit later than normal, provoked a snort from Jack.

'A liquid lunch, good job you've left your collar in your room'. David shrugged.

'That's why I never wear one Jack, doesn't do to let the side down right?'

'Well, David, we'll see you when you've finished, but meanwhile we've got work to do before the first session.' And with that they both walked off in the direction of the conference centre.

David remained nursing his beer and reflecting on the day he was having. The fact that he was about to see Madeleine again, and the main issue of the conference, which has supposedly been called to look into the way forward for the church in the seventies. It was, however, was much more concerned with promoting a particular way forward that would, with time, completely change the nature of what the church represented. David wondered how Fr Hamer was feeling about these changes, and strongly suspected that if he knew what David was up to at this very minute, he would not approve.

Returning to the conference centre, David entered the main hall to see Madeleine in an animated conversation with a small dark haired woman. Seeing David she called him across.

'David, hi, this Peggy.'

'Hiya David, great to meet you'

Her accent made it immediately clear that she was the much-heralded speaker from America. David knew that he was making the classic mistake, something that he wished he hadn't inherited from his mother but judging people on their appearance was undeniably his mother's trait. It was one that had over time, although of course she was the last one ever to realize the fact, robbed her of the opportunity on any number of occasions to make new and interesting friendships.

David, however, was able to hide his reactions more effectively than his mother and was learning to edit his responses more effectively than his Mother ever had hers. So he was able to return her greetings courteously.

'I'm looking forward to your talk', his response as the words left his lips sounded somewhat lame.

'Oh, that's fine David, maybe we'll catch up later, hang loose.' And with that she was whisked off to meet more important people. He and Madeleine then managed some small talk, before Madeleine was called to the top table. Jack Rogers did what came naturally, and began to talk over the general conference chatter, until nearly everyone had a seat and the accompanying hushes and calls for silence had quietened the audience, and everyone was listening to what he had to say.

To David much of it was so general, so removed from reality and so out of touch with the world he knew, that it was all he could do to listen without interrupting. But he knew that heckling would not be appreciated by this audience. It seemed that Jack's job was to set the scene for the conference and to do this, having gained the audience's undivided attention, he began with a story. It was the classic opening gambit, disarm your audience with a witticism, get them laughing and get them on your side. David knew a few jokes of his own, most of them a good deal funnier than Jack's. The joke was over, although what the pig was doing in the middle of a mountain road in the Rockies was never fully explained. The serious business of the conference was laid out. What kind of church do we want? What kind of ministry will that church need? It became clear as Jack's introduction rambled on, that all the questions were intended to be rhetorical, and the answers they begged were given in the word in the conference title, inclusive. An inclusive church and an inclusive ministry.

Listening, David realised that despite the claims that Jack was making, despite the reassurances he was giving implicitly throughout his introduction, it was clear who he wanted to include and who he wanted to keep out.

Sure he will ordain women, sure he wants everyone to join his church, as though it were some form of social club for the elite, but that inclusiveness was not on offer to David, or to those who attended the homeless breakfast. They would continue to be patronized by the Jack Rogers of the Church, because essentially, thought David, EBG is right, they are snobs to a man.

Catching sight of the Chaplain raising a hand in greeting and smiling encouragingly, David suddenly wished that he had not accepted the invitation, had not made the effort to attend, had not allowed his ego to get the better of him. He got up from his seat and headed out of the conference hall, out of the main doors, back to the pub he had just left. He'd had enough of Jack and the Chaplain for one day. Maybe he would be back for supper, he was hungry and maybe the American and Madeleine would be more interesting and relevant to the real concerns facing the church and world than the Chaplain's old college friend had been.

Clearly, his abrupt departure and absence had been noted, as Jack and the Chaplain looked across at him during supper with obvious disapproval, before turning back to their conversation. David had sat down next to a young clergyman, who introduced himself as Guy,. He was a vicar from a nearby parish in London, and they chatted a little airily about the conference theme. It soon became clear that they shared similar views, and not only about what was happening in the conference itself, but also about some of the main personalities including the Chaplain's good friend Jack.

Over the meal they shared their views that whilst the overall theme of the conference, with its focus on inclusion, was superficially attractive, it was clear also that that the real agenda was to begin to promote the idea of women's ordination in England. It was obvious that Jack's apparent commitment to the cause was clearly linked to his American wife's interest in what was happening in the Episcopal Church in the US, which was always ahead of the Church of England in theology, and in style.

David confessed that he had no experience of America other than a vague awareness gleaned from TV and films like Woodstock and Easy Rider and the music of Bob Dylan. His main reservation about America was the Vietnam War, which he had watched being played out on TV and in newspaper reports. But, he had to admit that in his experience, America had meant freedom and music and films. Guy smiled at this before explaining that he was sharing his supper with someone whose name was almost certainly on a list somewhere and who had been an active participant in an anti-war protest at the US Embassy just around the corner in Grosvenor Square. David was impressed that such an unlikely person had taken part in such a high profile rally, particularly one where the police reaction had been so extreme, but his reaction was dismissed.

'Oh, I was just on the edge of the crowd really. I held

a placard and shouted, but unfortunately for me, probably because I was wearing my collar, my picture appeared in a couple of newspapers. That was my five minutes of fame. I think the Bishop has thought that sticking me away in an inner city parish would keep me busy and out of harm's way. Anyway, now here I am attending a radical conference, what about you, what brought you here?'

David explained about the Chaplain, how he had extended an invitation, how he wasn't particularly interested in the topics under discussion, how he was sure that his own background meant that he would always be on the edge of things and that inclusivity was for middle-class people rather than the likes of him. Also that he was unsure about women's ordination but was here to learn and be convinced. Guy's reaction was very sharp.

'I knew Michael' he said. 'We were at college together, I never warmed to him, never liked him really. He was ambitious, but that wasn't the real problem I had. There was something, people talk you know, I suppose I thought it best to put it down to gossip and jealousy, but if there was anything in the gossip I ought to warn you to take care'.

David tried to press him further but Guy refused to be drawn.

'If you ever need a bed when you're in town', and he scribbled his address on a piece of paper, 'I'm not staying here, I'm just round the corner really, and I've got a meeting this evening that I can't get out of. I'll see you tomorrow, you can fill me in on the evening session'.

With that Guy collected his supper plate and tray and

headed out of the dining room. David was left feeling more troubled than ever. Gossip and rumour was just that, but there was, as the saying goes 'no smoke without fire'. Certainly, in his own experience, the Chaplain had gone from being cold, extremely unfriendly, clearly an enemy in the making, and a particularly well-connected enemy, and well placed to cause the maximum disruption to a career. Against this, David had no way of defending himself. The trigger for this change was, as David realised only too well, was the ill-advised confession. Maybe thought David he thinks he's somehow 'got something' on me that he can use, but why? What on earth use could I possibly be to him?

As he was lost in his own thoughts, a voice cut through to startle him back into the present. Madeleine sat down opposite him.

'How are things? I looked for you earlier, but Michael had said that you stormed out of the first session.' David laughed.

'Hardly stormed, but I did leave it's true. I couldn't make much sense of what it was all about, too early a start maybe, so I went for a quiet pint. Not that London beer is worth getting that excited about'.

'Well, I hope that you won't find it necessary to walk out of the next session. We're not trying to force the issue or scare people into supporting the campaign, but Sue will talk about what is happening in the States, which I think is really exciting, she's invited me over next year, which will be great'. David nodded.

'That sounds really exciting, but what are you planning

to say when you speak'?

'Oh, I'm going to unpick some of the bad theology which our opponents use.'

David reassured her that he would stay to the end, and that he was open minded, and probably didn't need persuading because he could see that there was a good case to be made.

Madeleine stood up. 'We'd better be going it looks like people are moving into the conference hall'.

David decided to pop into the loo first, always a sign that his nerves were getting the better of him. He then slipped in as he always did and found a seat at the back of the hall, on the edge of an almost empty row.

Before the speakers were introduced, Jack took them through, in what by now David recognized as his usual self-important style, an introduction which made light of an important issue. Pursuing grudges was clearly his stock in trade and the jokes were again targeted at the insiders and largely passed over David's head.

Having introduced Sue as the first speaker, he sat back and fiddled with a pencil in a distracted way, while Sue outlined the development of the campaign in the States. She began with a personal reflection about her own vocation, of being called to full-time ministry of both, as she put it, word and sacrament. Listening, David realised that much of what he was hearing, although from a different context, culture and experience of church life, reflected exactly his own growing sense of vocation. Sue, he realised was also an outsider, as a woman, just he as a working class man, was an outsider. But he had been admitted to join the club, and to enter the sanctuary. As Sue had expressed it in her talk, simply because he was male.

Somewhere, his own natural and well-developed instinct for fairness, and for what was right, told him that what he was hearing was right. The campaign was gaining momentum, and there was a particular group, and a certain Bishop in America, who was of the opinion that some form of action would need to be taken. That action would be akin to the civil disobedience that had transformed the civil rights movement. As she spoke, Sue became more impassioned, leading David to think, correctly, that if such action were to be taken she would be at the forefront of those women ready to be ordained.

Sue sat down to warm applause from a largely convinced audience, and Jack introduced Madeleine, taking the opportunity to describe her quite unnecessarily and somewhat patronizingly as an English Rose. Madeleine was obviously angered by Jack's introduction, and as she rose to speak her cheeks were flushed. Her presentation was professional, highly articulate, and very well-rehearsed, but it lacked the passion and anger that Sue had brought to hers. Nevertheless, again at the end, there was a positive response from the audience. Questions were then invited and Jack again indulged himself, misusing his position by asking almost all the questions himself, and answering some of them at length. This meant that the session overran by fifteen minutes, leaving the audience tetchy and irritated.

The conference centre had its own bar, and

most delegates headed downstairs for a drink and an opportunity to talk informally. David noticed that Jack, the Chaplain, and the two speakers were leaving by the front door, obviously heading for a meal or possibly back to Jack's vicarage for the evening. Puzzled as to why he had booked a twin room if he had no intention of using it, and wasn't planning to stay at the conference, David watched the group as they left the building. Preferring his own company to that of the delegates, most of whom seemed very churchy to him, he followed them out of the door and headed back to the pub he had used earlier.

The pub was noisy and smoky, but he managed to find a table in a corner and settled down, with his pint and a packet of crisps, to his favourite occupation, people watching. The rest of the evening passed by pleasantly and David reflected again on what he had heard from Sue and from Madeleine. He thought of the sense of his own outsiderness in relation to the church, and church people, and the sense he had taken from what Sue had said about being on the outside looking in. Uncertain as to how he could support the campaign, which was clearly gaining momentum, he decided that he should find an opportunity to talk at length with Madeleine who was clearly close to the centre of things. With that, he set off back to the conference centre, and bed, certainly realising that his early start was catching up with him.

Opening the door to the room he was relieved to see that it was empty, and just as he had left it. There was no sign of any other occupant, so he undressed, got into bed, and switching off the light he was asleep almost instantly.

It had been a day of new experiences and thoughts. The two speakers, the conversation with Guy, the bus ride and his early morning encounter with the two clients from the homeless breakfast began, in his sub consciousness, to coalesce into a weird and wonderful dream. The bus transformed itself from the industrial north of England to Atlanta, Georgia, a place he had never visited or even seen pictures of. Half the black women sitting in the segregated section in the rear of the Bus were women wearing clerical collars. Jack was driving the bus, chewing on a fat cigar and wearing a peaked cap. Somewhere at the front Madeleine was leading community singing and a marvelous gospel choir filled the bus with joyful music. The dream became deeper and richer and more profound. The homeless men performed a song and dance act to entertain the passengers, then David felt a hand on his shoulder and turning he saw the naked figure of the Chaplain moving to sit in the seat next to his. David tried to move away and realized that he was being forcefully held down, as the dream became a nightmare. He struggled to free himself only to realize that he was no longer dreaming, that he was in fact being held down. This was no longer a dream. Still confused, but now completely awake, David screamed into the pillow which muffled his cries. He realized that he was being held face down in the bed by a surprisingly firm hand gripping his neck. His assailant's other hand was pulling his shorts down and he could feel warm, stale breath on his cheek and the obvious sign that his attacker was extremely aroused. Managing to get a hand free David lashed out backwards and somehow his clenched fist connected with his attackers erect penis which caused him to curse loudly in obvious pain and release his grip.

This allowed David to break free and leap to his feet he turned to find that the Chaplain, naked in his dream was now here in front of him, naked in reality and nursing his now flaccid member which was bruised from the impact of David's fist. Angrily he demanded to know what was happening. Startled by the depth and violence of David's reaction, the Chaplain stepped back, trying as he did so to reassure David that everything was okay.

'I don't think okay is a word that I would use.' David was surprised at how calm he was feeling. 'You were trying to rape me, you bastard. What do you think I am? And why are you here? Why aren't you at your friend Jack's? I saw you leave, what do you think that you are doing'?

Grabbing his bag and pulling on his clothes David began to pack to leave, but as he was pulling on his jeans, the Chaplain suddenly attacked again, knocking him off balance and onto the floor. Now there was no pretence, and his attacker was clearly angry and aroused and meant to finish what he had started. This time David realised that he had to meet violence with violence if only in self defence. His first punch had been a lucky blow that had wounded his attacker, but clearly not fatally. David reached up for the table lamp by the bed and brought it down as hard as he could, aiming again for the aroused and swollen member. Again his aim was good and the chaplain again pulled back to protect himself from the attack. David took full opportunity of the moment and scrabbling to his feet and pulling his jeans on, he grabbed his bag and Jacket and headed for the door. Stepping out onto the landing he ran down the stairs into the entrance hall. The main doors had been locked at eleven thirty but David managed to find the night porter in the basement office and was allowed out by a side door into the street.

By now he was shaking, petrified by the experience, and uncertain what to do next. Searching his pockets he managed to locate Guy's address and telephone number and after some minutes' walking he found a telephone box that was working. Ignoring the cards offering sex in all its varieties, he dialled Guy's number. A sleepy voice answered, 'don't you know what time it is'?

David apologized, 'I can't go into the details but I needed to get out of the conference centre, I was attacked, he tried to rape me'.

Guy didn't wait for any more. 'Where are you, just stay there and I'll come and get you'.

As David waited by the telephone box he looked at his watch, it was three thirty in the morning. The night was very quiet, just an occasional whisper of traffic in the distance. He could hear his breath rising and falling too rapidly, his pulse still racing. Shock, he thought, and tried to consciously control his breathing. He saw a car turn into the end of the street, and suddenly realising that it could be the Chaplain, he drew back into the shadows. But as the car pulled up by the telephone box he recognised Guy, who opened the passenger door and invited him into the car. They drove in silence until Guy turned into a narrow passageway between two blocks of flats, he got out and opened an iron gate, driving in and parking the car by the door of his vicarage.

'Welcome' he said, inviting David in. They went into the kitchen, where Guy poured two mugs of coffee.

'God, David are you all right? You look awful'.

David realised that he was still trembling, and sipping the hot coffee, he described his experience. Guy's response was immediate.

'I'm not surprised, and I wish I had warned you earlier, or said more. I knew him at college and even then there were rumours that he had a sadistic streak in him, but he's always been very discreet. He always covered his tracks well, and when he met Suzie most people thought that it must have been malicious gossip and envy. Now it seems it was neither malicious nor gossip, what are you going to do'?

David made it clear to Guy that the whole experience had been deeply shocking. He didn't think that he would sleep, but if it was okay with Guy, he would just rest on the settee, and head home in the morning.

'You're not intending to report it to the police'?

'No', David explained. 'Who would believe me? Women get raped not men, and anyway I fought him off so it will be my word against his and it is unlikely that I will be believed any more than he will be disbelieved'.

'Well', offered Guy, 'if you want me to I will call the police, but I suspect that you are right. Now, if you're sure you're okay I'm going to catch up on my beauty sleep, busy day again tomorrow, so I'll leave you here, there is a spare bed made up, but if you prefer the sofa it's in here'. Showing David into the lounge he switched on a gas fire, 'hope this suits. There is more coffee or something stronger if you prefer'. David thanked him for his help and apologised again for the disturbance, and settling onto the settee was, despite himself, asleep in minutes.

After breakfast he rang the bus station and headed back to Victoria by tube, where he caught the express coach back north. The first thing he planned to do when he got back was to drive to Drissburgh and seek EBG's advice.

A fragment

Footsteps outside the
Window, the tread of
Feet on gravel, the
Visitors who pause
And go their way
Their unanswered knock
Echoing in the empty hall
Way of our hearts.
Left alone
We measure distance
Casting the stone
Into the heart's well
And counting the moments
Until the distant echo tells
How far we are apart
How lonely passions
Separate us.
This continuing
Drama of our love

EBG

Healing Days

Since David had departed for the Cathedral, life at St Agatha's had continued to run along a fairly predictable path. Without Bobby to hustle, intercede and act as a general go-between for Vicar and congregation, EBG had been exposed to more of the routine parochial infighting than he would have liked. He also missed his young colleague with the strange mixture of mature wisdom, and naivety that the young often bring not only to their enthusiasms but to their daily work as well.

In particular EBG missed sharing responsibility for the Sunday sermon, as an elderly member of the congregation had commented, 'that's the one thing the young man did tolerably well.' EBG responded quite forcefully that it was only one of the things that David did very well indeed. He was not sure that she noticed the emphasis in his response but EBG felt justified, a few days later, when the parish pump recycled the compliment in even more glowing terms, to the effect that David's preaching had landed him the plum job at the Cathedral, over the heads of all the other clergy. Because he was now back, ploughing as the Rural Dean put it, 'his lonely furrow, EBG had been unable to take days off or holidays for some time and the poetry had been painfully slow.

When David's call came, EBG was curious and he suggested a packed lunch and a walk by the sea, instead of the usual pub lunch. EBG's automatic suggestion had been quickly ruled out by David, who made it clear that what he wanted to say needed to be said in the most discreet way possible where there was no possibility of their being overheard. When David arrived, EBG, was in the middle of a trying conversation on the telephone with Hilda about some of the minuting of the previous PCC meeting. He gestured to David to help himself to coffee. As he observed his former colleague through the open door he could see that something was troubling him and that he was deeply stressed, and more than he had ever seen him before. It became even clearer once they had sat down that walk or no walk David needed to talk.

And talk he did, the whole story from the supper with Madeleine and Jack and the two Suzies. Then the conference, the trip to London, the twin room and then in some detail the events that had unfolded in the middle of the night. Then there was silence as David gripped his cup and stared into its rapidly cooling contents. EBG decided to let the silence do its work, so for some time they sat in silence before EBG suggested that the walk was in order as planned. It was a pleasant day outside, with high clouds drifting across a blue-grey sky. The leaves on the trees stirring in the light breeze as they passed along the path along the path. They passed dogs and dog walkers, some greeting EBG and one or two recognizing David greeted him warmly. EBG commented that after dying in office, leaving early was the next best thing if you wanted your reputation not only to survive you, but to even grow a little after you had left, at least for a while. David smiled and EBG could tell that his young companion was visibly more relaxed after sharing his story, and especially now that they were walking along the coastal path.

EBG was clearly disturbed by what he had heard. As he told David, he had known all along that something would happen, and that the Chaplain's feigned interest had been a set up all along. And when he had heard that the Chaplain knew all about David's affair with Gilly it had only been a matter of time before he was bound to put his knowledge to some use, some advantage for himself. But this was out of all proportion, completely and utterly unexpected and completely and utterly unacceptable. Now that they were alone on the path, EBG began to ask one or two questions about the attack. He heard again from David that the attack was unprovoked and that there was an element of subterfuge in the way that the Chaplain had reserved a twin room, which led to the events that night.

EBG then shared with his former colleague his own instinctive reaction to what he had been told. Before that, however, he had wanted to be sure that his young colleague really was coping with the emotional fall-out that inevitably followed such a traumatic experience. David responded reasonably positively. He had spoken with Guy a couple of times, and those conversations had been helpful. He had also telephoned the Samaritans who had been helpful, and because those conversations had been anonymous he had been plain and ordinary John Smith. He had been surprised to hear that male rape was far more common than he had realized. It was something that he had never heard of, never mind experienced. But the counsellor had explained that not only were men attacked physically as well as sexually, but that some so called physical assaults had sexual undertones that were never mentioned, because of embarrassment or fear of further repercussions.

EBG listened attentively before stating in a manner that brooked little contradiction, that he felt that it was his job now to act on David's behalf. Because he was shocked and angry at what he had heard, outraged in fact on his young friend's behalf, but he had the freehold of the parish of Drissburgh, and this put him in a much stronger position. Certainly stronger than David, but also stronger than the Chaplain.

He then explained carefully to David that if that was the role he undertook, then he couldn't personally offer David the emotional support he needed.

'You need to work this out for yourself', observed the older man. 'You need someone in your corner supporting you with the emotional fallout from this attack. Meanwhile, let me deal with the cause of the problem'.

'But what can you do'? David could not see how the matter could be made public without him paying an even higher price than his current upset. 'Surely he's got away with it, and he knows that'?

'Not necessarily'. EBG began to outline the beginnings of a plan which was forming in his mind. 'But to begin with I do need to involve another person, and for that I need your permission, to share the facts with someone you don't know'.

David was uncertain. In his view the fewer that knew

about the attack and the implications it had for him personally and his reputation, the better.

'After all', he explained to his mentor, 'when it comes down to it, it is my word against his, and who is going to take the side of a young and pretty junior curate, with just a couple of years' experience. You know how it is EBG, I am dependant for my future on a licence approved by the Dean and issued by the Bishop, which can be terminated at any time, and pretty much for any reason. If the Chaplain, who is the Bishop's principal and senior assistant in the Diocese, chooses to, he could have me out of a job in days, and there would be nothing I could do about it, because it would all happen behind closed doors'. EBG agreed.

'Which is why' he replied, 'I want to enlist help. I have a close friend since my curacy, which was some years ago as you can imagine. I've known him for, must be all of thirty years, he's a doctor, a GP, he's been in the same practice all that time. He took it over from his father, who's still secretary of the PCC. I served my title in that parish and even now if I need advice, Bill is the first person I turn to. But better than that, he is a personal friend of the Bishop, and the two wives socialize. Bill has always refused to sit on Diocesan committees; in fact he has been the scourge of various vicars, who wanted to use that as a steppingstone to further their careers. Bill, however, has always supported his local parish in his own way. 8:00 am communion, the PCC and the annual garden party which he hosts every year. I've already mentioned you to him and he'd like to meet you, but you have to agree to letting me share this business with him, otherwise I'll need to think again'.

It took EBG a few days to set up the meeting with his

friend. For David these were anxious days, wondering if he would be believed, if his story was credible, and what the Doctor would make of it. But when the meeting took place he was overwhelmed by the genuine warmth, obvious goodness and genuine sincerity emanating from a man who, in any other circumstances he would only have met in a professional capacity as doctor and patient.

Over tea in a comfortable, warm sitting room, David once again told his story. Starting with the supper and ending with his being met by Guy and returning to his vicarage for the rest of that night. The doctor then took David, quite meticulously and without betraying any emotion, back over the story in detail, making notes as they went.

Despite his emotional turmoil, which rose as he went through the events of that night, David responded positively to the highly professional, almost forensic approach adopted by EBG's friend who struck him as part psychoanalyst, part detective and David realized, part priest. All the ingredients of a first class GP, as EBG had promised him.

The doctor then retold the story and his diagnosis was exactly right. A highly predatory man, who had identified his victim. A victim somewhat wounded and weakened by the affair and subsequent confession, then created a trap, the conference, and then moved in for the kill, secure in the knowledge that he had the advantage to ensure that his victim, if not willing, would be compliant. Smiling, the doctor commented, 'this man you describe is what I would call a carnivore in an herbivorous world, you were lucky to escape. He raised a hand in anticipation of David's response, not unharmed, but you have lived to tell the tale. But what if he had succeeded? He was relying on the shame you would have felt to ensure that you never mentioned it again and thereby secure your unwilling collusion. Doubtless you would have ended up blaming yourself.'

David recognised and accepted the truth of the diagnosis. 'But', the doctor continued, 'after the diagnosis, the prescription'. Then turning to EBG, he continued, 'that's where you come in Edwin'. David blinked, he'd always known that EBG had a first name, two in all probability, now he knew one of them at least. EBG affected to be unaware of the slip, or perhaps he and the doctor had known each other for too long and too well for any but EBG's real name, or names, to be used between them.

'First', the doctor continued, 'the Bishop needs to be alerted as to this man's true nature. I agree with David here, there is simply nothing to be gained from the police being involved, it's one person's word against another, with no evidence on either side. Second, this chaplain needs to know now that we know. Thirdly, he needs to fall on his sword. I for one, and I am sure that you too Edwin, cannot standby and let this man continue to abuse the bishop's trust in future.'

With David's agreement, the two men, the immaculately attired GP with his diffident but commanding manner, his sheer goodness and commitment to truth, and EBG, a somewhat crumpled, older cleric in a slightly food-stained black shirt and an off-white clerical collar. They were an odd couple certainly, but they were both firmly standing in David's corner. Despite the mood of anger and confusion into which the Chaplain's attack had thrown him, David began to feel better about himself, and even better about the possible outcome. It would take time yet, and the first thing they needed to do was to make separate appointments with the Chaplain first, and then with the Bishop, whose diary was controlled by the Chaplain, or as the doctor commented drily, 'so he supposes'.

It all took nearly a week, during which time David had to conduct a campaign of avoiding action. Whilst the Chaplain did not attend the Cathedral services during that week and was preaching at another church in the Diocese on the Sunday. Nevertheless, as David knew at any time, he could turn a corner, drop into The Mitre or answer the telephone to find the Chaplain laying another trap for him.

Unusually, David realised that Suzie, the Chaplain's wife was much more in evidence. Having hardly seen her during his first year, suddenly every time he entered or left the house, there she would be, smiling and waving, with her shopping bags, books or briefcase, or crossing the Close on her way to or from her house. During this period there was only one truly terrifying experience. That was when David was awakened by his doorbell ringing at three in the morning. Looking through the security eye he could see the Chaplain ringing the bell and knocking. David to his shame, went back upstairs and hid his head under the pillows to drown out the sound rather than confront his aggressor.

This incident was, in all probability, David realised later, a direct consequence of EBG and his friend the doctor who had managed to tighten the net. The trap had been set in a confrontation David later learned from EBG, between his old vicar and the Chaplain. EBG kept the details purposefully vague, but the effect was dramatic. Whatever alternative course of action had been suggested or proposed was clearly much worse than the course of action which the Chaplain decided upon. He simply resigned. The Bishop accepted his resignation, regretfully and the Chaplain, leaving Suzie in the house, went on 'retreat'. The gossip in the Close was furious with people proposing a range of bizarre and preposterous theories to explain the sudden disappearance of the man who everyone agreed had a glittering career in front of him. David called EBG to thank him, only to be asked, 'Whatever for? We did nothing really',

Really thought David, sometimes I wish that my nothings could have such a dramatic and successful effect, my 'somethings' rarely make that much difference.

David then saw Suzie again on his way from a meeting in town and this time he had no choice but to fall into step with her as they were both walking in the same direction toward the Close. He noticed that she seemed to be tearful and as they walked he asked her how she was coping. It turned out that not only had Michael resigned as the Bishop's Chaplain, but his relationship with Suzie was also at an end. She was in the process of packing up her belongings and returning home to her parent's house. Her father, it turned out, was a country vicar in Gloucestershire. Her mother had been unwell for some time, and so it seemed to be the best solution under the circumstances for her to go home and offer some help in the house and parish.

'Of course when daddy retires we'll have nothing, but hopefully by then Michael and I will have sorted things out, or I will have a job. Anyway, sometimes you can't plan that far ahead, just take things a day at a time.' Thanking David for his concern and his offer of support, Suzie headed back to the house. As she walked away David looked after her retreating figure and thought, no, you can't plan anything. Life just seems to happen, sometimes good, sometimes bad, and sometimes bloody awful.

Remains

Everywhere memories
are seeping into the future
into earth and stone
Remains lie, deposits
of blood and feathers
bone rendering the earth
calcium rich
Underfoot detritus
crumbling to soil
enriching the land
The future comes
drawing down from
the deep reservoir of the past
secure in the promise

EBG

End Game

The streets in and around the old Elephant and Castle had been demolished for new high rise blocks in the sixties, and despite the publicity surrounding these examples of new urban living, the church struggled to maintain a presence. The traditional model of the visiting parson simply doesn't work when the older parishioners are too afraid to open the door, and conversations have to be shouted through letter boxes. Families found the strain of living in these streets and terraces in the sky too much to bear and as soon as they possibly could they moved further out to become commuters on the outer suburban estates or the new developments further down the river. Increasingly on his desperate daily rounds the vicar noticed steel shutters replacing doors, a sure sign of the drug dealers rapidly developing trade and more and more boarded-up flats. The tall red brick Gothic Church and its Rectory appeared increasingly anachronistic against the backcloth of urban change and decay. Despite the architecture, or perhaps because of it, the new developments were rapidly deteriorating and the local area looking more neglected and hostile than the slums they had been built to replace.

Guy, as the vicar of the parish, was certain that he should move. A new parish, he reasoned, would bring a new lease of life and the possibility that he could ply his trade with a little more chance of success. He was a good man. Open faced and generous with his time, an articulate preacher, and with a good loud voice that got through to the most hard of hearing of his elderly congregation. But he was being defeated by the uphill struggle of trying to maintain the church's presence in this run down part of London. All too aware of the lack of support, there were frequent calls from the Diocese, for outreach, mission, evangelism, but they were all, in Guy's opinion simply vain posturing without any additional resources or offers of support. Like David, Guy viewed the call for an inclusive church with scepticism. Inclusive for and of, whom. He had been a college contemporary of the man David knew as the Bishop's Chaplain in the northern Diocese, to which he had moved after a dazzling but brief time spent as a curate in what the media had dubbed an 'experimental' south bank parish, where he was never out of the media spotlight.

He had then returned again, very briefly, to their old college where he and Guy had collaborated over what he called an urban training centre. Here, young trainee clergy could spend time living in the parish, whilst continuing their studies, and offering some assistance to the vicar who in exchange for the dubious benefits this arrangement brought to him and the parish, had been appointed to the college's staff as Tutor in Urban Mission Studies. This experiment in making theological education contemporaneous and relevant and in tune with changing attitudes and styles in Adult Education nationally. This bold experiment, as it was called by the media, had earned the Chaplain even more accolades from the Church Press, who simply lapped up, accepted and affirmed his self-generated publicity. This was before the experiment could fail or be shown to be the triumph of style over substance that it was. So he had moved on again and appointed as Chaplain to the Bishop in the Diocese where David now was.

During his meteoric rise, stories had followed in the Chaplain's wake, but nearly always there was no real substance. It was all rumours, shadows, nothing solid that anyone could point to as firm evidence of inappropriateness in his behaviour. As so often happens, the Chaplain's patrons had put these rumours down to jealousy on the part of less able and less gifted clergy. Now Guy realised that the sinister rumours did have substance and he was aware that David needed continued affirmation and support if he was to overcome the events that had brought him to the Rectory in the middle of the night.

That David was grateful for the support he had received from Guy was not at issue, but as David explained, much of the practical response was being undertaken by people in whom he had absolute confidence. What he needed most of all from Guy, who had seen him at his most vulnerable, was pastoral support and friendship and this, Guy was only too ready to provide. He had warmed to the young man, and in particular to his northern humour and outspokenness, and so through regular telephone contact he had continued to offer David friendship and support. When the news broke about the Chaplain's resignation, and then his disappearance, Guy was puzzled but reckoned that it was none of his business. As long as the man's appetites were held in check, then 'out of the way' was in all probability the best place for him. David certainly, and Guy himself, even after ringing around one or two college friends, could find nothing out. No-one, it seems, knew what had happened. The man had simply disappeared off the face of the earth.

Time passed and despite the obvious shock, and the effect that the events of that night had on David's confidence, the daily telephone calls became weekly and Guy was confident that David was beginning to pick up the pieces of his life. He recovered his sense of humour, spoke compassionately about Suzie, the Chaplain's wife, who had now completed her move south to her family. In fact David had been able to offer practical support, helping her to pack, to sort out the things she needed to keep for the future, selling some furniture and recycling some through a furniture store which had been started to provide furniture and clothes to a charity for unmarried mothers. This was linked to the Diocese, which was changing its role from a straightforward adoption agency to that of providing support to girls who chose to keep their babies and raise them as single parents.

David, in his weekly call to Guy described his growing realization of how easy it would have been to become a victim. At one time he had been convinced that the attack had been his own fault. On another occasion he wondered if he had imagined it all. Guy patiently talked him through these aspects of coming to terms with what had happened to him. Guy offered reassurance, and patiently helped him come to terms with events, which whilst bad enough, could have been terrible. As they both agreed, whatever possessed the man to launch his attack, whether it was an aberration, or whether he felt that, because of David's confession he would be a compliant victim, the events had been a colossal misjudgment which had backfired. David's entirely justified response to the attack had given him the upper hand at the time, and which subsequent events had ensured that he would be free of any problems in the future.

The other person that David had kept in touch with during this time was Madeleine. It seemed that all she knew about what had happened at the conference was that Michael had apologised after supper and said that rather than going back with them to Jack's house, he would stay over at the conference centre as he had some work to catch up on. That the next day, neither he nor David were anywhere to be seen, and apart from some foolish remarks from Jack, which she had dismissed out of hand, no-one seemed to know why either of them had left the conference. The final twenty four hours were, she admitted something of a damp squib. David had decided to say nothing more about what had happened until in one telephone conversation, she amazed him by saying that she had heard from Jack that Michael had resigned, that he was living apart from Suzie, who had asked him to leave, and was testing his vocation in a religious house in the north of England. All this had come about as a result of unfounded allegations that had been made against him. It seemed that she had no idea about the allegations or who had made them, but David felt that the truth was more important and that she should, if she was to continue to move in these, in his view dubious circles, know from him that the allegations were not unfounded. Clearly it would be his word against the Chaplain's. At first Madeleine had refused to believe what David was telling her, but as he pointed out he had no reason to lie. In fact every reason to say nothing, but he was telling her because he felt that she needed to know the truth.

With time David began to recover and the emotional scars, which had been extremely raw, began to heal, and the continuing conversations with the two people who had in their different ways been part of the events certainly helped him to recover. He was delighted when Guy suggested that David visit for a weekend, and that Madeleine might join them for supper on the Saturday night.

The weekend was a great success and following Guy's invitation David preached at the main service on the Sunday morning. The supper party on the Saturday night had also gone well. Guy had invited one of his churchwardens and his wife, who were a younger couple originally from the north, and who knew the Cathedral. They also knew the city, which gave them a good starting point for an easy and relaxed conversation.

Over supper Madeleine was able to share her own news, which David already knew, that she had been invited to visit Sue in America and, what David didn't know, was that she was planning to fly out next month. She was planning, she said, an extended visit and for that reason had resigned from the parish where she was working as a Deaconess. To David's surprise he realized that the news, whilst good for

Madeleine, came as something of a disappointment, and that he was certainly going to miss her. At the very least he would miss the telephone conversations and her constant enthusiasm and zest for life. Perhaps, he thought later, what I like about her company is that I need a positive influence in my life after all that had happened.

Knowing that they were unlikely to be seeing each other for some time David had escorted Madeleine back across London to her home, for which she laughingly thanked him for his 'old fashioned courtesy'. This left him somewhat confused and uncertain as to whether he was being complimented, and was old fashioned a good thing to be? Or having his leg rather gently and sweetly pulled. Whichever it was their telephone conversations continued until the time that Madeleine was due to leave, and then she somewhat surprisingly accepted David's invitation to visit him at the Cathedral. Again the weekend was a great success and Madeleine was a hit with the residents of the Close when they met her over drinks at the Deanery.

The visit had coincided with one of the Dean's social occasions and when David offered his apologies, giving as his reason that he already had a guest for the weekend, the Dean immediately extended the invitation to include Madeleine. It was during this weekend, just before he was due to leave for the Deanery when the telephone rang, 'David, it's the Bishop' the voice on the other end began. David was dumbfounded, he immediately assumed that it was a joke, someone wanting to pull his leg. So his response was at best guarded, sensing David's hesitation his caller continued. 'No, really David, it is the Bishop.

I'm sorry to trouble you at this hour on a Saturday, in fact I think we are both due to be meeting shortly at the Deanery, are we not'?

David, still uncertain, agreed that it was a possibility, not that he knew who the other guests were, 'it's just that I'm catching up on some bits of office work, it's surprising how much there is now that Michael's gone. Well, the thing is, I wondered if you could spare me a moment or two on Monday. I know that it is short notice, probably your day off too, but if you could pop round? Shall we say eleven for a coffee'?

Still on his guard, David agreed, assuring his caller that he wasn't busy and that he could make the time as requested.

'That's fine then, see you later'.

David could almost hear the gales of laughter as his caller returned the telephone to its cradle. A practical joke obviously.

As they crossed the Close, Madeleine laughed at David's suspicious mind, 'what are you going to do'? she asked, 'will you turn up? Or are you going to stand him up? Thing is if it was the Bishop and you don't go, you'll never know what he wanted'.

Agreeing with her David continued, 'and if I do and it wasn't him, the secretary will soon send that one round the Diocese at my expense'.

Whatever the source of the call or the reason for it, David's cup, far from running over, suddenly appeared half empty. I'll bet, he thought, the Chaplain's decided that as he has got nothing to lose, he's left a note, or sent a message to the Bishop spilling the secrets of the confessional, and that will be it. Then, on Monday I will be trying to talk my way out of the mess I have got myself into and that will be the end, my career will be over. They will say, he was such a prospect but it all ended in tears.

As they entered the Deanery, they were greeted by the Dean with great warmth and charm. Madeleine was swept into the room and introduced around. The evening was clearly going well, as these occasions usually did. The Dean was a gracious host, his wife had prepared a buffet supper and a couple of Cathedral staff were there to help serve the food and pour the wine. Madeleine, as a new face, and a rising star in the church's firmament, was the centre of attention. Her involvement in the campaign to get women ordained was known to some of the guests, who were keen to quiz her about the progress the campaigners were making, and how much longer before there was any action.

After a while the Bishop arrived looking suntanned and relaxed as though he had been on holiday. David who had been chatting to the Cathedral staff for most of the evening, and whose glass, because he was close to the wine table, had been kept full all evening by the verger who was acting as wine waiter for the evening, almost without him noticing, was beginning to notice the effects of the alcohol. When he came face to face with the Bishop, who was looking for his first glass of wine, David's red face looked more sunburned than tanned.

'Aah, David sorry about earlier. I could hear in your voice that you weren't too certain that it was me, but I do assure you it was, me that is. Is Monday at eleven still all right for you'?

David grinned, what he realized was a foolish grin, but he was more than slightly tipsy by this point of the evening, and began to reply, but the Bishop without seeming to notice David's hesitancy, or his inebriated state, sailed off to greet one of the Cathedral Wardens.

Turning, David caught the Verger's eye, 'called in to see the top boss are we? Who've you been upsetting now?'

Epilogue

Far out to sea, let me explain the fleets
of warring nation's retreat
below in the lea of the island
echoes of ravaging pain
despair, shrieks of metal gulls, flap
mechanical wings drawn down by the scent of oil,
blood, water's indifference
By some definitions religion fails, lacking
as it does, impartiality and faithfulness
Its administration made more difficult by its need
for cult, ritual and a priestly class
Under such obligations it becomes clear
that only by maintaining silence
is justice established, only by loss
are we finally claimed

EBG

The Bishop's Move

Having spent the better part of his school days waiting outside the headmaster's office, David had come to regard any interview with authority with little or no enthusiasm. He always reckoned, based on experience, that the punishment, whether it was fair or deserved would be both painful and humiliating. He was in this, at least as far as his school days were concerned, usually right. The stinging bite of the leather strap on his upturned hand or the gym shoe on the tightly stretched and shiny school trousers were not however, on reflection as painful as the words that accompanied the punishment. These were if anything even more stinging in their aim of humiliating him and cutting him down to size.

As he waited in the hallway to be called into the Bishop's office, David looked back on that period of his life, and the schoolteachers he'd had the misfortune of being taught by. Many of them were ex-soldiers who having been demobbed in the immediate post war years, were encouraged by the offer of training and grants, to enter a profession for which most of them were entirely unsuited. Although they had never discussed, it his mother had mentioned briefly that his father had in fact refused the offer. He chose instead to go back into the dull, routine job in the factory where he had worked before the war. He had not progressed, preferring a life which offered limited, if secure, financial reward to the uncertainties of other occupations. David had always been uncertain about why his father had turned the offer down but was clear that if it had been because he realised that he would have been completely unsuited to the role of a teacher, then his father's decision to decline the offer had, in its own way, been a pretty heroic act.

In Drissburgh David had been required by the Diocese to undertake teaching practice in the local primary school. The experience had been a complete disaster. As soon as he entered the building, and on each occasion that he did, David was overwhelmed by a complete sense of his own inadequacy and fear of the consequences. His meetings with the head teacher and her staff were always cordial and respectful of his office, but as he entered through the doors of the school he was immediately returned, emotionally at least, to a time twenty years before. He was once again the nervous child who simply hated the buildings, which overawed him, to the smell which was a mixture of sweat, anxiety, simmering cabbage, polish and disinfectant. And emotionally at least, he became once again the small boy who had sat in the hall of his primary school and wept because he didn't have the confidence to approach the teacher, who he now realized, was in all probability kindness itself. She was selling the lifeboat stickers that all the other children were wearing proudly, and for which, in order not to be left out he had persuaded his mother to give him a penny or two to purchase.

The transaction barely merited that description even. Once the coins rattled in the collecting box, however small the contribution, the sticker was placed on the child's sweater. But for a small, terrified boy of five or six, the act of approaching the table was just too much. It required a degree of confidence he hadn't been born with, and it wasn't, he recalled, until the teacher saw him crying in the shadows at the back of the school hall, that she came to investigate. Putting a loving arm around his shoulder, she helped him deposit his coins and choose his sticker.

Over time, his confidence increased but his mother, who had contributed in the war effort, was not prepared to go back to being a stop at home mum. She worked all the way through his schooldays, in the low-grade office jobs that were all she was qualified for, leaving David at an early age to become what later was called a latch key child. In due course he acquired caring responsibilities for his two younger sisters. This included putting the tea, which was left ready to be heated up, into the oven for his mother's return.

These simple, limited and undemanding tasks always took priority over schoolwork, homework or preparation. Although with no TV in the house, David had become an avid reader of fiction acquired from the local Library, which he passed on his way to and from school. It had been a particularly proud moment when he took the reading test at the library. Alone and without any of the anxiety he felt at school, he read aloud confidently and was awarded his junior borrower's ticket. All this backfired on him in secondary school when he was told by the music teacher a certain Mr Rourke, after he had been hit around the head for singing tunelessly and flat, never to sing in his presence again. David was told to sit out the music lessons and get on with his reading. This he dutifully did until his second year in English, where the class were given a list of essential reading. Having read every book on the list and possessing neither common sense nor a sense of self-protection, David explained his dilemma. His reward for being the most well-read student in the class was to be punished by the English teacher for his effrontery and sent to sit in the corridor outside the Headmaster's office for a whole term. David reasoned that if the rewards for achievement were so poor, that he should leave school at the earliest possible opportunity which he did, with the headmaster's words ringing in his ears, 'Saxon, it would benefit neither you nor the school for you to remain here any longer than necessary'.

No, here he was again, outside the headmaster's study, in the same position, waiting. Although to be fair, he reasoned, the secretary did give me an encouraging smile and a cup of coffee, and that is most definitely an improvement.

But what was this all about? He was pretty sure that this was part of the fallout from the Chaplain's clumsy and aggressive assault. Was rape too strong a word, he wondered to describe what had happened that night? Every time he thought about it he came to the same conclusion. He had been given no warning, the grip on his neck had been fierce, intended to keep his face pushed into the pillow, possibly to prevent his calling out for help. The sense of helplessness he felt had been profound, and if his arm had not been free, enabling him to lash out, who knows where things might have ended.

As he thought the attack through again, he reasoned that Michael was not a nice human being. Even in the later stages of their relationship when David was at the Cathedral there had been an underlying sense of threat. There was a feeling that he could turn at any time, possibly turning the information David had given him in the confession, back against him. In the whole of their relationship, stretching back to David's ordination, there was a sense of power being used, manipulated and abused. David's suspicion of the Chaplain and his recognition that he would go to any lengths to remain in control of situations, ensured that David remained on his guard, which made his confession all the more reckless.

With hindsight, he realised that he had been daring the Chaplain to use the information in a game of double bluff, but there could only ever have been one winner. If the Chaplain had recommended that David be disciplined on account of his inappropriate relationship with a parishioner, his adultery, then the Bishop would have withdrawn his licence and David's career would have been in ruins. To then claim that the punishment was unfair because he had given this information under the seal of the confessional and that the Chaplain, by using the material was somehow in breach of his priestly obligations would have come to nothing.

So David had set himself up in a no-win situation where whatever happened he would lose; career, income, housing and further, he would have let down his friends. His old mate Pete, who often, when he had a drink would confide in David how proud he was of his achievement.

'From the gutters of Manchester to the Cathedral Close, what a journey' was the way he expressed it on more than one occasion. But he would have let down Fr Hamer, whose trust in him had never wavered. He would have been a huge disappointment to Harold McMillan his college principal, EBG, and most importantly to Gilly herself. She really didn't deserve the humiliation of appearing in the tabloids as the curate's Page Three Girl. All this to win a 'moral' victory. Something he had once read somewhere made him think that the right word was pyrrhic, whatever that meant.

So what awaited him beyond the door? The bishop's office was silent, like the crematorium chapel before a funeral with its plush carpeting. David thought that he should perhaps have removed his shoes. The pictures on the walls were extremely tasteful and reassuring. The secretary, who David knew by sight, had made him his coffee, bringing with it a chocolate biscuit, which David reasoned, could have been a good sign; but could equally have been softening him up for what was to come. Which was?

No doubt what had happened was that the Chaplain had created a kind of dossier on the more difficult of the new ordinands in his care, and that was now in the Bishop's possession. The secretary had suggested that the Bishop was taking a difficult telephone call from London, but in all probability he was even now mulling over the dossier.

The longer David waited the clearer he became that this was going to be a difficult conversation. On the

carpet, in front of the Bishop, 'it's come to my notice …
very disappointed … badly let down … can't continue
in a position of trust … suggest you move out today …
needless to say there will be a note on your file which will
ensure that … In future … any Diocese … Any Bishop …
should you apply for a job … Will know why you left this
Diocese and under what circumstances … Best for the
Diocese and for you … Should leave immediately.

As the imaginary conversation unfolded in David's
mind, he found himself wondering if he could protest,
challenge. After all, he reasoned, the Chaplain's departure
was a mystery. EBG obviously had the information from
other sources as well as David. Perhaps he and his GP
friend would speak for him, but then, of course EBG had
learned the truth from Gilly, and wouldn't compromise
himself or his friend, however highly he thought of
David. David, for his part wouldn't ask him to. Maybe,
David thought, I should join the Chaplain in exile, test
my vocation to the religious life in the same monastery.
It would, as he had joked with Neil about his own career
choice, be a prison sentence without any chance of parole.

At that moment the door opened and the Bishop
invited David into his study. Like the corridor it was
plush. Fitted carpets, which were all the rage, in muted
colours rather than the garish wallpaper favoured by
David's mother for the best room, which was why it was
hardly ever used apart from Christmas and other family
occasions. The study, again unlike David's parents' house,
was filled with ceiling high shelves stacked with books and
David was impressed. His own modest collection often

caused people to ask whether he had read them all. The same question formed itself in David's mind, how does he find time to read so much?

As if reading David's thoughts the Bishop smiled, 'I've read some of them, but in my position I sometimes have to rely on other people to do my reading for me'.

Ushering his guest into a comfortable chair, the Bishop asked, 'Now David, how are you enjoying life in the Cathedral'?

'Fine thanks, it's interesting, rewarding, I'm kept busy'

'Is the Dean treating you well?'

'Certainly. I had only seen him at a distance really, only at the ordination, but as soon as the Chaplain suggested the move, he called me and has helped me settle in'.

'Yes, it's a good community to be part of, unfortunately I can't be as involved as I might like to be, but that probably suits the Dean very well'.

David noticed that the Bishop's last comment, even though there was no change in his voice, had a subtle edge to it. Maybe, he thought, the rumours are true and there is a tension between the two men.

'How long is it now, since we made you a deacon'?

'Just coming up to three years,' David added a hesitant 'Sir' at the end of his reply, uncertain quite of the courtesies involved in chatting with Bishops, and aware that at any moment the conversation could veer off in a very different and much more difficult direction.

'Just occasionally', the bishop continued, without appearing to notice the hesitancy, 'someone comes along who we're rather glad to have in our team, a fresh face, new ideas, someone not out of the usual stable. I rather think that it enriches the diocesan gene pool, if you see what I mean'.

David was not entirely sure that he did, or where this was leading, but he nodded uncertainly. It was a very strange image, and not one he had expected. He was assuming that it was he that was being referred to, and there was no implied reference to his activities. It was not a bad image, 'since he has arrived he had improved the gene pool significantly' had a certain ring to it he thought.

But the Bishop continued, hardly seeming to notice David's loss of attention,. 'So then we are faced with the problem of how to keep those unusual candidates and not lose them to other Diocese or to other callings.'

It was then that David noticed the uncertainty in the Bishop's voice and mannerisms. Given their relative positions in the general scheme of things, in the Church and its hierarchy, David thought that the Bishop should really be more confident, especially when interviewing someone as relatively junior as he was.

'You see David, whatever people may think, Bishops really have very little power, except perhaps, very occasionally. We rely always on other people, from the clergy in the parishes, the Archdeacons, the Dean, of course, and his team at the Cathedral. But if there aren't enough stars in the Diocesan firmament then it doesn't shine too brightly. So we need to keep our stars'.

By now David was at a complete loss. He could no longer follow the conversation or see where it was heading. Surely, he thought, as the Bishop stood up and walked across to his desk, this couldn't be leading to a reprimand, it was all going too well.

The Bishop returned with a folder, the dossier, was David's immediate thought.

'Before he left, Michael brought your file up to date, I have it here. He speaks highly of you, that much is clear, despite your differences, he thought of you rather affectionately, I believe'.

There was no affection shown at the conference, thought David, aggression certainly and an image of the Chaplain's bruised erection came into his mind uninvited, causing him to shift uncomfortably in the comfortable armchair.

'So, David', the Bishop continued, I have been giving some thought to what we can do with you. I've been giving some thought to what is brewing in the Diocese. Unfortunately, you realize that the traditional pattern, and we are very traditional in this part of the Church, is two curacies before you can become a Vicar. In any event it has to be three years but if the other clergy see someone coming up too quickly on the inside rail they get twitchy. They are surprisingly jealous people clergy, David, you need to watch out for that'.

He paused and reread the file, perhaps he's looking for the bit about my confession thought David. By now the Bishop's nervousness had transmitted itself to David who was beginning to wish that he had not accepted the coffee.

'The thing is David, I need someone here, with Michael's sudden, and I might say quite unexpected departure. I find that I miss the support that a Bishop's

Chaplain brings to what is, all in all, a rather lonely office. The girls help of course and make sure that things run smoothly, but I need someone at my side whose advice and experience can ease the burden. What I don't need, and this is by no means a criticism of Michael, just a simple observation, but I don't want someone who will constantly chip away at the authority which is properly mine'.

As the Bishop went on David noticed an interesting shift in the centre of gravity of the conversation. From the rather fearful, about-to-be-carpeted young man waiting outside the headmasters office David felt that he was now the counselor, and that the Bishop appeared to be asking his advice. Although David realised that the spell would be instantly broken if he uttered as much as a word. Clearly that was not required from him.

Closing the file and placing the folder on the side table next to his chair, the bishop looked up quizzically at David. He removed his reading glasses and played with them thoughtfully before speaking again.

'You must be wondering what all this is leading up to, and why I have asked you in. I have already overrun my time, and any moment Alison will be knocking on the door to say that my next appointment is waiting. In fact I believe I did hear the doorbell a few moments ago. So, David this is my proposal to you, that you come and work here with me, as my Chaplain. You'll bring a fresh approach, EBG says that you have a wise head on those young shoulders of yours and the Dean agrees. So what say you, I do hope that you will accept my offer'.

All that David could recall later about the next few minutes was agreeing and thanking the Bishop for the confidence he was showing in him. He left the study and bumped into Neil, who had arrived for his exit interview. He later told David that he looked as though something truly terrible had just happened. David walked out of the Bishop's house into the Close, whooping, throwing his hat into the air, uncertain later whether he was wearing a hat or not, then laughing uproariously. At that point the Dean, halfway between his house and the Cathedral stopped and raised his arm in greeting.

From Madeleine

Dear David

It was wonderful to receive your letter, I am so pleased for you and that your obvious gifts have been recognized. I am delighted that you will succeed Michael, he was a wonderful man in so many ways, not the least his support for us in our campaign. Whatever your views on that issue you will be a worthy successor.

The Bishop will be fortunate to have a strong, knowledgeable right hand man and at some point in the future a Bishop might even appoint a right hand woman (sorry I couldn't resist that!)

The States are an exciting place to be right now (does that sound too American?) and I am working as a Deaconess in a church in Philadelphia, the City of Brotherly Love! But in Philadelphia, the Bishop with his crew cut and bearing look every inch the military Chaplain he once was but is very keen to support the ordination of women. Sue and her friends are very close to him at the moment. One of the candidates is 86 would you believe, and they have drawn me into their group. Now we are to be ordained next month in the Cathedral.

The Bishop's view is that the Church won't move until it is pushed and so we are planning a major act of civil disobedience. Seven of us are to be made priest on the Sunday after next. It is of course the BIGGEST secret and by the time you will read this letter it will have happened.